The

Job

Post

K. M. Welch

NFB
<<<>>>
NFB Publishing/Amelia Press
119 Dorchester Road
Buffalo, New York 14213

For more information visit
Nfbpublishing.com

To Mom and Dad, for all the stories you read and told.

1

I KNOW IT'S NOT possible, but I swear it moved. The heat is making me hallucinate. Or the stench. Perhaps the heated stench. Where the hell is he? I've been sitting next to a dead goose stuffed into a black trash bag on the side of the road for over an hour on the hottest day of the fall. Each minute the bird leaks a stench that would peel wallpaper. Each minute feels longer than an hour. And there it goes again, the bag moved. I'm losing my mind.

The day started out normal, had a nice cup of coffee, drove in with the windows down and sat at my desk for a whole five minutes before the phone rang. The call seemed easy enough from a kind and normal sounding resident. They saw a dead goose in the lake on their morning walk and wanted to let someone know as their daughter was having her homecoming pictures taken by the lake later that afternoon. I thanked them, hung up and called the dog warden who handles all things animal in the town, dead or alive. Warden picked up on the first ring, said he was on his way and to meet him at the waterfront. Nice day for a walk by the lake I mused. Oh, was I wrong.

"Good morning, it's Shelly, right? Caught me at a good time, just got back from break and was about to head out on my rounds. How's the job treating ya?"

"On a day like today, I can't complain. Have to apologize I didn't catch your name, the phone list they gave me has you listed as Warden, that's it."

"Well that's what they call me." He smiled after that and kept staring at me. No additional name offered. The warden seemed like a nice enough guy, a little socially awkward, later end of middle aged and a very robust gentleman.

"Well Warden it is then, I'm Shelly. Nice to meet you and thanks for swinging over. Looks like our feathered friend is just about dead center in the lake. I unlocked the canoes for you and you can have your pick of the paddles and lifejackets. Let me know if you need anything else!"

"Well hold on now, you're going out there with me."

"I am?"

"I don't know how to canoe and my heart is not up for strenuous activity these days."

"Umm, ok. So, do you want me to go out and get the goose?"

"Oh no you can't get the goose, you're not trained or certified."

"To scoop a dead bird, I need to be certified? You're kidding me, right?"

"Nope Missy, Health Department Regulations. If I let you scoop the bird I can be out on my sweet ass. So, here's what we are going to do, I'll sit in front and bag the bird, you paddle us out there and back. Now I have a breakfast meeting to get to so let's hop to it and all."

With that he proceeded to walk to where I had the boats lined up and attempt to find a lifejacket that would fit his easy 300lb body.

"You've got to be kidding me."

The lake that held the deceased bird was Big Lake, one of the Town's seven lakes, hence the Town's namesake of Seven Lakes, and happened to be the largest of the seven at roughly 75 acres. Big lake was the only developed waterfront in town and boasted a boat launch and boat rental area alongside a small sandy beach all of which sat surrounded by pristine rolling parkland, woods and trails. On the other side of the road the landscape is made up of slightly more developed green space with a few ball fields, picnic pavilions, a tennis court and the Conservation Outdoor Education Department where I gleefully accepted the seasonal caretaker position a week ago.

I straddled the canoe stern and tried my best to steady it as the warden climbed to the bow. We both broke a sweat as he sat down. Part of the boat was still on shore.

"All set?"

"Let her rip Missy!"

"It's Shelly, not Missy thank you very much, and if we're going anywhere you need to help me rock this thing out of the muck."

His tad bit of extra weight had sunk the bow firmly into the earth creating a suction that was not going to give up without a fight.

What felt like an exuberant amount of time later the boat reluctantly let go and we were on our way. Sort of. I can only imagine what we looked like with the bow riding low and the stern visibly out of the water by at least 3 inches. The living geese were laughing. Every honk had a distinct snicker attached.

"We don't have all day, give it some muscle there dear. Dead goose dead ahead, ha ha no pun intended."

My eyes rolled so far back I heard my grandmother's voice calling from beyond the grave 'Eyes gonna get stuck if you keep it up'. The longest paddle of my life so far and I was a wilderness canoe guide for a year out of college.

15 minutes later thankfully we had reached the cause of the adventure. I did a few side draws and slid neatly alongside the now belly up goose.

"Ok Warden, do your thing."

With a move full of theater level flourish, he fluffed the garbage bag he had tucked I don't want to know where in the air, leaned over and proceeded to tip the boat sling-shotting me into the lake and rolling himself onto the bird.

When I re-surfaced I didn't even register the cold water, the disbelief mixed with outrage was a very effective barrier to the temperature.

"Oh, come on! You have got to be kidding me."

I let out a growl as I swam and collected the paddles. I turned to lay into my skipper when I noticed his panicked pale face.

"Help me, I... I... Can't swim... I can't touch... Fish..."

"It's ok, take a breath, you're floating, you have a lifejacket. Now, now...there there..."

I patted him gingerly on the shoulder as I swam around to get back to the boat.

"Don't leave me! You can't leave me...Missy I..."

"It's Shelly. Now shut up and help me or I will leave you and the bird out here to bond." His eyes stayed wide but at least his mouth closed.

"Here's the plan, stay calm and we will be back to shore in no time! I'll lean on the left side of the canoe while you, on the count of three, push on the other side and hoist yourself back in the boat."

I was very proud of how positive I sounded as in my head the mantra was no way this is going to work, I'm going to spend all day swimming a guy, a boat and a dead bird back to shore.

Ten attempts later Warden was back in the boat exhausted, winded and cold but at least safe from the dreaded fish. I pulled myself back in, re- positioned the canoe, bagged the bird and started back for shore.

As soon as we ran aground the Warden mumbled a thanks, asked me to wait with the goose to adhere to lord knows whose protocol and went to get his truck. I put the boats away, rung out my clothes as best I could then heft the goose over my shoulder looking the part of a very morbid Santa.

A short five-minute stroll and I was at the side of the road waiting for Warden to arrive. That was an hour ago. An hour and 15 minutes ago to be exact. The longer the goose baked in the bag the more my temper rose.

"I'm giving him 5 more minutes. That's it. That's all you get bird and there I go talking to a trash bag....I swear..."

I cut my rant off as I saw a dark green pickup slow down and pull up.

"Finally, where the heck have you been?"

I yelled my question over my shoulder as I stood and hefted the bird up.

"Well I'm not sure that's any of your business as you appear to be homeless and living out of a trash bag."

I snapped my head around and found not the warden but a smirking guy behind a pair of aviators wearing a well-loved baseball hat leaning out of his truck window.

"I was just joking, your uh, hmm staff shirt gave you away, you must be the new hire. You could stop glaring at me and introduce yourself."

I was seething. If I could shoot lightning bolts from my eyes I would have incinerated him and his stupid truck right then and there.

"Ok then, well obviously we got off on the wrong foot, my names Levi and..."

"And I am busy at the moment and in no mood for rude men who have nothing better to do than drive around in the middle of the day."

"I wasn't being rude."

"Have a wonderful day sir, this conversation is over."

"Now wait a second, can I ..."

"Over."

"You're being a little unreasonable."

I went from seething to fuming to erupting, that was the kind of morning this had turned into

"I'm being unreasonable?"

Someone on a bike snapped their head around as they jumped at my volume and tone and nearly crashed into the wood rail separating the trail from the road but I didn't care.

"Relax lady, geez would you just at least put this on please?"

He tossed a flannel shirt out to me looking a little sheepish.

As soon as It touched my hands I threw it right back at him knocking what left of his smirk off his face.

"Why in the world would I want your shirt?! I have asked you to leave me alone, I..."

"You're wearing a white shirt and it's a bit revealing at the moment."

I opened my mouth but nothing came out. A quick glance down and I realized he was right. If Performance T-shirt actually meant 'will cling to every curve creating a perfect mold when wet' then this company had nailed it spot on.

"Look I'm going to go, I have to get back. You keep the shirt. I can get it back... or not. He added the last part as I seared him with the last of my dignity mixed with fury.

"Nice meeting you, I think."

With that he drove away.

No sooner had he left than the Warden pulled up. He took one look at me, turned bright red, mumbled a thank you as he took the bird and placed it ever so gently in the bed of his truck and left.

As his taillights rounded the bend I whipped the flannel shirt as hard as I could at the ground and let out an exasperated scream. Then I felt silly yelling at a shirt and put it on as I didn't need to make anyone else turn red in embarrassment at the sight of my fairly visible chest. Shrugging it on, I headed back to the office wondering how I would return this shirt to a strange man who I hoped I would never see again.

2

LEVI WAS STILL grinning as he pulled into his parking spot. He was just going to say hi and pass along the warden's message. He had run into him at River's, the local coffee spot, said he had a near death experience and needed to wash the cold from his bones and asked Levi to spin by Big Lake parking lot to let the caretaker know he would be a few minutes late. He failed to mention that the caretaker was a she, that she was soaking wet sitting by the side of the road, pissed as hell and had heart stopping eyes. The rest of her he had no doubt would keep his heart racing but he only allowed himself a quick glance as that t-shirt was showing off most likely more than she cared to. Fortunately, those green eyes with hints of gold made it near impossible to tear his gaze away.

Unfortunately, she barely let him get a word in let alone a second to hear his message from Warden. Looking back on it, he should have been a bit more patient and let her get whatever it was that was bugging her out then started a conversation, but patience has never been his strong point. And now she had his favorite shirt. Whether either of them liked it or not he would be swinging by again soon to at least grab that. A man can't live without his favorite shirt.

"Hey Levi, wasn't sure you were going to show that pretty face of yours today. No rush to actually start earning that paycheck you get. It's not as if we are 16 calls deep this morning and it's only 10:36 am."

"Aw Sal, you missed me over the weekend. Didn't know you cared so much. Got you a mocha frappe thing, River says hello."

He gave Sal a wink as he set down her coffee. Sal, short for he wasn't sure what as she always said Sal is more than enough to anyone who asked, was his right, left, top and bottom hand. When he started with the county 10 years ago as a Park Manager Sal took him under her wing. She helped him navigate the political hoopla then and when he was promoted a few years back to District Ranger for the entire county parks and forestry system, he had asked her to move with him and be his assistant. In reality, they were more like partners. She handled the administrative necessities of managing the parks and he dealt with staff and the round the clock calls that ranged from serious to downright ridiculous.

The smartest thing he had done in his career to date was to talk Sal into sticking with him. Sighing deeply, he stared at the calendar. Less than four months and he would have to find out what it would be like to run this place without her unfaltering, no bullshit, everything organized to the last centimeter, diligence. Sal and her husband were retiring and traveling the country in an RV with their three dogs. Her last day was circled in red. With stars, and a smiley face. Problem was he was happy for her, she had earned every bit of retirement but it terrified him to lose her. He sulked a little in his coffee over it all as his computer woke up. The beep from the front desk transfer shook him out of it.

"Must be a full moon tonight, crazies are coming out of the woodwork. Sending a call over to you, a tourist who swears they smelled big foot near their campsite last night. Have fun with this one kiddo."

Levi smirked a little, he could hear the giggle in her voice as she patched the call through.

3

THANKFULLY SHE KEPT a spare set of clothes in her car just in case. Never had it crossed her mind that she would need it to due to a dead goose but such was life she mused. Re-living the event as she finished bagging up her wet clothes, she burst out laughing at how silly it would have looked from shore. The whole thing was a bad comedy skit. Her mood darkened a little as that guy filtered through her head.

What a jerk, I mean really what kind of guy pulls up to a stranger who clearly had a crappy morning and tries to make small talk? And didn't have the decency to tell me I was practically naked? Am I right?"

Luna looked solemnly back, saying with her deep brown eyes I hear you sister, preaching to the choir.

"Thank you, at least someone has my back around here."

Luna thumped her tail against the floor and rolled back onto her side ending the conversation. One huge perk to the new job was that she was able to bring Luna to work with her. It may have been the deciding factor to take said new job, but she would only admit that to Luna herself.

A few years back things were rougher. She had struggled to wade through ending a dead-end relationship, being stuck in an emotionally draining job that did not come close to making up for the stress through financial compensation. Her apartment at the time was cozy, but not in the best part of town. In the part of town she could afford was a more accurate description, but she felt it was livable until her neighbor's apartment was broken into. No one will ever know for sure what happened but the theory was whoever broke in did so because they thought the place was empty. Her neighbor startled them enough that one panicked and shot her. The forced entry, what was taken vs what was left behind and the poor but fatal shot told a tale of inexperienced thieves, not criminal masterminds. She woke the next day to police knocking on all the doors in the building trying to piece together what had happened. Fear took hold that day of her. Every creak, every shadow was danger lurking near. It was crippling in the sense she only went to work then straight home not wanting to be in the city at night which didn't even make sense to her as the thing that triggered the fear happened feet from her front door. Then one day things started falling into place starting with a lump of fur.

Thirty-six steps was what it had taken to get from the front of her building to the curb where she parked her car. Thirty-six steps and roughly 10 seconds. One morning half way through her dash to the perceived safe haven of the car she froze and spun around. A furry softball sized lump was whimpering and shivering next to a garbage can. She picked up the pup staring into her tiny but inquisitive eyes and felt the pup's tail thump against her arms. She never made it to work that day, or the day after or ever again for that matter.

Something snapped free inside of her that day, the fear began to ebb as she took back control of her life. Without any internal debate she hopped into her car, found a vet and after a clean bill of health stocked up on puppy supplies. Back at her apartment giddy to be doing something instead of hiding, she packed everything she owned in two hours flat. Sent a quick, not apologetic in the least email to work saying she could no longer work there, not her most professional moment, and hit the road.

After a couple of years of seasonal jobs, side jobs, freelance work and a dash of creative self-branding, she and Luna had found their way to Maine. Doing a bit of sight-seeing along the southern coast she stumbled across the job posting for Seven Lakes Conservation Education Seasonal Caretaker. 'Quiet town seeks Passionate Outdoor Professional' was the flyers wording. Just a few towns inland and to the north of her current position, it was as if the universe had it all planned out from the beginning. At least that's what she thought when she interviewed and accepted the position.

"What were we thinking dogoo? We should have fact checked a tad bit more before signing on for a season, eh?"

Drying her hair as best she could with an extra T-shirt she rubbed Luna's belly with her foot. Catching a look at herself in the office window reflection she let out a deep sigh. No amount of T-shirt toweling was going to help here.

"My hair has seen better days, far, far better days."

Giving up she tipped her head over and bundled up her lengthy red mess of hair into a haphazard bun and opened the office back up for the day.

No sooner had I sat down to check emails and attempt to drink my already cooling coffee when the front door banged open knocking all of the neatly placed informational print outs off the bulletin board, sending them swirling around the office like angry colorful birds. Parting through the paper birds like a knife stomped in a giant of a man with an incredibly thick, shades of gray beard that came to a perfect triangle point half way down his chest.

"I need to speak to whoever is in charge right this second!"

"Well that would be me, what can I do..."

"No, not the office girl, the director! Now!"

He threw his hands in the air as though he was signaling a touchdown. I really thought about saying the director was at lunch and I would be happy to take a message. Just for a second.

"Well you're out of luck. By default, I'm the Director, office girl, occasional plumber and handyman for the Center. Everyone is gone for the season except me, seasonal caretaker at your service. How can I help you?"

He looked eerily similar to a Halloween decoration with his angry eyes and mouth frozen open as he paused while processing what I just said.

He didn't seem dangerous, just furious. Even so, I took a slow causal step sideways to the back of the desk where I had a trusty baseball bat tucked away. No matter where I worked, a baseball bat blended in really well and never looked overly aggressive. Over the years living on my own I had learned a woman can never be too careful. Luna on the other hand, who lives with more of a gypsy outlook, chose that moment to stand up, yawn, stretch and saunter over to his feet where she sat on top of his boot and gazed up patiently.

The instant their eyes met the angry man melted into that of a cooing high-pitched fan girl.

"Well look at you pretty girl! Where did you come from? Awe there, there, how 'bout an ear massage. Oh yes, you are a looker. Sweet thing you."

That was Luna. Always knew how to make an entrance, timed it perfectly every single time to bail me out of something.

I cleared my throat politely to remind my visitor I was still here and wondering what he wanted.

"This is Luna, Luna meet..."

"Harvey, my name is Harvey White."

He glanced up as he spoke this time with a hint of a smile playing at his lips.

"Sorry for the rude entry, I've just had it up to here with this shit, oh sorry sweetie didn't mean to swear in front of you."

He of course was addressing Luna again at this point.

"Walters, the guy who was running this place kept saying he was taking care of it but I went out there again today and it's the same story. Sick and tired of it for crying out loud."

"As crazy as it sounds, I only met Walters twice, briefly. Once when I interviewed, then again when he hired me a few weeks ago and basically handed me the keys and a few files. I would love to help you but you're going to have to walk me through whatever it is that you're sick of."

He took a deep breath and slid into a chair as he exhaled, keeping a hand on Luna.

"The meat. The rancid horrible meat."

"Ah, well that sounds, hmm, well bad?"

I wasn't sure where this was going.

"Almost a year it's been happening. Someone keeps filling the garbage can to the park that's right across from my driveway to where it's overflowing with meat. One day it will be empty, the next thing I know I'm waking up in the middle of the night to some critter trying to get at it and when they can't get through the bear lid, they start nosing around the yard trying to get into the hen house or the kennel where I keep the team's food!"

I must have been staring with a blank look on my face, as he paused and gave me a 'I am wasting my breath with this one' look. Truth be told I felt I was pretty quick with most things but I was having a hell of a time following what was happening.

"Ok, so your team's food is in a kennel that is just outside the park?"

"I run sled dogs."

He said the next part very slowly to drive home the point that I was not up to the task of solving this in his mind.

"My sled dog team lives in the kennel and that is also where I store their food."

"And the meat..."

"Is being dumped in the garbage at night. It's rotten and a violation!

And no one will do anything about it! Each time it happens I risk my dogs getting hurt by a bear, coyote, skunk or all of the above, not to mention it reeks to high heaven for days after and has to weigh over 300 lbs. because I can't move the damn thing! And I shouldn't be the one moving it, it's on park property!"

This did not sound like anything I wanted to deal with and hoped to hell that it was something I didn't have to deal with. What were the chances this would be a quick look into it and be done? Maybe I could walk the line in between, find out whose problem it was, pass it along and tell my dog loving friend it was being handled. If my subconscious could slap me it would have, I am not that lucky.

"Is there meat in the garbage now?"

"YES! Haven't you been listening? For crying out loud, what do we pay you people for?! If this is our tax dollars at work I might as well start burning my money for heat!"

"I was listening! It's a lot to process. Rancid meat in a can is not something anyone has a handy fix-all for. For the love of, I don't know what, I am trying to figure out how to help you!"

I must have looked crazy enough with my hands waving around my head trying to make my point and my eyes wide and bulgy because he stopped and just stared at me for what felt like eternity.

"Alright then, let's see what you got. Follow me."

With that statement, he stood up and strode out the door so fast its thwack against the door frame shook the entire 10 x 10 department, knocking cobwebs from behind the 1970's ceiling tiles into my horrible, office-coffee-maker coffee.

Sitting, staring at the door, I weighed my options. I let out a long sigh.

"Come on Luna. This day can't get any worse and we need a coffee that doesn't taste like burnt leather."

Luna stretched, shook and waltzed out the door to the work truck as I taped a 'Be back in an hour' sign on the door and pulled it shut.

"I hope we're back in an hour," I muttered as I opened the cab for Luna and leaped in beside her. Harvey honked his horn rather aggressively and sped off a few feet before slamming on the brakes and honking again. His arm waved frantically out the window signaling for me to get a move on and follow him.

Shifting into first gear I couldn't help but think this was a bad horror movie and I was walking right into the b grade plot.

4

Harvey White had left another message on his machine about meat. Always about the rotting meat near his kennel. Problem was each time he went to look into it, someone had already taken care of it leaving him with nothing to go off of. Harvey swore up and down he never moved it but mysteriously it leaves without a trace. If Levi had to put money down it would be on Harvey taking care of it himself and stirring the pot just because. The last time he went to take a look, after taking his call, their conversation escalated rather quickly to shouting when he tried to explain he couldn't do anything if Harvey wouldn't leave everything where he found it and wait for him to get there. Overpaid lazy rent a ranger was the insult that caused him to burst out laughing which led to Harvey losing his head and really laying into the verbal barrage. He was supposed to be the professional, he should have let the old man vent and found a way to help. Coming out today was his way of making peace. He just hoped that whatever was in the can had been left this time so he could hopefully do something about it.

Technically, the can in question was not his problem. It would fall on the hands of local police as his property was technically in town, as remote as it was, and not park or forestry land. The local police force consisted of one Chief of police, who was more often drunk than sober, and his assistant who had her hands full doing the job of two people.

Jackie was good at her job and could go anywhere. Her kids and family kept her where she was for the last 20 years and he bet at this point, she was just waiting for the Chief to step down, allowing her to officially take over. Levi hoped that that happened as he believed she would make really positive changes given half a chance. Towns like this only survive when everyone looks out for everyone else. It takes a community to raise a kid they say but Levi always thought it takes a community to run a community as well.

"Well this should be interesting."

His eyebrows shot up in surprise as he parked his truck at White's and a smile escaped as he registered Harvey had not only called him but apparently the now dry mystery woman caretaker.

"Good afternoon Harvey," he called as he hopped down out of his truck and grabbed his notebook and a few pairs of gloves.

I couldn't believe it. I had just stepped out of the truck when his voice had my head snapping around like a deranged owl.

"You, what are you doing here?!"

"You know Levi? Perfect! Both of you can figure this out finally! Meat's over there, just follow the stench and flies. I have to go feed the dogs. Come up to the house when you're done."

And with that he strode away before I could firmly inform him this creep was following me.

I was winding up to let him have it. I took a breath and opened my mouth to yell when Luna jumped out of the truck's open window and sauntered over to say hello.

"Luna, get over here!"

It came out more of a hiss and growl. Already flustered, I could feel the heat creeping into my face. Being a redhead has its perks, being able to hide your emotions is not one of them.

"Hello pretty eyes."

The creep was down on his knees crooning into my dog's face. So much for Luna's judgement of character. Clearly, she had zero skill in that department.

"Looks like your human is a tad upset at me. How about we start over."

With the last statement he spoke not so much to Luna as he said it while gazing directly at me. I wanted to stay mad. I had my jaw clenched and eyes set in mad mode. Luna's tail thumped metronome style on the ground as he rubbed her belly and the sincerity in his smoke gray eyes had me relenting a little.

"I'm Shelly and this is Luna."

He gave her one final rub, stood up and extended his hand with a hint of a smirk that he quickly bit back.

"Levi. Nice to meet you officially, and sorry about earlier today. The plan was just to introduce myself."

"Let's let earlier be, oh I don't know, done. I'm, hmm well I'm sorry as well. Could have been a little nicer."

It took some serious effort to choke out the meager apology and had my face turning red again. It didn't escape my attention that the redder my face grew the more his eyes smiled. I didn't realize someone's eyes could smile let alone down right chuckle.

"What were you doing anyway sitting with trash on the side of the road?"

"Went for a swim with the Warden."

"You went for a swim? With the Warden? In a T-shirt in October..."

The redness was now taking over my whole body. Levi cut himself off and threw his hands up in defense.

"Right, moving on."

I rolled my eyes and shook my head to clear out the negative thoughts that started to swirl again. Pondered for a minute if the rolling of eyes was counterproductive to a head clearing and dove into the next chapter of the day.

"So, I know why I was summoned here, why did Harvey feel he needed both of us?"

"He's been trying to get someone out here to look at his 'meat' issue for ages. Anytime he called I couldn't tromp right over and by the time I would get here, he'd have it all cleared out and nothing for me to go off of."

"So, you're a meat detective?"

The sarcasm was not missed by Levi as I gave him my best quizzical look.

"District Ranger for the Parks and Forestry Division for the county. Not as glamorous as a meat detective but I get my own Forestry Truck and all the syrup I can eat. Someday I'll reach my dream of being a meat detective, but until then, Levi the Forester at your service."

He finished with a mock bow that had Luna wagging at warp speed.

"Ha, ha, very funny."

I couldn't bite back my smirk. This aspiring meat detective was growing on me.

"This seems like a case more up your alley but I'm here and a little intrigued. What is the deal with this whole ... mystery?."

Levi filled me in on as much as he knew. Someone had been filling up the 50-gallon garbage can near Harvey's property with rotting meat, randomly over the course of the last six months, or longer. It would be there for as long as a few days or sometimes only a few hours.

"Chief of police made it out for a few of the drops but didn't find anything to point a finger at anyone, and other than an annoyance to Harvey, wasn't a big enough issue to call anyone else in."

He paused, took his hat off and ran a hand through his slightly shaggy hair and shrugged his shoulders.

"At this point I'm with you, more intrigued than worried, but Harvey has a point about his dog's safety and anyone who happens by here. As we head into fall this meat will for sure attract the coyotes and any other critter looking for an easy meal. Wildlife mingling with locals is never a good thing. For that reason alone, I am hoping to figure this out."

As he spoke I watched the flies swarm around the can. A whole horde of them swirling up and down as they moved trying to find a way in.

"I can smell it from here. It's like a train wreck that you know is going to be horrific but you can't turn away. Alright, I'm going to take a huge breath and hold It as long as possible. Ready to investigate?"

Levi held up a hand to stop me.

"I have a better idea."

Levi sauntered over to his truck and rummaged through the glove compartment.

"Here, wipe this under your nose. It will block out most of the scent."

"Vapor Rub?"

"Don't look at me like that, it really works! Trust me."

"How do you know it works? You just said you've never made it to a meat dump."

"Part of my, oh so glamorous job is to scrape roadkill out of the way. Trust me, if this can block the smell of a three -day bloated rotting deer in the sun, it will block this."

He tossed the container over and returned to his truck to dig something else out.

"Well I guess that makes sense. Vapor rub it is."

I applied an overly generous amount that had my eyes watering and brain tingling and handed it back to Levi who applied nowhere near as much as I had. I consoled myself with the thought that he deals with super stenches more often, most likely has a tolerance to it all.

"Want Luna in the truck?"

"Yes, please. Can I roll the windows up a tad? She has a slight tendency to leave whenever she feels like it. Never goes far, but she doesn't need to be a part of this."

He nodded, rolled the windows up and moved some things out of the front seat for her to sit comfortably.

"Hop on up pretty girl."

He smiled at her when he said it and gave her a friendly rub as he shut the door. Hated to admit it but this guy may not be the creep I thought he was.

Walking over to the garbage can, I looked around. It was a very secluded corner; the only sign of housing was the start of Harvey's gravel driveway but even that took a bend quickly and was mostly hidden by the trees. The other side was all forest aside from the slightly widened shoulder that we were parked on.

"Is this Harvey's property that it sits on?"

"No, his property line ends about 10 feet from the road on that side. The edge of his driveway where the Kennel sign is, is actually town property. Town owns 10 feet on either side of every road."

"Really?"

I wasn't sure if he was pulling my leg, I would have to look this up later I thought.

"Yeah, I think the idea was in case any culverts have to go in, gas lines, that sort of thing, the Town wouldn't have to get permission from every homeowner to make needed improvements. Technically, when you look at the map, the Town property line falls about 15 feet short of the garbage can, the County Forest line doesn't kick in until a mile or so down the road and the Center's property line is a wiggly one that runs 30 feet from the shore all around the lake, making this area a no-man's land."

"What's the Center?"

I had been meaning to sit down and really memorize a local map but it hadn't been a priority at this point.

"What's the center?"

He was looking at me with an are-you-serious sort of look.

"Shelly, you uh are the caretaker of the Center, aren't you?"

I should have been embarrassed but at this point on this particular day not knowing where I worked was the least embarrassing thing to happen.

"I was just testing you."

Shrugging it off I made a mental note to devour the map when I returned.

"The locals call Seven Lakes Environmental Conservation Area the Center. Originally, it was supposed to be built in the center of town but wetlands got in the way and it migrated to where it is now 40 some years ago. I'll give you the 10-cent tour when we're done here, free of charge and I'll even throw in a cup of coffee from River's."

"I can find my own way around, thank you for the offer."

I tried to make myself look dignified and in control as I said this, but It came out sounding a bit haughty and not convincing as I wiped vapor rub tears from my eyes.

Levi let out a laugh and shook his head.

"I get it, you're an independent woman."

He made the quotes with his fingers as he said independent.

"You're new in town and if I know Walters he left you next to nothing to work off of in terms of what's what. Getting a cup of coffee with the District Ranger would be networking, nothing else."

He said the last bit with a smirk and looked as though he was going to elbow me in a chiding fashion but thought better of it.

"Come on, you don't even know where you work Shel."

"It's Shelly. I don't need..."

Oh what the hell. My day can't get any worse and the coffee in the office tastes horrible. I had tried to muster up a solid argument but couldn't.

A little local insight would be helpful as I was going to be living here for the next 6 months. Besides, a good cup of coffee sounded like heaven.

"Ten cent tour, nothing else, twenty minutes tops."

"Deal."

We had reached the garbage at this point. Levi crouched down to look at the ground.

"No tire tracks, grounds pretty soft still from the rain the other day. Nothing out of the ordinary other than it's full of wrapped meat."

Levi was walking slow circles around the can looking at the ground for something to help with the puzzle.

"So, whose can is this? It doesn't have the logo on it like the ones by the office."

Levi paused and looked thoughtfully.

"Doesn't have the Towns logo or the Forestry either. Hmm. Good question."

"Who's been emptying it?"

"Ah, that's a good question too. I assumed the Town, but now that you asked I'm not positive."

I smiled a little in spite of the stench, and gave myself a mental pat on the back. May not know where I work I thought, but I'm a better meat detective than you sir. I took a long stick and started poking at the contents.

"What are you doing?"

"Seeing what's in here."

"By stabbing it with a stick? What's that going to tell you?"

I opened my mouth to answer but nothing came out. I had no idea what it was going to tell me.

"Well... It's firm-ish."

Levi blinked and stared at me blankly then slid on a pair of gloves and proceeded to cut open the bag. He reached in and pulled out what I supposed was a hunk of meat. Instead of looking gross and full of maggots as I had braced myself for, it was a neatly paper wrapped bundle complete with a small piece of tape. Something you would get at your local butcher for Sunday dinner not rancid mystery meat.

"I wasn't expecting that."

"That's what I was just thinking."

I inched a little closer as Levi cut open the paper wrapping. Carefully he pulled back the wrap and out oozed horrible meaty juice with a few maggots. I bit back a gag and retreated a few steps.

"Now that's what I was expecting, ugh."

Levi shot a wink my way and then proceeded to pull out a few more wrapped packages, cutting each open and peeking at the contents. He stayed in his catcher's stance squat in silence as he pulled out a notepad.

"Maybe Harvey knows who's been emptying it."

I didn't know what else to do and started walking up the driveway to his kennel. Levi glanced up from the notes he was making.

"Be up in a minute."

He paused for a second just as I was rounding the corner and yelled up to me.

"Harvey's house is the smaller building, the kennel is the thing that looks like a house."

5

Levi wasn't sure quite what to make of all of this. As he talked it out with Shel- er Shelly, he corrected himself mentally, what seemed odd became downright strange. Had that sixth sense making that nagging feeling in his stomach when something's wrong. He had learned to trust that instinct over the years. Was a firm believer that Mother Nature had given him a healthy dose of intuition, just had to be willing to listen to it. The times he hadn't he had paid the price, could feel the scar on his shoulder blade as he thought about it.

Nothing was left behind or pressed into the earth to give a clue as to who had been here. Best place to start was to figure out the answers to Shelly's questions. He tucked his notebook into his back pocket and started up the driveway after her.

He could see her about fifty feet ahead of him. She was smart, a worldly smart, not a know it all smart, and independent to say the least. He may have teased her about it earlier but it was a trait he admired, needy damsel in distress was not his idea of good company. As he followed behind her, walking a little faster to catch up he grinned, didn't mind his current view one bit either.

6

Just as Levi had described, at the top of the gravel drive sat two buildings. One looked like a cute house, white with blue shutters, window boxes that had end of season flowers still blooming with a blue metal roof. The other was a clapboard structure that resembled more of a dilapidated shed. Someone had installed a few windows into it on the side facing the driveway and gave it a touch of home with a welcome mat that read wipe your paws.

"Shed or dog palace?"

"Shhh."

Levi chuckled as he whispered his shushes.

"Don't let Harvey hear you say that or you'll be on his list and get the cold shoulder for the rest of the year. For certain will not be invited to his holiday mixer."

"Holiday mixer in his shed, I would be devastated to not get an invite."

I placed the back of my hand on my forehead and made a dramatic swoon over the thought. Harvey chose at that moment to exit the pup palace.

"Meat got to you didn't it? Come in, sit down. I'll get you something to take care of it." I started to stop him to say I was fine, just goofing around when Levi gently elbowed me in the rips to stop.

"Just go with it, I've never gotten an invite into the Kennel. I want to see what's inside."

He wiggled his eyebrows Groucho Marx style as he sped up to catch the door behind a vanishing Harvey. I couldn't help but laugh. Oh, what a day and it wasn't even lunch time yet.

As soon as we entered, we both stopped dead in our tracks. Which was a good thing as no sooner had we entered than Harvey yelled from around the corner to take our shoes off or put the boot covers over our shoes before we entered. Apparently, his kennel was chemical free and he took no chances with what may be dragged in on shoes. I couldn't help but wonder if he made his dogs wear dog booties inside.

The room that we stepped into was one big open space, any walls that may have been there when the house was built were gone. Each wall was lined with large kennels that had walls that went up far enough to keep the pups in their own space, but stopped about 6 feet up leaving the tops open to the vaulted ceiling. The whole set up reminded me of a mini horse barn with stalls built for dogs. The interior was painted a crisp white, the center of the room had a durable woven light blue rug that took up most of the floor space. A wood burning fireplace was in the center and had two giant toy boxes overflowing with dog toys on either side. A set of blue wingback chairs were tucked in the far back corner and looked as though they stayed there until dragged out for human use. I assumed human use, but looking around... maybe not.

"Ah, Harvey? Where did you go?"

Levi looked as stunned as I felt as we stood rooted to the doorstep in our pull-on booties.

"Come straight back towards the fireplace, there's a door on the left."

As we strode past the dogs, each one came to the door, their big husky tails thumping the ground.

"They are all so quiet. I've never been to a kennel that wasn't a roar of noise as soon as someone walked in."

I was in awe of the dog's mild manners. We reached the door and turned into a little kitchen area and found Harvey pouring something that smelled like fall into three mugs.

"Your dogs are so calm, I thought Luna was well mannered, but your crew takes the cake."

Harvey smiled and handed each of us a mug and motioned for us to sit around a well -loved but sparkling clean farm table.

"They know this is their home, their quiet spot to relax. When they get outside, a whole 'nother story. As soon as they see their gear, they start singing, wrestling, and get all worked up. They love to run."

"So, you train sled dogs?"

I took a sip of the warm liquid and then a hearty gulp as it was a delicious warm cider-y concoction.

"Train, breed and race. Family business since the 30's."

You could hear the pride in Harvey's voice as he talked about his dogs and business. It was an interesting story about how it started out as a delivery service during the rough months of winter when trucks couldn't get around and eventually evolved from hobby to passion to being one of the top breeders in the world. The gruff person I encountered earlier was replaced by a gentle story teller. After over an hour that seemed like minutes and another cup of cider, Harvey cleared his throat changing the subject.

"Enough about all of that, what did you two find out and more importantly what are you going to do about it?"

Harvey stood and refilled mine and his mugs as he waited for a reply. As I waited for Levi to say something I couldn't help but snuggle into my chair a little, this kitchen is very, very cozy I mused. I looked up and locked eyes with Levi. He had a strange expression on his face, one I couldn't read, but it felt like a good time to wiggle my eyebrows at him like he did earlier.

Levi bit back a laugh and cleared his throat.

"No answers at this moment but a handful of questions to start us off. Do you know who's been emptying the can when you call it in?"

"No idea. Sometimes it sits for a full day, others I call about it and run out for a bit and by the time I get back it's empty. Never seen anyone fill or empty it."

He had a handful of additional questions for Harvey about his daily routine, neighbors and other things that stuck out as odd but nothing striking came up. Levi thought about that as he glanced at Shelly, who had just finished her third cup. Harvey, being an impeccable host, stood up to refill it again this time Levi intervened.

"Well thank you for inviting us in, Harvey, time for us to go. Luna's waiting in the car and we have a few other people to talk to about this. Give me a call on my cell if you see anyone empty it."

"Yes, thank you Harvey."

My body at the moment had a mind of its own and walked over to him and gave him a hug. Harvey's face turned red as he sputtered out your welcome. I spun around to face Levi, "Let's hit the road Jack."

I attempted to walk out the door but tripped on Levi's boot and almost face planted into the floor. Levi caught me by the back of my coat before I smashed into the floor. As he stood me upright I burst out laughing, patted him on his shoulder and sauntered out the door humming.

Levi cleared his throat, "Harvey, what was in the cider?"

"Oh, just a little rum, takes the chill out of the bones this time of year."

"How much is a little?"

Harvey looked a little put out at the question.

"I don't measure, just go by feel. Tasted perfect, didn't it?"

Levi glanced at the counter and saw a half empty fifth sitting there next to the cider. Oh brother, this was going to be an interesting afternoon. He yelled a thanks and a reminder to call him as he trotted out the door after Shelly.

SOMEHOW Shelly had gotten down the driveway to the trucks by the time he caught up to her. She was sitting next to the tire with Luna standing watch.

"Levi, what was in that drink?"

The feel-good feeling had passed on the walk down the drive as whatever was in there hit her empty stomach. She had her elbows on her knees with her head resting in her hands.

"Ah rum, a lot of rum. I didn't know it was in there or I would have warned you."

She glared up at him looking a little green. Levi scuffed the ground with this toe feeling a little sheepish. It wasn't his fault she drank it, he reminded himself.

"I hate cider. Just pretend to take a few sips to be polite."

"Didn't taste any rum, just cider. The ground is spinning. Please go, Luna and I will camp out here."

"You're going to camp here, with zero gear, in October? Next to a can of rotting meat?"

At the mention of the meat I turned a solid shade of green and threw my hands up covering my mouth. I stood up quickly and stumbled over to the bushes. Levi made a lunge to help but Luna knocked him back and gave a low warning growl.

"Easy, pretty girl, just trying to help."

Up until that point he hadn't really noticed how big Luna was. Easy 80 lbs. and looking much larger with her hair standing up.

This day couldn't get any worse. I turned around to see Levi with his hands in the air being rooted to the spot by a growling Luna. God, she loved that dog. Taking a breath, she stood up, placed a hand on a friendly tree to steady herself and gave a quick whistle to call off Luna. Luna turned her head and gave a glance to say, are you sure?

"Yes, let him go."

Luna trotted over to her and she transferred her hand from tree to dog.

"As you can see we are just fine. Have some food in the truck, we will re-group and then head out."

Levi glanced into the truck that belonged to the Center. It was a bare bones 1975 Ford pickup that had nothing in the front seat.

"The truck looks pretty sparse. Show me what you have and I'll be on my way."

She looked at Levi and then the truck. Oh Shit, she brought the work truck not her truck. This is the Tuesday from hell she thought.

"Look, I appreciate your help but I do not need you to do anything. We are both adults, we are good."

Taking a breath, she let go of Luna and attempted to walk strongly to the truck to make her point. Three steps in she was drifting to the left when the ground shifted and she ended up on her hands and knees.

"I'm fine, the ground is uneven. Harvey should have that fixed, it's a hazard."

She was scrambling to get up as soon as she wiped out. Levi hoped he wouldn't have to force her into his truck, no question about it if he did he would be stopping at the emergency room to treat a dog bite. He couldn't leave her there and she sure as hell couldn't drive. Stubborn women gave him a headache.

"How about this. I owe you a cup of coffee and I could use some lunch. We can swing back to grab your truck after."

She looked ready to argue. Thinking quickly he threw in that they could stop by the Town Hall to ask about the garbage can and check on the normal pickup route and maybe even snag a few garbage men to chat with about the mystery meat, see if they had seen anything as they emptied it. Still silent. He opened the truck door and made an after you gesture.

Her head hurt, her knee hurt, her hand hurt and she wanted to vomit again. Food and coffee would help. She sighed and dragged herself and what was left of her dignity to the passenger side of his truck.

"I don't need any help."

"Duly noted."

"Stop smirking."

"Not smirking."

He climbed in and shut his door. Luna hopped up in the middle and they both waited patiently for her to follow suit.

"Please drive slow."

I shut my eyes and rested my head against the cool window. When I noticed we weren't moving I opened them again and saw Levi had a rag outstretched towards me.

"Why do I want that?"

He eyed me carefully before answering.

"You have some pine needles and well fur stuck in your vapor rub. I don't care if you leave it. It gives you that woodsy run with wolves look."

I glanced in the side mirror and saw my horrible furry, dirty mustache.

"Shoot me now, please."

I took the rag and closed my eyes again to Levi laughing, thankfully attempting to hide it, and backing the truck out of the drive.

7

WHAT SHOULD HAVE been a 40 minute drive felt like 10. The truck slowed to a stop, gears shifted into park. I had my head leaning on the passenger window. I was enjoying the coolness on one cheek while the other was being toasted by the heater. I opened one eye and read the large sign over the cozy looking building. River's Café. My mind was all yes cute coffee shop let's go, while my stomach was sticking firmly in the no way no how camp.

"I may just wait here, with Luna."

Added to not feeling well, I also realized I had left my wallet in the work truck. Having Levi drive my drunk butt was one thing, needing him to pick up the tab was too much for one day. Time to throw Luna under the bus I thought.

"Luna was stuck in the truck too much today, I'll wait with her. Take as long as you need."

Levi glanced over, thinking her color looked a little better. He contemplated his next move.

"Tell you what, you two snag one of the outdoor tables and I'll meet you there. How do you take your coffee?"

"No thank you, I am all set."

"It's not a problem and River's has the best brew this side of the Mil-lonecket. Even have a good mocha concoction, so I'm told, if that's more your cup of tea. Or tea, she has tea."

"Nope. All set."

I stared out the side window to make my point. The silence was start-ing to become awkward.

"How about.."

"I said no thank you, no means no."

I snapped rather snippy, glaring at him over Luna's head. Luna, who is afraid of nothing, does not like conflict and chose that moment to lay down which would have been fine, except I had one hand braced on her shoulder and lurched forward ruining the effect I was going for.

Levi looked more than a little exasperated.

"Fine, have it your way I'll get you something and hopefully you will hate it."

He said the last bit louder and more sarcastically than he intended as he stalked away from the truck. This woman was ridiculous, can't take a friendly gesture.... He let out a forceful sigh that had a bit of a deep growl to it.

No one was waiting as he walked up to the empty counter. He was stand-ing for no more than a few seconds when River popped her head out of the kitchen.

"Hey Levi, twice in one day? Rough Tuesday?"

River teased him a little. She had known him since she set up shop five years ago. He was one of her first customers to become a regular. A few years older than Levi, although no one would ever guess as she had that youthful beauty that made people think for sure she was in her twenties when really she only had a few years to go before hitting the big 4- 0, she enjoyed his company.

"You could say that."

He forced a smile then went to order but nothing came out.

"Ah, I'll have a large black and..."

Oh hell he thought. She was already grumpy and feeling crappy, what do I get her when she doesn't want anything?

"Make it two. No, just one and a cup of tea."

"Ok, what kind of tea?"

"What do you mean what kind, just tea, you know hot tea with the bag on the string."

River gave him a look then spoke slowly.

"Yes Levi, we have hot tea. All kinds of hot tea. Black, Chia, Earl Gray, Green, Breakfast, Vanilla, Herbal, Caffeinated..."

"Oh for the love of... never mind I'll just take the coffee."

Exasperated, he started to fumble with his wallet trying to get out of there as quickly as possible.

"One or two my dear."

"Two! Just two black coffees!"

"No tea then?"

River couldn't resist, she hadn't seen him this worked up in ages.

"River, just two coffees. Please, I beg you."

The teasing calmed him down a bit, he let out a long breath.

"Actually, do you have any cream and sugar to go?"

Options, taking her options would be a safe bet.

"So, who is it that has you all worked up?"

She was filling a bag with a handful of creamers and sugar packets as she poked at him a little more.

"Know it's not Sal, she wouldn't touch a plain cup of coffee, even from here. Definitely a woman, you would not go to this trouble for a fellow man."

When his face flushed a little she knew she hit the nail on the head.

"Ah so it is a woman! Good for you, spill it."

She leaned over the counter expectantly.

"River it's not like that, it's... she's a professional....got called out on the same call is all and she needed a lift back to town."

He was flustered to the point he kept shifting from one foot to the other lifting his arms up and down as he didn't know where to place them. He needed to get out of here.

"Thank you, I gotta go."

He slapped a ten on the counter and started to back out the door.

"Keep the change."

River laughed out loud, it was fun seeing Mr. Cool as a cucumber a bit rattled.

"Bye handsome, have a good day!"

For whatever reason, River's farewell put him in a more of a foul mood. He was stomping by the time he got to the picnic table.

"Here, coffee. Cream and sugar in the bag."

He sat down abruptly and took a long slug.

"Thank you, you didn't have to."

She was a little annoyed he had gotten her one, but also thankful, which made her more annoyed with herself. Dumping a healthy dose of cream followed by a dash of sugar, she stirred it up and took a deep breath. It smelled heavenly. Taking a tentative sip her taste buds did a jig and her stomach didn't blanch. Victory she thought and took several sips with her eyes shut in silence.

He was staring at her, waiting for her to say something. She was just sitting there sipping, eyes shut. He opened his mouth more than once to break the silence, but stopped himself. Not sure what else to do he slugged his coffee down and waited.

"This is really good. So, where do we stand with the mystery meat?"

"We?"

I narrowed my eyes a little over my coffee I had cradled in both hands.

"Yes, we. I'm hooked on the whole mystery meat. Maine Mystery

Meat, or maybe Malicious Meat of Mystery, Mushers Meat Mayhem..
Or..."

"Really? Are you done?"

"Alliterations make the world go round my fine friend."

"Oh ho, so I'm a friend now!"

He jerked back as he said it and feigned shock with his hand over his
heart.

"Har, har. Catch me up, what did we learn with our visit to Harvey's
house of dogs?"

"Meat shows up and disappears randomly, has been for over 6 months,
and Harvey is not the one to empty it nor does he know who does. I
looked through most of the can and it was filled with individually wrapped
butcher style packages but none of the packages had a price tag or store
sticker on them. All of them were about the same size give or take a little
bit, only real difference in some of them was the color tape holding the
package together. Some were blue, others brown and a few black."

"What if someone just bought way too much meat and didn't know
what to do with it?"

"Multiple times? And that's easily 300 lbs. worth of meat, who the hell
would over buy that much?"

"A hoarder? Maybe they can't stop themselves from buying it and
then realize they have way too much?"

Levi smiled and shrugged.

"Possibility."

I thought about all of this as I took another slow sip.

"Well it shouldn't be too hard to find out who the can belongs to and
that should tell us who is emptying it."

"Shouldn't be."

Levi stood up and drained the rest of his coffee, glanced up at the sky
that was starting to sprinkle rain.

"When I get back I'll make some calls, see who's doing what."

He started walking back to the truck.

"Do you want to come with me or should I drop you two at the center?"

"Actually, if you don't mind, can you spin us back to the truck?"

His silence irked her for most likely no reason other than the day had sucked and she had the start of a pounding headache thanks to Harvey's over hospitality.

"Never mind, we'll walk."

I let out a short whistle that had Luna jumping up and trotting ahead of me.

"Hey! Just wait a sec."

Levi trotted a few steps then stopped as it began to really rain. He jogged back to his truck as he fished his keys out of his pocket grumbling to himself about stubborn women.

I slowed to a stop as his truck pulled up alongside us. We had made it to the corner before he caught up. It was now pouring out and for the second time today I felt like a drowned rat. Luna looked up at me, also a drowned rat. I turned and glared at him. It was childish, but that was the mood I was in.

Levi took one look and decided to keep his mouth shut. Years ago Sal had beaten it into him that the best thing to say is nothing when you get 'that' look from a woman. He wasn't always quick on the uptake but this for sure was one of those times. He leaned over and opened the door without a word.

Luna took one look at me and leapt inside and shook all over the dash and Levi. I bit back a laugh as I climbed in and resisted the urge to follow her lead and add to soaking the inside. He pulled a tattered woven blanket from somewhere and handed it wordlessly over. As I wrapped it around us I vowed to stare straight ahead no matter what. I was officially in a mood and I didn't care one bit. Shitty, rainy day from hell.

8

Levi pulled up next to her truck and threw his into park, waiting to see what this exasperating but comical duo would do next. He kept his silence as she opened the door, Luna nudged his arm then leaped over her to exit and use the outdoor facilities. She had stared straight ahead the entire ride, he kept glancing over on the drive. He was impressed with her stone-cold stare as she attempted to untangle herself from the blanket, not softening one bit. She bumped the visor in the process and all the maps he had tucked up took flight throughout his truck. He couldn't contain it, the look on her face threw him over the top. He started to laugh and couldn't stop.

"I'm glad you think this is so funny. Why the hell do you have a thousand maps, this is agh!"

I laid my head on the dashboard in defeat. I took a deep breath.

"I'm going to go now, before anything else happens."

He was still grinning as I turned to look at him.

"You can stop laughing now please. My humiliation limit has been hit. Goodbye."

"You're welcome, and I hope we do this again, you are...very unique."

"100% positive, that is not really a compliment."

I swung myself out and shut the door and started walking but stopped mid-way to the truck.

"Hey, do you see that?"

Levi rolled his window down.

"Decided to say thank you after all?"

"No, you jerk, do you see that?"

I pointed to the now empty garbage can.

"Huh, well there goes any digging."

He got out and walked around looking for tire tracks, anything really.

"I don't see anything that tells us, anything."

"We were only gone for two hours?"

"Tops"

"For it to go midday it must be on someone's route, don't you think?"

"That would be my guess."

He walked back to his truck, hands stuffed into his coat pocket.

"I'll call you with what I find out."

He pulled out his phone and leaned with his elbows resting on the hood

"What's your number?"

"You can call the center."

"I thought we were friends."

He grinned up at me from under his hat.

"Business acquaintances."

I glanced over my shoulder as I climbed in and gave him a withering look, whistling for Luna. He was still smiling as I drove by.

9

THE REST OF the day was mercifully uneventful, the night even more so. When I was greeted by the blinking red light on the answering machine at the center the following morning I hit play, very optimistic that today was going to be a good day.

First message wasn't so bad, Mrs. Tullan wanted to know if the beach was still open for swimming. Nope, it was now October, last day was in August, easy call back. Next was from Levi, saying he made some calls and to give him a buzz when I got in. I decided to call that one back after lunch, no reason to tempt fate and ruin a fairly good morning. The last was just a number left by a polite voice asking for a return call when we opened, the message had only been left a few minutes before I walked in. Why I called that one back first, I'll never know.

The voice picked up on the first ring.

"Hi this is Shelly calling from..."

"What the hell took you so long to call back?!"

"Excuse me?"

"Absolutely unacceptable! I'm going to write a letter of complaint, waste of resources letting inept individuals be in charge!"

"Ma'am, I"

"Well you could at least apologize! Or do you think you're better than me?"

"Whoa, hold on lady, apologize for what?"

I had no idea who this was and she was on the other end screaming at me. The universe was mad at me. The only logical explanation I could come up with, the universe was pissed as hell at me.

"Do you think it's just fine to waltz into work and open whenever you please? We have an extremely tight schedule that must be kept."

"Hold up a second, I am the seasonal caretaker and yes I can open up whenever I want because the center is technically closed for the season! There are no set hours, it's October, mid -October!"

"Mark my words I will have your job by the end of the day, this behavior is completely out of line!"

I laughed out loud. At this point it was either that or cry.

"You can have my job! Please take it! Just do me a favor, would you please tell me what horrible thing I did or didn't do?!"

Silence. My outburst was rewarded with silence for a few seconds then a very prim voice coolly answered.

"The bocce courts are atrocious. Not a single one is lined and we start in 15 minutes."

That fact that there were Bocce courts was news to me but didn't feel this was the time to share that thought. I have this under control.

"Which courts are you referring to?"

"The only Bocce courts in town."

She drew out the word only. So much for being in control. I filled my cheeks with air and let out a long breath as I stared at the ceiling.

"Look, I started a few weeks ago. Nothing was left about Bocce courts or that they needed anything done to them. Who are you, where are you and what do you need?"

The angry Bocce enthusiast was Betty Ann, the un-official programmer for the unofficial Bocce Club. Each summer they ran a seasonal Bocce league that ended with a round robin playoff. Apparently, this summer the playoffs were cancelled first due to monsoon style rain, then oppressive heat, followed by a large portion of the players being out of town for a bus trip to Canada and on it went until the makeup day was pushed until today, October 17th.

Betty Ann had booked the day back in August with Walters, and apparently had a permit. It had been promised everything would be ready. Ready it was not.

I had told her that I would get everything set as best I could and should only take 20 minutes. After rummaging through the storage shed I scrounged up two cans of white marking paint and a rake and realized 20 minutes was almost gone. I called Betty Ann, told her I would be there in 5. Ten minutes later I called back for directions as I couldn't find the stupid bocce courts. Finally, 15 minutes after that I was just about to the large mob of bocce players.

"Ok, sorry about that. I'm Shelly, and Betty Ann is...?"

"Over here young lady."

I looked around, then looked down. Betty Ann was maybe 4-foot-tall but what she lacked in height she made up for with presence. She had to be in her 80's, but marched me over to the courts like a drill Sergeant.

"These need to be raked and lined fast. Properly."

I looked from her to the three long rectangles she was standing next to that were filled with a coarse gravel mixture, and back again.

"This will get done so much faster if you tell me where you want what. I have no idea what lines you need for this."

Betty Ann's face puckered and sent me a glare that had me hold a little tighter to the rake. I took a cautious step back.

"Oh, don't worry about Betty Ann, she's more bark than bite."

A woman in overalls with a bright orange shirt with little flowers printed all over it wearing Birkenstocks walked up and poked Betty Ann in the ribs.

"Bets, go set the tournament board up, I'll handle this."

My eyes widened when she called her Bets. I had just met this petite cannon but would bet she did not tolerate being called Bets.

"Fine, make sure it gets done right and soon. We are already over an hour behind schedule."

With that "Bets" marched off.

"Don't mind my sister, she gets a bug up her you know what over her schedule. I'm Ruby, you said your name was Shelly?"

I shook Ruby's Hand, but kept an eye out for the slightly shorter, angrier sister.

"Full disclosure Ruby, I have no idea what I'm doing. Tell me what you need and I'll do it."

Ruby smiled and hooked her tiny arm through the crook of my elbow and started towards the first court.

"First on the to-do list, remove goose poop. Bocce balls don't like to roll through poop, the group won't play with goose poop on their balls."

I looked around, all three courts were covered with poop. It was as if the geese decided this was the community privy and I did not have a shovel. I was starting to hate geese.

Another player volunteered an old play bill which I wordlessly took and then spent the next 30 minutes using it to scoop and fling goose poop off the three courts. What made it even better was the 30 plus mob that made up the peanut gallery each had advice as to how I should fling the poop.

They also added a comment or two about the length of my jeans, messy bun and that I really should get on with finding a husband or wife, they didn't judge anyone in these parts they assured me.

"Alight Ruby, poop free and raked to level. What's next?"

I could feel the sweat trickling down my back.

"Just the lines and we're done."

"Easy enough, where do you want it?"

"We need the Pointing Foul line, Hitting Foul Line and the Center Line on each."

"Ah, ok the center line goes in the center?"

She nodded in approval and at my silence that followed went and stood at each end where the rest of the lines should be. Another 15 minutes and they were ready.

"Thank you, Shelly, you're more than welcome to stay and play. You can take one of my turns, you look like a solid bocce player."

"Thanks Ruby, I should be getting back but I appreciate the offer. Besides, you all look pretty intense, I would not want to bring down your game."

"Tell you what, swing back in a few hours and have some food. We wrap up with a potluck picnic and we could use someone to take a league photo. Last year we tried to use Ryan's self-timer on his phone but all we ended up with was shots of his lower region as he was attempting to set it up. Still not sure if that was an accident or not, horny old that goat he is."

"Well on that note I'm going to go, but I'll swing back to snag a picture for you. Two o'clock you think?"

"Perfect!"

And with that she turned with a wave and opened up a bright red case that housed an even brighter set of red bocce balls. This really was the big leagues, I mused.

10

Luna greeted me with a hearty nuzzle upon my return. I had left her not knowing what I was walking into. She gets along with just about everyone provided they are nice. It's been few and far between the times she felt uncomfortable enough with a person to cause her normal gypsy self to be on guard but I never wanted to put her in a situation if I could avoid it. Had I spoken to Ruby initially she would have come along for the ride. I rumpled her ears and gave her cold nose a kiss.

"If we wrap things up here in time you can come with me for a picnic. I have a feeling you would woo many samples away from them."

I didn't have a ton to do, what I told Betty Ann was the truth and a large part of why I agreed to take the job in the first place. The Center wasn't open, I didn't have to clock in according to any schedule but my own. The biggest thing was to stop by daily, check on the various buildings to make sure everything was working over the winter, no burst pipes that sort of thing, and secure. Meaning making sure kids weren't using the place to make out, smoke pot or more.

Other than that, there were three or four pages of little odd jobs to take care of that mostly was routine off-season maintenance. Things like staining the railings on the porches, putting new skid plates on the canoes, and preventing mice from making camp for the next 6 months and eating everything.

A handful of reservations for the various buildings were scheduled through the end of December that I would have be on site to open up for, clean and close behind, and the surprise season's end of Bocce, but that was it.

The job didn't pay a lot, but it came with housing, a cute log cabin on the outskirts of the town that backed up to a sizable creek. More importantly, it gave me a reprieve from rushing into what I was going to do next. I had six months to enjoy a winter in the beautiful woods of Maine while I figured out what I was going to do with my life come summer.

I finished what I was calling coffee. Next time I was near a larger city I was splurging on a Keurig. The ancient relic that was left for me to use made everything that percolated smell eerily like musty socks. Pushing the moody thoughts of what to do with my life away I held the door for Luna as we went outside.

The sun was shining, it was a beautiful fall day and perfect to scrub a summer of play from fifty plus lifejackets. I stood, stretched and snagged the boat house keys from their hook on the wall below an incredibly large mounted bass.

"Come on my girl, we have work to do that will start with a paddle on the lake."

Luna happily trotted out into the sunshine. I smiled into the sun as I fished my sunglasses from my vest pocket. Life really couldn't get much better than this moment.

11

LEVI WANTED TO bang his head against a wall. His entire day had been spent fielding phone calls and filling out reports. One of his new hires, a kid just out of college with a forestry degree and his CDL, had been texting while driving a work truck. Ran right into a massive white pine instead of making the slight turn that the road took. The truck was totaled, but worse, a group of tourists who were documenting the start of their hike on the opposite corner where the fire tower trailhead was, caught the whole thing on camera. Had it uploaded on every social platform Levi knew of and then some he didn't know existed before the kid had a chance to call the wreck in.

Levi learned about it from his supervisor who saw it on YouTube, never a good phone call to start your day with. It was damage control from there on out. Hoping to distract himself he had called Shelly mid-morning to talk about what he found out about the garbage cans but got the machine instead. It was getting on to late afternoon and he still hadn't heard back from her yet. It bugged him that her not calling back yet had him checking his phone all day. Usually he throws the stupid thing on his desk and forgets about it until it rings. He let out a growly sigh as his office phone lit up with a transfer call from the front desk.

Sal only sent on the calls she couldn't solve on her own or the ones that had her laughing to the point of tears. For the most part he didn't mind taking the calls she passed on for that reason, but today none of the many that came through were funny. God damn cell phones and stupid kids.

"Hello, Levi speaking."

He let his head drop onto the desk when he heard the voice of the mayor come through the line.

"Yes sir, I...no, I do not think it's the least bit funny, either. I will be... no idea how many calls... ok. Yes. He....no...goodbye to you too jackass."

"I hope he hung up before you said that."

Levi moved his head just enough so one eye could glare up at Sal.

"Ha! Nice try mister, save it for someone who will give a damn. Here, I brought you a fresh cup."

"Today is a nightmare."

"Oh, it's not that bad. By Friday we will all be laughing at the video online and everyone will move on to the next stupid thing someone does."

"He wants me to can the kid. Said it's bad for the town's reputation to have tourists afraid to hike with reckless county workers driving 'amuck'."

He took a sip of coffee.

"What the hell does he mean by amuck?! The kid was stupid, without a doubt, and I could see suspending him for a week or so, but get rid of him all together?"

He let his hands drop and kicked the garbage can out of frustration. Then straightened it up when he saw Sal scowl at him.

"It's election year honey, every politician is grasping at anything they can to make a point, look like they are making a difference."

Sal looked pensively out the window as she cradled her cup of tea in her hands.

"You know what may work? Suspend the kid for two weeks then have him re-apply a few tiers down as one of the seasonal trail groomers for the cross-country trails and winter interpretative rangers. Make it clear he is on 6-month probation and with exemplary behavior he can earn his position back. You were saying just the other day we need another on call CDL driver for snow season but couldn't swing the salary for even a part timer. The money you'll save having one less forester will cover that and the kid's new position. Give the mayor until tomorrow then stop by and tell him how you were thinking about his speech about doing more with less and learning from mistakes, tell him it inspired you to come to him with this. If you do it right, by the end he'll think it was his idea and be using it on the campaign trail."

Levi grinned at her feeling lighter for the first time in hours.

"Sal, you are the most gifted, intelligent woman I have ever met."

He paused as all of what she said really sank in.

"Hey, how often do you manipulate me into doing things with your mind games?"

Sal just smiled, patted his knee and left.

He stared at her retreating figure then looked at his calendar. What in the world was he going to do when she left?

12

I THOUGHT ABOUT calling Levi, but after scrubbing the lifejackets and stopping by the Bocce party I just wanted to head to the cabin snuggle up on the back porch with Luna and something warm to drink. Driving back, I started thinking about the rotting meat and the absurdity of it all.

"The whole thing sounds like an eerie Stephen King novel doesn't it?"

I glanced at Luna who was already asleep in the passenger seat. I hit the brakes as the one light in town turned to red. Silly things were still on timers, no one else was at the light. Waiting on ghosts I mused. On a whim, I turned my blinker on to signal to the nonexistent vehicles around me and veered right towards where I thought the Forestry Department was located.

LEVI held the door open for Sal then locked it behind him. Finally, the clock mercifully turned its hands to 4:30pm. No one had to answer any phones or emails until tomorrow. Only emergencies would come through to his cell and he prayed everyone made good decisions tonight.

"Of course, someone rolls in two minutes after closing. Levi, you want me to send whoever this knucklehead is off while you make yourself scarce? Easier for me to shake them than you, no one wants to talk to me about all of this."

Levi glanced up and saw a familiar redhead with tri color dog in tow exit an ancient pickup truck.

"No, I can handle this one, night Sal."

He was grinning and jumped the last two steps on his way over to her truck. Sal made her way to her ancient Bronco and smirked as she watched him check his stride so as to not lope over to this woman she had yet to meet.

"Oh, I don't think you have anything close to a handle on this one kiddo."

Shelly was leaning back against the hood of her truck, arms crossed with one foot resting on the bumper. Her hair was down and blowing around her shoulders in the wind. He was a little tongue tied by the time he got over to her, felt like a high school kid trying to talk to a pretty girl at lunch. Not one to shy away from beautiful women, it boggled and pissed him off a little. This one had him oozing the charm of a tween. Thankfully Luna sauntered over and gave him a chance to collect himself.

"Hello pretty girl, nice surprise to see you today."

She had her front paws on his leg and was leaning into his shoulder scratch. Dog ecstasy.

"Hey Levi, we were driving by and thought we'd swing by to see if we could catch you. Day got away from us, we didn't have a chance to call you back until now."

He glanced up from his kneeling position.

"No worries, I forgot I called you, actually."

Lie, a total lie, he thought as he continued to rub Luna down. Safer to keep his hands busy with her legs being mere inches away from him. Legs wouldn't be so bad except they connected to her butt. Her butt was one thing he was trying incredibly hard not to look at, at the moment.

"So, what did you find out?"

Levi gave Luna one final ear rub then stood up and leaned on the truck next to her.

"Not a lot but it makes this more of a mystery than before. The Town doesn't empty the garbage can, neither does the County, Center or the Forestry guys. Here's the kicker, no one knows who it belongs to and the little patch of land it sits on, as I said, doesn't belong to anyone. Like I was saying back at Harvey's, everyone's property line in the area falls short of that patch. I thought maybe by default it was the state's but when I checked in with the Town Assessor he couldn't find anything on it. Maybe the last patch of earth no one officially has a claim to."

I mulled that all over as I stared at the clouds. A brisk breeze blew through the parking lot sending a shiver through my vest.

"Yesterday it filled and emptied within, what six hours or so? That's not a huge window for it to be a random coincidence."

"It's really strange is what it is."

"What's your next move now that it's gone?"

"Wait until the next time then hang out in Harvey's driveway and see who empties it I guess. I called the Chief of Police to see if they had anything as I know Harvey has called them out a few times but he wasn't in. Not expecting a call back either, he's not known for his communication skills."

I tugged my collar up a bit as the wind gusted by.

"Maybe I'll stop by the police station tomorrow, see if they know anything. I have to hit the post office, it's next door. I sent Walters an email this morning asking if he knew anything and specifically if he knew who was supposed to be taking care of the garbage can. I don't know him well at all but I am guessing it will be a while before I get a response back. I'll let you tell Harvey the good news, not sure I'm ready for another visit yet. Thanks for keeping me in the loop, let me know if you find anything else out."

I turned to go, opening the truck door for Luna. Levi shifted over resting his arms and head on the window sill of my open door.

"You ah, want to grab a bite to eat? Moe's has killer potato skins and the best chowder I have ever had, hands down."

"Ah, well..."

I looked at Levi and then back to the truck trying to decide if I should and If I did what that would mean. Did I like the guy? Seemed nice enough, but wasn't sure I wanted to cross that bridge now or if ever. Was this just a platonic after work when our paths crossed kind of thing? I was horrible at reading these situations. I had mis-read the signs or lack of on more than one occasion. As if he could read my mind he interrupted my internal debate.

"Not as a date or anything. I just figured you didn't know a lot of people yet in town being new, and I was heading there anyway."

He said it jokingly but looked slightly deflated. I felt like an ass. There goes my face turning red again. Luna nudged my arm then, giving me the comfort of her cold nose pressed into my hand.

"I wasn't thinking that, just trying to decide with Luna if I should run her home and by then what time it would be. Wouldn't want you to wait on me..."

I trailed off as he gave me an 'I call bullshit' glance.

"Not to worry Moe's is pro dog, even have water bowls for the outside tables. Think you can handle a brisk breeze? Food is worth it, I promise."

He wiggled his eyebrows teasingly.

"Since it's not a date you can buy the drinks, pay back for driving your drunk butt around yesterday."

"I never will hear the end of that, will I?"

I sighed, rolled my eyes and caved.

"Moe's it is, I'll follow you over."

13

Sɪᴛᴛɪɴɢ ᴜɴᴅᴇʀ ᴀ heat lamp with Luna curled up on the bench beside me, taking a sip of an exceptional locally brewed beer, I couldn't help but think this was one of the best nights I had in a while. Levi had been right; the food was outstanding. The atmosphere cozy, and I had to admit the company was pretty good as well. I hadn't laughed until tears came to my eyes in ages. In the few moments of silence I realized just how much I needed a night like this. Something to break the wake, work, repeat cycle.

"Here you go, little different than the last one but I think you'll like it. Called Honey Badger Rye. Same brewing company from up North."

"Thank you, Mmm smells good. What did you get?"

"Something with a little more body to it, SledHead Red."

I raised an eyebrow at him quizzically.

"Really, that's the name?"

"How is it any weirder than Honey Badger Rye? You didn't even bat an eye at that."

He had a point. I just took a sip of said Honey Badger and changed the subject.

"So, why forestry?"

He shifted in his seat stretching his legs out under the table so his boots were resting on the bench next to us.

"Felt like a good fit. Grew up not far from here, and practically lived in the woods as a kid."

He shrugged and paused, reflecting.

"I wanted a job that didn't have me chained to a desk all the time. Forestry was something that really interested me, everything about it from harvesting for products and replanting for preservation. These days I find myself stuck at a desk more than I like but I get out enough that It's not the end of the world and, this will sound cheesy, I can make a positive impact in this position. I'm not clocking in to follow someone's plan for the day, I'm the one making the plan. That alone is worth a few days of riding a desk each week."

"Never wanted to leave and go somewhere you weren't born and raised?"

"Right out of high school I went out west, spent almost a year traveling and doing odd jobs to get me to the next point of interest. Then I started looking at schools and no matter how many I looked at or toured, the top three were all in Maine. This will sound... hokey... but these woods are like no other. They have stories to tell and then secrets they'll share with no one. You can be near noise, humans, civilization and walk ten feet into the forest and all of that disappears. The moss, the trees, the everything that makes up the woods so cohesive and dense it blocks out everything else and swallows whatever, whoever steps in. The only place I have ever found that can make you feel utterly alone and safe at the same time. Once I realized how much I needed this place, it was an easy decision to stay."

He paused, staring at me with a small smile, eyes reflecting the soft glow of the patio's string lights.

He shifted forward so his elbows now rested on the table and leaned in closer.

"Your turn, why.... What is it that you do actually?"

"Hey now, uncalled for."

I laughed and swatted his forearm teasingly.

"No, no, not like that."

He laughed and flashed that smile again.

"I know you're the caretaker now, but that can't be the total of your career. And that it sounded ass-ish, let me try again."

I held up a hand to stop him.

"No please don't dig yourself deeper into the pit you started. Fair enough question."

Now where to begin I wondered?

"Well, I went to college for social work and minored in art therapy. Spent a year after graduation working at my Uncles Dude Ranch out in Wyoming."

Levi choked on his beer as he laughed at that.

"What's so funny about that?!"

"Nothing, just trying to picture you as a cowgirl."

"Laugh it up, but it was crazy hard work. Taught riding lessons, guided week-long canoe trips, did guest service things when he needed me to and everyone was expected to help with the daily chores of a ranch. Loved every minute of it but wanted to use what I went to school for. Missed the east coast so I accepted a job for a non-profit doing social work in inner city Boston. Loved it at first, had the naivety of being fresh off the boat, was going to make a difference and all that. After a year or so things got dark, lost the shine of a new adventure. Years after that I couldn't leave work at work, was always thinking about what I was doing, should be doing, could've done better. No matter what I did It always felt like I was letting my clients down, most of them kids living very adult lives. One day my neighbor was killed during a robbery, that was the lowest point."

I paused, thinking about if I should cut it off at that but the beer had me loosened up a bit so I kept on.

"I sat there, for a while, in the low. Then one day on my way to work, I basically tripped over a tiny, matted pup who couldn't stop shivering."

I glanced at Luna and ruffled her fur at the memory.

"That was it, decided enough was enough, packed up all my stuff and Luna and went south, then west again and looped back north. Worked for a few trekking companies taking people on canoe trips, backpacking adventures, that sort of thing. In winter I taught skiing, basically took seasonal odd jobs that felt right for the last five years or so. Soo, to answer your question.."

I paused and started laughing to the point it was hard to speak.

"I don't know exactly what I do per say."

I took a long slug of my beer and shrugged.

"How's that for an answer?"

"Still can't picture the dude ranch."

"Another lifetime anyway."

"Do you want another beer?"

"No, I'm good. Anymore and driving would be questionable, I would take a water."

"Two waters coming up."

I closed my eyes enjoying the warmth from the heat lamp, the folk rock that was pouring out from inside, felt my toes tapping to the beat.

"Are you sure you're alright to drive?"

I opened one eye, Levi was standing over the table holding the waters.

"Yes, very sure. Just enjoying the moment, that's all."

He didn't move, just looked down at me questionably.

"Sit, we will drink our water and then I'll walk a straight line for you if it will make you happy. Really, I'm fine. I would never drive impaired, would walk a hell of a long way home before even thinking about doing that."

Levi sat down and figured she was stubborn enough that that statement most likely was true. Still, he figured keeping her talking for a bit longer wouldn't hurt, just to make sure.

"How far of a drive home do you have?"

"Not far."

I smiled sweetly back at him in the silence that followed.

"Not far? That's it? Not going to give me anything else to gauge other than not far?"

"Mmm, no."

"Normal people would say oh it's only a 5-minute drive, or I'm off of Summerset. Something a bit more descriptive."

"If I did that you'd know where I live, easy."

"What's so bad about that?! I'm not asking for your address for Christ sake, just making sure you get home ok."

"That is the exact advice that every momma gives her daughter. After a few drinks dear, make sure you tell the man you recently met your address. Nothing bad could ever come of that."

Levi rolled his eyes and shook his head.

"As for the second part I have no doubt in my mind you could figure out where I live with a few, not the exact address, hints. Small town, you know everyone in it and where they live and have for your entire life."

"You're the most stubborn person I have ever met. And ridiculous. You're lucky I like your dog, the only reason we're sitting here."

I burst out laughing, I couldn't contain it.

"She is my better half that's for sure, I will give you that."

Levi raised his right hand and placed it on his heart.

"I swear, on my heart or honor, whatever it's supposed to be, I am not a psycho, serial killer, weird dude that looks through a woman's window at night or anything like that. Just a good guy looking out for his present company. In fact, I'll tell you where I live as a sign of good faith. 1742 Gunther Hollow Rd, big old white/grayish farmhouse with a quarter of a fence up by the road. See? That wasn't so hard. And I'm not one bit worried about you sneaking over to peek in my windows tonight."

This guy cracked me up. I was starting to hope that maybe this was a date. Time to change the subject.

"What's a lone guy needing a big old farmhouse for?"

I cocked one eyebrow and gave him my best interrogation look. I hoped it was as effective as it felt.

"Are you sure you're ok to drive? Got something in your eye?"

I gave up on my interrogation look and gestured for him to continue. He gave his head a little shake then continued.

"It's a fixer upper. Honestly, I have no idea what I'm going to do with it. It was a bank auction house that no one bid on, real fixer, fixer upper, I drove by and it looked so sad the way it was sitting there but could be beautiful."

He took a sip of his water.

"I don't know why I am telling you this. You're going to think I'm bat-shit crazy. But I could see a family there someday. The place lit up, dogs and kids running around."

"So, do you have a family or are you just thinking down the road?"

"I didn't say I saw my family in it, just that it would be a good family house for somebody. Just taking it one day at a time, fixing things as I go. Living there as I fix it makes it a good investment, it's a really nice spot. Outskirts of town, backs up to forest land, and a great fishing pond about half a mile in."

"Sounds cozy."

"Well, it will be one day. Drafty's a better word for it now. I have a tarp as part of my roof currently, but hopefully this weekend that will be taken off the to-do list."

"You were not joking about the fixing part."

I finished my water, stretched and stood.

"Do you need to do a sobriety test?"

"If you say you're good, I'm good, smart ass."

As Levi walked us to the truck, I noticed the parking lot was pretty empty at this point. He glanced at his watch.

"Holy crap, didn't realize it was this late."

What was going to be a quick bite turned into four hours that felt like thirty minutes.

"Thank you for the dinner invite, you were right, getting out and checking out the town was fun."

"You are welcome. Drive safe, and do me a favor. Text me when you get to wherever it is you're going, let me know you two got there ok?"

"Hmm if I do that then you'll have my number."

"That would be terrible."

"Horrible."

Levi pulled out his phone, looked like he was going to say something then thought better of it.

"What's your number, I'll call it quick then you will have mine."

Wouldn't kill me to have a friend in town, I told myself and rattled off my number. Besides, this one did not send serial killer vibes off in the least. Numbers traded, I was ready to hit the road.

"Have a good night, Levi."

"You too, Shelly."

He double tapped the door of the truck as he walked away. Took a glance back after a few steps and waived.

"You know Luna, I am really regretting that this wasn't a date."

With that thought I pulled out of the parking lot and headed home.

Levi watched her pull out, made a mental note she took a left, and sighed. Thought to himself as he pulled out she'd better text or he'd be up all night wondering if she made it home. If he was going to be up all night because of a woman that was not the reason he wanted it to be for.

14

THE BRAKES MADE a grinding sound at the red light. Rolling my neck back and forth to loosen the kinks out I made a mental note to find a parts store. I couldn't remember the last time I changed the breaks. Had to be an easy 60,000 miles or so ago. The light changed, I eased the truck up into third gear then quickly down shifted and swung into the parking lot on the right. The local police station was nothing to write home about. It was an old brick building that was in desperate need of a power wash. The small sign out on the front lawn along with the one police cruiser were the only reason that I could tell anyone would be able to discern that this was in fact the police station. I pulled up in front, threw it in park and sat for a minute contemplating what I was doing.

Should I go in there? Was this really MY job to be doing this? Life would go on if the case of the mystery meat was left a mystery. It wasn't a life or death situation and I was not some character in a book. Ruffling Luna's ears I let out a sigh. The other part of me was incredibly curious. I glanced at my phone, thought about texting Levi that I was stopping by but then thought better of it. True to my word I sent him a one word text 'home" last night and had gotten a one word 'good' in response. This was the strange period of any new friendship where you didn't want to come across as crazy by over texting but not sure what that level was yet.

A small bell dinged as I swung the door open and stepped into the small waiting area. It was as if the 70's was taking a stand inside. Yellowed linoleum floors met up with yellowed knotty pine walls that continued overhead with yellowish drop ceiling tiles capped with buzzing fluorescent lights. Being small however had its upside, the only option I had was to walk straight ahead to the long desk that cut off the public from whatever else the station had behind it. No one was at the desk. No one was any-where in sight. I stood there not sure what to do for five minutes or so thinking someone, anyone had to swing back to the desk soon. It was a police station for Pete's sake.

"Hello? Is anyone here?"

I yelled to the back as politely as I could muster thinking that is where someone must be. No answer. Impatient, I boldly lifted up the Formica counter top half door topper that acted as the desk gate and walked on through to the back. The first door I passed was to an empty room and I mean empty. Cold dark dreary, not a speck of anything in it. My brain registered that that was a tad weird as I kept on going. The next door had a neat looking office inside, a clean desk, a few kid drawings on the wall but no person. I was this far already, might as well keep going. The hall-way came to a T. To the left was another short hallway that then turned right, to the right was another shorter stretch of hallway that looked like it had another room off of it. As I was deciding which way to take I heard a quick laugh that turned into a coughing fit coming from the right.

An older man was sitting in an office chair, back to the door with his feet up against the windowsill talking on his cell phone. The desk tag said Chief of Police. The office reeked of stale cigarettes. Standing for a min-ute not sure if I should interrupt this phone call I decided it was a good thing I was not an ax murderer as the Chief was oblivious that I was there. That thought lead into good god what would happen if an ax murder came to town and this was the police force that would have to take them on? I knocked on the door frame. The chief of police half jumped, half fell out of his chair as he spun around.

"Who the hell are you?!"

His mouth hung open giving him a pit bull scowl as he glared at me.

"Yeah, hello to you too. Sorry to interrupt, I was at the desk out front for a while but no one was there."

Silence. This wasn't awkward at all. I cleared my throat.

"Like I said, sorry to interrupt, I'm the new caretaker of the Center, Shelly is my name, I had a few questions about...I don't know... a case is what I guess you would call it. You have taken a few calls about it from Harvey White?"

He continued to glare for a moment more.

"I gotta call you back."

He clicked his cell shut, slid his chair up to his desk and clasped his hands in a way that made a triangle but still allowed him to point his two fingers at me.

"Before we go any further let me make one thing clear. THIS is a police station. Not a library, not a café, not a place you just stop by. Unless you are a POLICE officer you do NOT pass the lobby. Unless you're a criminal on your way to the clink. Are you a criminal turning yourself in?"

"Ah, no...I"

"Then you have NO business being back here!"

He stood as he forcefully spoke this last part, sending his chair wheeling backward and bouncing off the wall. I don't know if it was the look on my face or his chair bashing back into his legs that took him down a notch or what. He adjusted his tie, took a breath and sat back down gesturing for me to do the same. Even though my mind thought it was in my best interest to leave, my pride had me sitting down. No way in hell this douche was getting the satisfaction that he scared me off.

"Now, next time you need something, wait like everyone else out in the lobby or call 911, understand?"

"Duly noted."

I hoped my reply sounded as sarcastic as I meant it to be.

"Since I am back here already, can I ask you a few questions?"

He stayed silent but gestured with his hand to get on with it.

"Ok, well Harvey White called the center the other day about rotting meat that is being dumped outside his property in a trash can and he wants the Center to take care of it."

I paused thinking now would be the perfect time for said chief of police to add to the statement I just made. He just sat. In silence. Now I was getting pissed. I leaned back in my chair, throwing one leg over the other striking my best cop show pose for questioning.

"He also said that he called your office a number of times and that someone came out to investigate. I wanted to see what you guys found and what we should be doing about it."

"We?"

"Well yeah, we as in the Center and Harvey. Technically it's not on anyone's property, this meat dump site, which I'm sure you know, but it's a hazard to anyone on the Center's property or Harvey's if it attracts animals. Would you be able to tell me what you found out? Do you know who is dumping the meat or even who is emptying the cans?"

The Chief drummed his fingers together as he stared at me. I stared back waiting.

"Look, Sally."

"Shelly, my name's Shelly."

"Shelly. Any police investigation is confidential. But I will tell you this as you seem to be trying to help out our... wonderful community. Harvey White is an eccentric old man who has nothing better to do than call the police for every creak he hears. The can is on a state highway route and is emptied on a schedule regardless of what is in there."

"Highway? It's in the middle of nowhere."

"Scenic highway, sweetie. This is Maine."

I ground my teeth together to keep the thoughts in my head from spilling out of my mouth.

"Who is putting it in there? Who knows, again it's Maine. Lot of people live up here who do things their own way. It's not a crime to fill a garbage can. Harvey is a cranky old man who lives inside his mind of how it should be, not how it is. It was nice of you to follow up for him, good job and all that jazz but leave the police work to the police. Now if you will excuse me I need to be going."

"So that's it? You're not looking into it anymore?"

He stood up, grabbed his hat and ushered me out the door.

"As I just said, leave it to the police."

"Who aren't doing anything about it."

He pulled and locked his office door, muttered something before turning to face me.

"Any police investigation is confidential. Whether we are or are not doing anything is confidential. Have a nice day Sally."

With that he strode down the hall and turned out of sight.

"What an ass!"

"Yes, he is."

I jumped, heart thumping as I was pretty sure I was alone.

"Um, hi?"

I slowly walked forward until a head popped out of the other office making me jump again.

"Hi, sorry I didn't mean to scare you, but he is an ass. I'm Jackie, the deputy of this lovely establishment."

Forcing what I hope was a pleasant smile, I held out my hand.

"Shelly."

Jackie smirked as she shook my hand.

"You sure it's not Sally?"

"So you heard the whole thing."

She nodded and walked back into her office and pulled a chair out for me.

"Like I said, he is an ass who, if I have any Karma coming my way, retires soon. So Harvey had another meat adventure?"

"Yes, yes he did. Do you know anything about it?"

Jackie booted up her computer as she talked.

"I was called out the first time, Chief was out on one of his 'Patrols'. I spoke with Harvey, checked it out. Other than the can of rotting meat, nothing was throwing any red flags. Took some notes and said I would follow up with him in a few days. Honestly with it being the first time I thought it was some out of state hunter who came up for a guided hunt, ended up with more meat then they knew what to do with and dumped it. Can was empty a few days later, nothing for a month or so then Harvey called again, left a message with dispatch, same thing.

I have a friend who works in the police department, a few towns over. They have the same demographic so I gave him a call to see if he had anything similar pop up on them over the years. He didn't but he remembered hearing something similar from someone else in another department, and said he'd give me a call back.   Went out on another, more pressing call, then swung back to the office to snag a trail camera, figured I would put it up for a few weeks and see who was doing the dropping. Chief asked what I was doing with the trail cam and after I gave him the run-down said that he had already taken care of it. Harvey was a crazy old man, yada yada, yada. Had one of the seasonal guys over dealing with it as we spoke. Said we had better things to do than waste our time playing garbage warden."

She swore softly as she smacked her monitor to get it to turn on. She clicked open a few files then grabbed a post it note and pen.

"So long story short, I never went out other than that initial call. My friend got back to me with the name of an officer across the state who was having a similar problem. I gave his name to the Chief but betting a case of beer he threw it out. Here is the name and number, good luck and let me know if you need anything."

She handed over the post it note with the name and number scribbled on it.

"Thank you, I appreciate it."

"Not a problem. Question for you though, how did you get back here anyway? He never lets anyone past the front. Hell, I'm pretty sure it irks him that I come back here."

I smirked and shrugged.

"Well, no one was at the desk when I got here so I took a stroll and ended up in his office. Seemed to have worked out in the end, eh?"

Jackie grinned and shook her head as she walked me back up front.

"You are something else, Shelly. I have a feeling I will be running into you again."

I thought about her final sentence as I climbed back into my truck.

"Luna, I am not sure Jackie expecting to run into me again is a good or bad thing."

I tucked the number into my inner coat pocket and pondered my brief but weird visit to the police station as we drove home.

15

LUNA LET OUT a low warning growl from her sunning rock, seconds later I heard the crunch of gravel under tires. Heard the vehicle stop, door open and close then Luna's growl fading into rhythmic tail thumps, friendly visitor. A few seconds later a pair of boots appeared in view followed by Levi's face peering cautiously at me under the truck.

"Hey there Shelly...ah...what are you doing?"

I handed out my socket wrench and rolled out from under the front of the truck.

"Changing my brake pads, a few other things."

I plucked the wrench out of his hands and started to wipe it down before placing it carefully in the tool box. I hated when tools were tossed haphazardly into a box. How the hell was anyone supposed to find anything that way?

"Why?"

"Why what?"

"Why...are you... changing your breaks?"

"Oh, I don't know, I was bored, thought I'd try something new?"

I did my best valley girl impression and batted my eyes as I said it.

"Do you have something in your eye? I got a first aid kit in the truck, I think there's some eye wash in it."

"No, I'm...just never mind. I'm good."

A minute passed by that was awkward to say the least, he just stood there staring at me opening his mouth to say something every few seconds but nothing came out. I couldn't take it anymore, I burst out laughing.

"You should see yourself Levi."

Chuckling, I started to pick up the rest of my tools.

"I'm working on them because they need to be changed. Caliper on the driver's side was hanging up."

"You do know we have a body shop in town, by the gas station?"

"Yup, that's where I got the parts from."

I patted him on the shoulder as I walked by.

"Oh, come on, don't tell me you're one of those guys."

I sat down on the cooler after grabbing two waters out and offering one to Levi.

"What do you mean, one of those guys?"

"Women can't work on anything with wheels guys."

He laughed, crossed his arms and leaned back against the hood of the truck.

"No, no issue whatsoever with you being a mechanic. You ahh... just caught me off guard. In a good way."

I raised my eyebrows at him as I took a sip.

"And I was trying to decide if I could bluff by pretending to know what a caliper was. What the hell is a caliper by the way?"

"I will teach you young grasshopper. Maybe, if you're nice."

"Pretty sure Mr. Miagoe did not offer his knowledge on "If" basis."

"Sure, he did. What do you think that whole wax on wax off thing was? Bonus points, by the way, for knowing the Karate Kid."

Levi tipped his baseball hat in half salute.

"Other than wanting a lesson in auto care, what are you doing here?"

"Got your text yesterday, said you had some more info on our meat. Was driving by the center and thought I would take a chance to see if you were here. What's up?"

I ran him through my interesting experience with the sheriff and Jackie as I put away my tools. Stretching to work a kink out of my back I realized how quiet it was. Glancing up I locked eyes with Levi who quickly cleared his throat and looked over my head to the sky. I craned my head around to see whatever it was he was looking at but nothing seemed to jump out at me. Shrugging I turned back around.

"So? What do you think of it all?"

Levi scooted over a bit, giving me some truck to lean on.

"Honestly? I have no idea. Could be something shady or could be people just being their weird selves. Sheriff's always been an odd duck and lazy doesn't even begin to describe him. Most likely he called it all off so he wouldn't look bad for not looking into it more."

He trailed off as he shrugged his shoulders.

"Or?"

"Or it really is nothing. Just some rotting meat that ends up in the garbage can. Whoever is leaving it, I for one, am thankful they are using a garbage can. Can you imagine if they just dumped it on the side of the road? Contained is bad enough, free to be dragged around by who knows what?"

Levi shuddered as he thought about it.

"Or it's something."

I crossed my arms thinking about all of it. It just didn't sit right saying it was nothing. Levi nudged my elbow with his bringing me out of my circular thoughts.

"What are you thinking over there Red?"

"Eww, no. Don't call me Red. Red's like, a name for your truck or... or a rooster."

"What?! No, Red's kind of like a cute, endearing nickname."

"Do I look like the cute endearing nickname type?"

"Ahhh... well... so... I don't know how to answer that without digging myself into a hole."

Finally, I thought, now it was his turn to turn a little red. I let him suffer for a few more seconds in the silence as I glared at him before a smirk snuck out.

"How about you just call me Shelly. That is my name."

"Fair enough... Shel."

I rolled my eyes at him, picked up my tool box and started to place everything in the cab.

"Joking, just joking. Shelly. So, what were you thinking?"

"It's not going to hurt to..."

I reached into the glove box where I stashed the post it note from Jackie.

"Give Officer James a ring, see what he thought of all of this when it was happening over by his neck of the woods."

Levi rubbed his chin as he looked at me. I couldn't read him yet. Wasn't sure if he thought I was crazy or if he agreed that something just wasn't right or what. He looked at this watch, muttering something to himself before clearing his throat.

"Let's do one better. Should only take about an hour, hour and a half to get there. What do you say we stop by in person? Easier to get a feel for someone when you can see them answering your questions."

"Now? As in right now?"

"No time like the present. And if we leave now, we can chat with him then grab some dinner from the Crab Shack before heading back. You thought Moe's had good food, wait until you try a crab cake."

Chewing on the idea of it for a second, my stomach started to protest loudly that it needed food.

"What the hell. Why not? I'm in, just let me pack up and lock up."

"Cool, I'll be in my truck."

He opened up the crew cab and called Luna over who happily hoped in. Few minutes later I climbed up.

"Alright, ready to roll."

Levi flashed me a grin and started backing out of the Center's drive.

"So, what are we going to talk about for the next hour and a half?"

"How about you explain to me what a Caliper is and how you know how to fix them."

I laughed.

"Well it all started a long, long time ago..."

16

LEVI DID NOT under sell the Crab Shack. Finishing my last bite, I tossed my napkin in triumph on the table then stretched out on the picnic bench letting my arms dangle down to the ground. Levi let out a snort of laughter.

"You ok down there?"

"I'm letting the grease absorb into my body. I ate too much."

"See? Told you it was worth the stop. Used to take all my high school dates here before I realized that high school girls did not usually want to eat that much greasy food on a date."

"Sounds like you were a real Casanova back in the day."

"Yup. Used to have um lining up around the hall to say hi to me."

I laughed hard at that one.

"That would be what, all of 5 girls? That went to your school, lined up?"

"Hey, don't go picking on my wonderful small town."

He threw a napkin over the table at me that bounced off my nose. Still laughing I swung my feet around and sat up. As much fun as I was having, we had a mission to accomplish.

"Alright, alright. What is our next move?"

"Next move? What are we, in a Bruce Willis movie?"

"Oh, come on, live a little! We could be cracking a major mystery."

"Or driving around asking about rotting meat that is only... rotting meat."

"You're just as curious as I am, admit it."

Levi took a long draw on the straw of his milkshake as he stared at me.

"I am curious, just keep it in mind it may be nothing."

I gave him a mock salute.

"Yes, captain sir."

"Shut up."

He threw his last napkin at me as he started to clear the table.

"Pick that up please, you really shouldn't be throwing garbage on the ground Shelly, it's called littering."

He winked as he walked by.

FIFTEEN minutes later we pulled into the police station. Levi reached behind his seat and pulled out his Forest Ranger Ball Cap and tugged it on his head.

"Ready Eddy?"

"Ready Betty. Do I get an official hat to wear?"

"Ah no, sorry I only have one."

"Are we going in good cop bad cop?"

"Yeah no, not going to happen."

"Then what's our game plan?"

"We are going to walk in and ask what happened with their rotting meat case. Nicely, like normal human beings."

"Sounds like a solid plan. Let's go."

A bell chimed as we pushed the door open. Walking in I felt like I was back at Jackie's station, everything looked pretty much the same except for the bright travel Maine posters that were hung up on the back wall.

A young officer walked up to the desk a moment later, she was smiling, warm and friendly. I wanted to trade our police station for this one. This one was already way better than ours and I had only been in it for 15 seconds.

"Hello! How can I help you two?"

Levi leaned a little on the counter, standing sideways as he chatted with her. I bit back a laugh as the officer fluffed her hair a little as she talked. I couldn't say I blamed her, Levi was a good-looking guy and could turn on the charm when he needed to and he was easily working with it turned up to at least 8 at this point.

"You know", she began then paused as she leaned in "I have always wondered what a day in the life of a forest ranger was like."

Okay, time to speed this along before it leaves PG territory. I cleared my throat, loudly, making her jump a little.

"Sorry, frog in there. So back to that police report you said you had filed? Any chance we could get a copy?"

"Yes, give me a few minutes, it's back in the files somewhere."

She gave me a firm, professional stare, then Levi a smile and a wink as she spun into the back part of the building. I crossed my arms and gave him the look.

"What. Why are you looking at me like that?"

"Why? We're supposed to be getting Intel and you're taking your time flirting at the counter."

"What?! I was not flirting. Just having a conversation, you know, like humans do occasionally. You should try it sometime."

I scoffed.

"Really, not flirting one bit. Trust me, you would know if I was flirting. Well, most women know when I'm flirting. Especially when it's with them."

He gave me a pointed look.

"What the hell's that supposed to mean?"

He grinned and shook his head. The officer reappeared with a file in her hands at that moment ending my next retort before it came out.

"Ok, here is what I could dig up. There may be more in another file depending on who filed it and how but I doubt it, as Officer James is very consistent with his file processing. Like I said earlier, you can read it here but I can't release it to you."

"That makes sense, thank you for digging it up. Ok if we step over there and leaf through it?"

Levi gestured to two chairs in the corner.

"Absolutely. Give me a shout if you need anything."

"Thank you, Officer..."

"Tara, you can call me Tara."

"Thank you, Tara, really appreciate it."

As we sat down I had to bite back another laugh as I caught Tara watching Levi walk away.

"Pretty positive you were flirting, and judging by the way she is mooning over you she thought so too."

"What, you jealous Red?"

"Oh no, not in the least and do not call me Red. We've been over this."

"Not flirting."

He flipped open the folder before sticking it in between us so I could read it at the same time.

It seemed like your basic police report, not that I really knew what was or wasn't, but it was written with just facts. Straight forward statements that told somewhat of a story. It included a few pictures that were taken by a resident who complained about overflowing garbage, not great shots however. All were a bit blurry and it looked like whoever took the photo had a habit of covering part of the lens with their thumb.

"Hmm look at this Shel, says here that an officer from Fort Kent came down, met with James, said they had a similar thing going on up there and felt it was the same group of young adults bouncing back and forth causing trouble."

"Ok, but why would a group of young adults do that?"

"Good question. Doesn't really get into the why, but looks like a week after they met he called again to say they caught the group. According to James's report they haven't had trouble since. Last entry was well over a year ago."

"If they caught the group doing it, then why is it happening by Harvey's place? And for what, like six months now?"

I pondered that thought as Levi pulled out a notepad from his jacket pocket.

"What's that for?"

"Well, Tara said we can't take the file with us but didn't say we couldn't copy the name and contact info of the officer from Fort Kent, Officer... Pickins."

"Thinking we should give him a call?"

"Exactly what I was thinking. Weird though, James has his name listed but nothing else. Forest service obviously isn't the police but whenever we file reports we include names, phone and email- if they have one, of anyone we officially talk to."

"Well can't be too many officers in Fort Kent by the name of Pickins, right? How many police stations are we talking about anyway?"

Levi looked at me and smiled.

"One. There is one police station in Fort Kent."

"Really? Only one? A place with the name of Fort you would think it's well, bigger. But Ok then, that settles it. We, and by we, I mean you, call them up and ask to speak with Officer Pickins, get the low down on the gang they busted. Easy peasy."

"Come on Nancy Drew, let's go make a phone call."

We walked back up to the counter where Levi handed the file back.

"Thank you, Tara, for your help."

She gave me a quick glance to acknowledge my thank you before turning her full attention back to Levi.

"If you need anything else, here is my card. Cell is on the back."

I rolled my eyes, I couldn't help it. They have a mind of their own.

"Actually, would you know when Officer James will be back on shift?"

"He is out for a while on personal leave. No return date set."

Levi stuck his hand inside his jacket pocket pulling out a small card.

"Here is my card, if he calls to check in or anything, would you have him give me a call?"

Tara's face fell a little when the invitation to call only included Officer James. I hated to admit that this lady was starting to irk me. A few more seconds of "polite conversation" as Levi put it and we were on our way out the door.

"I bet you $10 she calls you just to call you."

"Do I win the bet if it's only a text?"

I gave him a shove towards the bush we were walking past.

"Can't keep your hands off me now, eh Red?"

Levi pulled out his phone and answered it before I could throw a witty remark back. Which was good, it gave me time to think of one instead of just turning various shades of red. He hung up no longer smiling.

"Everything ok?"

"Ah no, actually we gotta run. Call just came in, a group of teenagers were hiking and messing around up on Castle top ridge, one fell off the cliff face. Think he's alive but can't get to him. Can you drive? I got to make some calls."

17

I got us back to the forestry department in far less time than it took us to get there. Having a truck with flashing lights on the top makes for much safer speeding. Levi hopped out, ran into the building and came back out with a ready pack, radio and what looked like climbing gear. He was talking into his phone still, coordinating with the crew he had already dispatched to the scene when he jogged by Luna and I. I gave him a good luck wave that he caught out of the corner of his eye and did a quick reverse back over.

"Shit, sorry forgot I gave you a ride here. Go into the office and grab any of the keys hanging for the trucks and take it to the center. I'll have someone drop me off to grab it later or tomorrow. Are you ok with that?"

"Go get outta here, we will be fine. Text me when you and the dumb kids are all back safe."

His radio crackled and the sound of another ranger came through. Levi mouthed a thank you as he hopped into this truck and took off sending gravel airborne for a few feet.

"Come on Luna, let's go see what truck we get to take home."

We walked in taking a quick glance around before shutting the door behind us. While looking for a key rack a face popped out from behind a file cabinet door, I let out a shriek that I am not proud of. Luna started to bark, ready to take on whoever it was.

"Dog don't push me today."

Sal's stern voice made Luna stop and drop right into a sitting position.

"You ok over there?"

"Jezz, you scared the absolute crap out of me. Didn't think anyone was here."

"Why are you here? I was just about to close up."

"Umm, Levi had to run out on that call."

"Yeah, I know, I was the one who called him in."

She was giving me a you are not so bright are you look.

"Right, well I was riding with him when you called. My truck is back at the center. He said I could borrow a forestry truck to get back."

"You were riding with him? As in he picked you up? In his truck?"

I could feel my face turning to match my hair then Sal broke out in a huge grin.

"Well that's the best thing I heard all day. Come on, I'll give you a lift while I interrogate you. I'm Sal, and you are?"

I didn't know what to say to that statement other than my name in response. Sal held the door open and gestured for us to exit. Feeling a smidge of dread, we hopped into her Bronco.

TWENTY minutes and 20 questions later I was positive that this was the scenic route back.

"So why were the two of you out in Sherman?

"Rotting Meat."

"Harvey again, still? Always going on about his meat."

Sal dragged out the word meat when she said it. I had to laugh. I liked this woman.

"How is life at the center treating you?"

"Not too bad, pretty quiet, and to be honest a bit boring. Not that I am complaining, just different than I thought it would be."

Sal made a hmph noise.

"To be completely honest, after the first day of working there I was surprised some retired couple hadn't jumped on it years ago and hung on."

"I always thought the same thing, but year after year we end up with a new seasonal caretaker. Hell, there has been more than a few times in the last 7, 8 years the person working splits before spring even hits."

"Maybe they got bored, stir crazy?"

Sal gave me a I don't think so look.

"The other thing I have noticed again, over the last 7, 8 years are the individuals they hire. Always women, always young and single in the way as they have no family tagging along. And another thing? None of them had any business being in that position in the first place."

"What do you mean?"

"They were nice enough but better suited to strolling a mall than maintaining a trail. Outdoors people they were not."

Sal let out a laugh.

"One of them I remember called 911 when they saw a racoon eating the groceries they had left out on a picnic table. That call made the police blotter in the paper. Honest to god, I would bet good money that not one of them had ever spent time outdoors other than a walk around a paved trail in a city park."

"Geez, they must not have had very many options to pick from if they ended up with someone like that for the job."

"That's the funny thing, I know a handful of people who applied for it over the years. Locals who knew what they were doing."

"Why would Walters pass on them? A local with skills seems like a shoe in for this job."

Sal paused for a second before answering.

"Like I said, they seem to hire a certain....type."

I thought about that for a second then it hit me.

"Wait a second, are you saying that's why they hired me? That I'm that type?!"

I didn't know if I should be hurt or offended or both.

"You are a young woman and single but you seem to actually be a good fit for the job."

"Oh, well thanks. I think."

I pondered that for a second as we swung into the drive.

"Alright, here we are."

Sal put her Bronco in park next to my truck.

"Thanks for the lift Sal, appreciate it."

Luna gave her a nuzzle as she hopped from back to front seat.

"You're welcome kiddo, you too, dog. Hope to see you around some more Shelly."

I waved as she backed out. Luna let out a yawn yowl as she stretched.

"I agree Luna, a stroll before we head in sounds perfect. We sauntered off along the path weaving around to the lake Luna sniffing and chasing red squirrels, me thinking about everything and nothing all at once. Then it hit me. What if they hired me because they thought I wouldn't be able to do the job? Why on earth would you hire for that reason? More importantly, what the hell does that say about my interview skills?! As we neared a fork in the trail I whistled to Luna to swing right. I had a lot to think about, thoughts worthy of an extended stroll.

18

THE NEXT MORNING, we set out on a mission. What Sal had said really struck a nerve and I wanted, no needed, to prove to myself that I wasn't hired because I fit the city bimbo bill. We hit the center a little past sunrise. It had turned into one of those nights where you just keep tossing and turning with too many thoughts bouncing back and forth.

"Alright Luna, let's see what we can find."

I stretched my arms like I was going into a boxing class then unlocked and flung the door to the office open for us. Luna's excitement about our crusade lasted about 10 minutes then she ditched me to sleep in a sunbeam coming through the window.

"Ok guess I am now on my own. And I'm talking to myself, maybe I fit the type around here more than I thought."

I started with the file cabinets, closets, random desk drawers. I looked through boxes stashed around in weird spots. But there was nothing. And by nothing, absolutely nothing. No staff files, no timesheets, nothing to say this place had people working here. Standing in the middle of the room, hands on my hips, I slowly spun a circle trying to get the nagging feeling in my brain to connect with the rest of it. Then it clicked. What was really mind boggling was the lack of the other things. No files on old programs, or flyers and brochures. Not a news clipping of an event or old schedule. Other than a very, very small file that had a handful of permits for the rental buildings on the property from the summer and a few into the fall, the place was pretty barren. A year-round place like this that had been in operation for over 30 years should have buckets of that kind of crap. With that realization the office suddenly had a weird sci-fi theme going on sending a shiver through me. I took that as a sign to use the bathroom.

Coming out of the restroom I happened to look up and noticed a small framed out square in the ceiling. Hopping up on a chair I gave it a test shove and it moved. What the hell, I'm already this far down the rabbit hole why not? I climbed into the attic storage area and realized it had no lights or if it did, they were not by the small entry hole in the floor. I retreated to get my headlamp from the truck. With the headlamp in place, take 2 began.

As I looked around I felt like I struck gold. Boxes and boxes galore. I blew the dust off one box and found it filled with photos of people swimming, boating, riding horses, sitting around campfires that told stories of laughter and good times. Another set of boxes had summer camp program flyers, advertisements for campers and staff. A trunk had moth eaten table cloths folded neatly inside. I spent the better part of two hours up in the attic rummaging through things. I kept thinking this is what a place like this should look like. The differences between what was downstairs and the memories in the attic were stark. I heard Luna whine from the bottom of the chair.

"Coming down girl, hold up."

I took a photo that had a lineup of teens in it each holding up a fishing pole and what looked like a bass. As I started down the makeshift ladder I paused as I realized all the stuff up here was from years ago. As in an easy two decades. Not one bit of it was recent. I ruffled Luna's ears before tucking the chair back and placing the photo on top of a bookshelf in the office. Something weird was going on. Nancy Drew I was not, but I knew that much.

An hour later, I was back in the office and I had a pile of pencils at my feet. So far, I have been able to twirl one back and forth between my fingers six times before it flung elsewhere. Originally, I had sat down to think. Then while thinking, I started twirling my pencil. Which led to how many times can I do it before it falls. After I hit three in a row I was hooked, determined to hit 10. That was 20 minutes ago. I was back up to four with my current pencil when it flung out and bounced off the windowsill.

"Ok, enough of this."

Luna's head shot up at my sudden voice.

"The question is, what to do?"

I drummed my fingers on the desk looking at the calendar. I was a month or so into my new job and bored. The only real thing I had left to do was help Harvey with his meat and I wasn't so sure that was my problem. It was more just something to do to stay busy. On a whim I called Walters to see what else he may need done while I was here for the next 5 months. The phone rang, and rang, then went to voicemail. The other three times I had called, the same thing happened. I didn't bother to leave a message. None of the others were returned. Feeling annoyed at being ignored I grabbed the cell phone someone had tucked into the mailbox the other day with a note that they found it by the beach. It was dead when I got to it and threw it on the charger earlier to see if I could figure out who it belonged to. On a whim I snagged it, hit an emergency call and dialed Walters. He answered on the second ring.

"Walters here."

"Hi, it's Shelly. From the center. The seasonal caretaker?"

There was a long pause on the other end.

"Hello? Walters? You're still there."

"What do you want and what number are you calling from?"

"Oh ah, this is a cell that someone turned in. Lost and Found, mine was dead."

Bit of a lie but I didn't feel bad one bit as I was starting to think this ass hat was purposely ignoring my calls.

"Did you get my other messages?"

"Not sure."

"Ok then, well just wanted to check in on a few things."

I could hear him making an annoyed sigh on the other end. The sound made me want to kick him in the shin. If only I could through the phone line.

"Well since I finally got in touch with you I'll go over all that I left in those messages that you're not sure you got."

I sounded snarky but didn't care one bit and dove right in.

"The list of things you had to do over the next 5 month or so? It's done."

"What do you mean it's done? There were easily 20 things that need-ed to be completed on it."

"More like 40 and yeah they are done. Complete. Is there another list you want me to start working on?"

"No way that you can be done. You must have rushed through it all. Go back and make sure you take your time. I didn't hire you to do half assed work."

This guy is a serious ass.

"Look, I can assure you all the things were done correctly and well. Honestly? What you had listed a high schooler could have handled."

"Oh, so you think you're better than a high schooler?"

"What?! What kind of comment is that?"

"Enough! Just go back and do it again." I took a breath and counted to 10. Be the bigger person, be the bigger person.

"Ok, whatever you say. I saw a bunch of Christmas lights in the attic do you want me to..."

"What were you doing in the attic?!! That place is off limits! To Everyone!"

I had to hold the receiver away from my ear as he shouted the last part.

"Dude, chill...just chill out! I was looking for things to do and saw the attic so I took a look. Nowhere, anywhere does it say stay out of the attic."

"Just do your job! Nothing else!"

"Fine!"

There was a long stretch of silence as both of us took a few breaths to calm down. Luna was standing at attention looking worried. She did not handle yelling well.

"Anything else?"

I cleared my throat.

"Yes, one other thing. I've been working with Levi...." I paused for a second realizing I had totally forgotten what his last name was.

"Well Levi from Forestry on the rotting meat issue that's been happening by Harv."

"That old timer is half senile, has no idea what is fact or fiction."

The words spat out with force and dash of disdain.

"Again, just do your job. Hanging out with Harvey is not your job."

"So, when he calls to complain I should just ignore it?"

"Yes! No, just...if he calls again, call the sheriff. It's his job to deal with the mentally ill, not yours."

"I really don't think..."

"DO YOUR JOB! Thinking is not part of your job!"

This guy was really starting to tick me off. Who the hell did he think he was?! Then I heard the dial tone in my ear. I couldn't believe it. He hung up. He hung up on me.

"What is wrong with him?! No wonder no one ends up coming back! I was upset while on the phone, now I was pissed. I grabbed the notepad

I was using the other day to brainstorm ideas of things to do to get ready for the spring season, ripped off my ideas and smashed them into a ball, then threw it as hard as I could at the wall. Luna of course trotted over and brought it back, dropping it at my feet. I dropped down next to her and let out a laugh sob into her neck. A few deep breaths had me feeling better, then my phone rang.

"What?" My greeting came out a lot harsher than I intended it to. One of those minds not connecting with the mouth moments.

"This a bad time?"

It was Levi. Rolling my eyes to the ceiling I wondered if Karma would ever allow me to act like a normal human being in front of this man.

"No, just fine. Sorry for the harshness, not directed towards you."

"Well that's a plus. Feel sorry for whoever it was supposed to be for."

"You don't want to know. So, what's up? Did you get all the kids out ok?"

"Thankfully yes. The kid who fell is ok, sore as hell with a broken leg in about 5 places, but he will live. Hopefully the whole thing put the fear of god into the rest of them including all teens in town. Whoever thought Castle Hill was the place to party had to have been high. In fact, I am sure they were. The kid that fell? Doctors think the only reason he only has a broken leg was the fact he was stoned out of his mind. When he fell he most likely didn't brace for impact. Was too relaxed and saved himself a dozen other possible outcomes from his stupidity."

I let out a snort.

"I'm not sure that's the example you should lead with when presenting to a high school class. All I heard was if you're stoned enough you can leap off cliffs without dying."

"Har, har, thankfully our high schoolers are smarter than our caretakers."

"Hah! You really think that thought hasn't crossed the minds of every high school kid who has for sure heard the story by now? All who are most likely at this very second currently taking a hit in mom and dad's basement turning that tale of stupidity into a legend?"

Levi groaned.

"Why can't kids be smarter? It would make my job a hell of a lot easier."

"Smarter than what, when we were kids Levi?"

"I was an angel. Gold halo and everything."

"For some reason I highly doubt that."

"Moving on."

Levi cleared his throat before switching to his next topic.

"After I finished the boat load of paper work that goes hand in hand with rescuing stupid kids, I called to talk to Officer Pickens."

I had been leaning back in the office chair with my feet propped on the desk. The mention of Pickens had me leaning upright, eager to hear what he had to say.

"The Fort Kent Police department does not have an Officer Pickens working for them."

"Did he move?"

"That's what I asked. Get this, not only do they not have Pickens working for them, they have never had an Officer Pickens working for them. As in ever. I had the poor dispatch lady go back 20 years through files to make sure."

"Well that doesn't make any sense. Why would James write in his report that he met Pickens if Pickens doesn't exist?"

"I'm wondering who it really was that James met with."

"You think someone was pretending to be a police officer?"

"That's exactly what I am thinking."

I let that thought sink in for a second.

"Why? Why would anyone do that? Hell, if you're right the guy acting like Pickens is either really good at impersonating a cop or Office James is a really crappy cop."

Levi let out a short laugh on the other end.

"Yeah I was thinking along the same lines, Red."

"Are you thinking we need to track down this James guy? Grill him for some answers?"

"Reel it in Nancy Drew, no one's grilling anyone. But yes, I think that is what we need to do."

"How are we going to do that? Isn't he on personal leave for the next, however long?"

"I have an idea. What are you wearing?"

"Excuse me? "

"No, not like that. I have a friend who has a friend that knows James. Says he lives about 20 miles outside of town, but most evenings he can be found a little farther out at the Last Chance."

"Last Chance, what is the Last Chance? A strip club?"

"Shelly! I can't believe your mind works that way!"

I could have cut the sarcasm with a spoon.

"With a name like Last Chance it could be anything."

"Well it's a bar. And the last chance to grab food for about 100 miles, hence the name."

"That was my next guess."

Thank god we were on the phone. I could feel my skin turning red again. Levi snorted.

"Tell you what, pick you up in 20 minutes at the center? We can grab a bite and a beer and see if we can't bump into James and see what he remembers about Pickens."

I didn't say anything right away, trying to decide if my jeans with a hole in the knee and favorite gray sweatshirt would work for whatever this was turning into. I must have been silent for too long, next thing I know Levi is awkwardly stumbling through his next statement.

"Hey, so this is not a date or anything. Just let's figure out what's going on. To help Harvey kind of deal."

He sounded a little hurt.

"Yeah, for sure. Totally get it, I was just trying to decide what to do with Luna."

"Bring her along. Nice night out, we can eat on the patio they got over there."

"Well ok then, see you in 20."

As Levi hung up I couldn't shake the feeling for a second time that I was wishing this was an actual date and kicking myself for not saying so.

19

THE RIDE TO the Last Chance was beautiful. The sun was just starting to set as we left the town line sending streaks of yellowish orange across the lake. A few stars were starting to poke out, not a cloud in sight. Mother Nature had the stage set for a crisp postcard northern night. I smiled as I rubbed my hands together. Nights like these made my heart happy. Luna also loves a good fall night and let out a content sigh as she draped her head across my lap warming up my hands with her thick fur. It was a quiet ride but not an awkward one. Both of us lost in our own thoughts, me mostly daydreaming as I watched the world outside the window change into sunset tones then dusky hues.

"Well this is not what I expected."

Levi pulled into a parking spot close to the patio. The Last Chance was a Picasso of a building. It had what I assumed was the bar adjacent to the patio area that was roped off with caution tape and a wet paint sign. The other side of it was clearly an addition with a mini mart store front. Next to that another addition that appeared to be a laundromat with a family video on one side.

Levi pulled on his ball cap and smiled.

"It's like I said and its name sake. It's the last, and I mean last, stop for food, supplies, clean laundry and a movie for 100 miles as you head more north. One stop shop for folks around here."

"You know? It has to be kind of freeing to live around here, to know that this is the last stop before you head home. After this point you're on your own, no pressure to go anywhere because it isn't there."

"I suppose so. Never have to worry about being sent on a last-minute milk run."

"And that too. Smart ass. Anyhow, how will we know it's James if we see him?

Levi pulled out his phone and opened it up to the police website and zoomed in on an officer's picture.

"This is Officer James."

He looked like a cop. Short buzzed almost blonde, but not quite, hair with a nose that looked like it had been broken a few times and never got back to where it was supposed to be.

"Should be easy enough to spot at this place, not like there's going to be a huge crowd to wade through."

"I'll say."

I glanced over really taking in the caution tape for the first time.

"Looks like the patio is a no go."

"Yeah, it does, what do you want to do Red? Your call."

Looking around it seemed like a fairly chill place. Glancing down at Luna her tail started to thump in her let's go for it. Smiling, I ruffled her ears and started walking towards the door with Luna at my hip.

"Uh, Shelly? What are you doing?"

"Improvising."

"Shelly, wait up, what?"

I stopped before the door, hooking my arm through Levi's.

"We walk in close to one another, head for a corner table, Luna rides our coattails and gets to have whatever we slip her under the table."

Levi looked skeptical.

"Come on Levi, live a little. What's the worst that could happen?"

Letting out a laugh Levi held the door open and we, all three, waltzed inside.

WHERE the outside was a cut and paste appearance, inside the bar was downright cozy. Large logs lined the walls, the ceiling was brightly lit with strand upon strand of white Christmas lights that cast the rest in a warm yellow light with just the right amount of shadows near the tables that flanked either side of the bar. It was also the kind of place that when you walked in, every head turned to look at who entered. I felt Levi's pace falter a little and tightened my grip on his hand as I made a causal bee line for the farthest table. Luna knew the drill and kept plastered to my side until we hit the table where she disappeared underneath.

I sat down, relieved to see most of the heads had turned back to something other than us.

"I don't think anyone noticed. Feeling like we are in the clear!"

Levi gave me a very skeptical look.

"Do you really think no one noticed an 80lb. dog walking in the door? When everyone in here looked at us as soon as we entered?"

"Feeling good about this. We were smooth, practically spies."

I shushed him as the waitress walked over. If I had to guess she was in her late 50's, had a sleeve of tattoos and a no-nonsense vibe that radiated off of her.

"What can I get you?"

"Two pints of whatever you have on tap please and a menu?"

Levi looked to me as he ordered, I nodded in agreement.

"Menu is written above the bar, let me know when I come back with the beer. Anything for your dog?"

Levi smirked, giving me a I told you so look as he nudged my boot under the table.

"Ah, can she have some water? Please?"

So much for us being spies I thought. The waitress gave a nod and headed back the way she came.

Levi was still smirking. I threw a balled-up napkin at him, hitting him in the chest.

"Alright, alright. World class espionage is not my strongest skill. So now what?"

"We eat, drink and wait. See if he shows up."

An hour and a half later Luna had moved up from under the table to stretch out on the bench and was cat napping. The food was outstanding. I was down three games to zip in darts. My abs hurt from laughing the majority of that time but no sign of James. Finishing up my third pint Levi raised his empty glass silently asking if I wanted another. Funny how easy it is to communicate without ever speaking if you're open to it. Made me think we are not all that different from animals when you really break it down. With that philosophical thought I shook my head realizing if I was into deep, deep thoughts that I had better call it quits on the alcohol. And I had to pee. I sent a flurry of hand singles in his direction to say I was headed to the restroom. He looked puzzled, but gave me the thumbs up as I danced by to a CCR song someone had just selected from the jukebox.

Few minutes later, feeling much more comfortable and yet again amazed at how much one person can pee after a few beers, I hopped up onto the bar stools to snag a couple of waters to bring back. The tv above the bar had a fishing show on. Some guy was holding up the largest bass I had ever seen.

"Holy hell that's a big fish."

The guy a few stools down grunted in agreement.

Looking over to my fellow fish watcher I realized I had just found James.

20

"JAMES? OFFICER JAMES?"

He glanced over, gave me an up and down kind of look then returned to this fish show.

"Who's asking?"

"Me. I mean I'm Shelly."

I was starting to wish I had spotted him two beers sooner.

"We were hoping to run into you..."

"Who's we? Got a mouse in your pocket?"

He was still staring at the TV as he spoke.

"That's funny, real funny."

I said it as dryly as I could. The bar was not huge by any stretch of the imagination making it easy to flag Levi over. Figured at this rate some additional help would not hurt. As Levi hopped onto the bar stool next to me I mouthed who the guy next to me was.

"James, I'm Levi. Can Shelly and I buy you a drink?"

He turned from the TV this time giving us both a look over.

"Look, you look like a nice couple. I'm sure as hell not into that kinky crap with the three of us climbing into a bed together. Let me watch this in peace, please."

I almost spat the slug of water I had just taken as he politely refused to go to bed with us. Instead I had a coughing fit as it went down the wrong tube. Levi gave my back a few whacks as he leaned over to talk to James.

"No, no, wrong impression there James. We are not looking to take you home. Just wanted to ask you a few questions about the case you signed off on a while back about the rotten meat being left in the public garbage cans."

This time when James turned he slid off the bar stool and signaled for the bartender to ring him up.

"Who sent you?"

"Sent us? No one sent us."

James settled his tab and started to get his coat on. He was just going to leave, our only lead. Without thinking I stood up and grabbed his arm.

"James, please. Just a few questions. It's happening again and we're trying to figure out what exactly it is."

He Looked from Me to Levi and back again before sitting on the edge of the stool. His body language was shouting that he was not staying for a lengthy chat.

"If it's happening again my advice is to stay out of the way. Forget about it."

"What about your report? It said you met with Chase Pickens who found the guys that were doing it."

Luna had materialized by my side, sitting sentinel as she eyed James up and down.

He held out his hand for Luna to sniff before he started rubbing her ears.

"I met with a guy who said his name was Chase Pickens. A guy who also said he was a cop. I was overloaded with cases at the time, he said he solved it I said hallelujah. Never checked to see if he was who he said he was, just took his word for it all and signed off on it on my end."

Levi cleared his throat and leaned around me to make eye contact with James before he started talking.

"So, you don't think Pickens was a cop?"

"He wasn't a cop or named Pickens. Pickens doesn't exist in the entire state of Maine police force database. Actually only five men in the state with that last name, two are dead, one is a baby and the other two in their 80's. Only thing I do know is he drove a big black extended cab truck and had phony police plates on it, not that it registered with me at the time. I did think it was strange that a cop was driving that around on duty but not enough to look into it."

"How did you know the plates were phony?"

"I made a mental note of the plate when we met. I'm not always the best cop but always a cop. A few weeks after I thought the case was closed we heard of it happening again on the police scanner a few towns over. I tried to get in touch with Pickens but the phone number I had for him was no longer in service. Ran his plates, no records found."

The next statement I made just fell out of my mouth.

"You didn't do anything then, just walked away?"

James' expression hardened as did his body as he glared at me.

"Lady, just stay out of this. Whatever this is, it's not worth it."

Levi leaned farther over drawing James's attention off of me.

"I'm with Shelly on this one, what did you do when you found out he was a fake?"

He stood this time, buttoned his coat and tugged his hat firmly on.

"I went on vacation, my partner followed up on it."

"Can we get a hold of him? Your Partner?"

"Sure. Chester O'Rourke. Find him at 7341 Lewis Rd. Leave me alone, and leave this alone too."

With that he strode out the door, letting it slam behind him.

I leaned over the bar, grabbed a pen and a coaster jotting down the name and address before I forgot it.

"I think we may have struck a nerve."

Levi nodded in agreement as he sat back down.

I signaled the bartender over.

"Can we have two more pints?"

He flipped the bar cloth over his shoulder, leaned on the counter with both hands, pausing to make sure he had both of our attentions.

"I think it's time for you two and the dog to go."

Suddenly the Last Chance wasn't feeling so warm and cozy.

Levi put a twenty on the bar, told him to keep the change. We grabbed our stuff and walked out the door.

"Levi, I feel like someone might throw something at us any minute."

I kept glancing back to make sure that that notion was really only in my head. Levi didn't say anything but kept a quick pace back to the truck. Luna hopped back in the truck and once we were both in, I hit the lock button.

"That was not how I thought that would go down."

"You and be both Red, you and me both."

"Now what do we do?"

"Still have that coaster?"

I pulled it out of my coat pocket, handed it over to Levi. Levi glanced at his watch.

"Only 8:45pm. Got time for one more stop to 7341 Lewis Rd? Lewis Rd. is only about 5 minutes from here."

"As long as we don't stay here I'm game."

"You aren't kidding. Last time I bring a date to the Last Chance."

Levi smiled at me as he pulled out of the parking lot. I rolled my eyes but deep down liked the fact that he called it a date.

"You know, he didn't even blink an eye when he thought we were asking to sleep with him. Do you think that happens a lot?"

"Well he is kind of handsome, I guess."

"Really? You Levi, think Officer James is Handsome?"

"Hey, don't get any ideas. He is totally not my type. Too copish and not female. But I can admit that he is a good-looking dude."

I let out a snort of laughter.

"Shelly, I am a modern man and fully comfortable with my sexuality."

"I don't know what to say to that."

Levi Grinned and kept driving. A few turns and a few minutes later he pulled over to the side of the road.

"What's wrong?"

"That's a good question. We're here."

"Here? This isn't a house, Levi."

"No, it's a Cemetery."

I leaned over the driver's side peering out the window. Sure enough, over a wrought iron gate was the address just below the gothic style words `Lewis Rd Cemetery.'

"What the hell is going on Levi?"

He didn't say anything, just stared at the fence then leaned over and pulled a flashlight out of the glove box.

"Well, we're in it this far. Let's see what we can find out."

With that he hopped out of the truck.

21

"Levi! What are you doing?!"

I half shouted, half hissed it out trying to be quiet. I don't know why, but being in or near a cemetery made me act like I was in a library. Trying not to disturb whoever, or whatever, was nearby. Levi couldn't hear me partly because I was trying to be quiet and the other part as he was already across the road holding the man entrance in the gate open and beckoning for me to follow.

"Oh my god, this is nuts."

I puffed my checks full of air and blew them out forcefully before opening the door for Luna and I. We jogged across the road and stepped through the gate, jumping as it clanged shut behind us.

"Easy there Red, just the gate."

"Shut up Levi. This is a bad Idea."

"What, walking through here at night? People are allowed to be here at night."

He gave me a sidelong glance as we walked on the gravel path.

"Don't tell me, are you afraid of ghosts?"

As he said the last part he put the flashlight under his chin to illuminate his face. I punched his arm and walked a little faster with my arms crossed.

"Hey I'm just teasing. Ha, ha. But really, you don't believe in ghosts, do you?"

"Yeah I do. Because they're real. So should you."

"Ghosts are not real."

"There are paranormal things that happen every day everywhere."

I took a look around as I said it, positive we were being watched. Had the hair on the back of my neck standing up.

"Yeah so people say. Doesn't make them true."

I stopped at the fork in the path, stood for a second listening to the creaking sound the trees make when it's cold out but not yet frozen.

"My grandpa Ted lived for years in an apartment above a shipping yard. It was his shipping yard, third generation to own and operate it. One night a guy who stopped in once or twice a year to get fuel and gossip stopped in and was talking to my grandpa while he filled his tank. He finished up, went to grab his wallet and ran into Zeke, the caretaker/ night watchman who had been working there since his mid-twenties up by the front. While he was paying he mentioned that he had seen Ted, said he looked a little off and wasn't saying much. Zeke gave him his change and apologized that he had to break the news, but Ted had passed away six months ago. That guy swore up and down that he spoke to Ted. Would not believe Zeke for one minute that he had passed, thought it was a trick Zeke was trying to pull over on him."

The wind picked up just then making leaves crackle as they danced across our path. Luna stood up and pressed herself against my legs as she gazed into the dark beyond the flashlight beam.

"What are you trying to do, scare me? I got to say, that's a hell of a story."

"True tale, promise. We never saw my grandpa after he passed. Not me, my mom or my dad. Sometimes lights would be on down there that you knew you shut off, or a cabinet door open that was latched when you left. But he never re-appeared in front of any of us. For a few years others who knew him from this or that but didn't know that he had passed would stop by, grab some fuel and would swear up and down that they spoke with Ted in the yard."

"That's just crazy."

Levi quickly added "I don't think you're crazy, just never really believed in ghosts that's all."

I shrugged.

"I think spirits are around us, not attempting to scare people like in the movies, but around. You just have to be willing to be open to the idea to notice them I think. A friend of mine's Gran used to say that they just wanted to be acknowledged then they would leave you alone. She was always saying hi to someone we couldn't see, or saying things like I see you, now run along. The air would sometimes feel colder around us when she did or a scent that you know didn't belong would float by suddenly then disappear. She insisted that as long as you're respectful, they will mind their own. Never questioned it growing up, just believed every word and to be honest? I still do."

Levi kept glancing over his shoulder as I spoke.

"Did my ghost story scare you?"

I bumped his shoulder with mine. He flashed a smile then shook his shoulders out.

"It was a good story. Not sure if I am 100% on board with team ghosts, but I will try to be respectful from now on just in case. You feel like we're being watched?"

"Yeah, got that feeling too when we walked in."

I glanced down at Luna. She was alert and staring out in the darkness but not acting like someone was out there. The wind was at our backs, pushing the scent of anything that may or may not be out there watching us away from her keen sense of smell.

"Let's keep moving."

"Okay, but where are we going? This place is huge, Levi."

I spun a slow circle looking around at what I could see in the glow of the flashlight. "Should we really be wandering around in a cemetery at night? What if there's a fresh grave and we don't see the pit and fall in."

"The odds of that happening are really slim."

"But there's still a chance."

"Don't you want to find out why James sent us here to speak with Chester?"

"I do but I also don't want to be buried alive."

Luna let out a low warning growl at that moment.

"See? Luna agrees."

"So now what do you suggest our next move is?"

I pulled out my phone.

"Ah young Obi wan, let me show you the power of Google."

I typed in Chester Ruke, Maine. Only thing that came up was a listing for used tires at a place named Ruke's. Levi was leaning over my shoulder.

"I think you typed O'Rourke wrong, try it with a Capital O and R with a comma in between the two."

This time a few links popped up. One for Nora O'Rourke's Facebook page, one for the police department where he worked and one link that led to the obituary page in the local paper.

"Levi, read this. Says Chester died in a hiking accident, leaving behind his wife Nora."

"You know what? I remember hearing about that on the news. If I remember right, said he fell over 100 feet onto some rocks on the coast. His wife thought he had gone out before sunrise to try and photograph it from the top of the trail. I guess he had a habit of doing that in various places around the area. I'm trying to remember when that was."

I looked at the dates listed at the end of the short article.

"Says here he died a few weeks after James signed off on the final report. Why would James send us here, why not just say hey Chester is dead by the way? Why send us on a goose chase?"

Levi stared at the article as he thought, took another look around before motioning for us to start heading back to the gate.

"What if he didn't think it was an accident?"

"Like someone murdered the guy? Levi, you really think that's a possibility?"

"James didn't want to talk about it. Maybe he's just not a sociable guy, but to lose your partner and then send us out here? I agree, why?"

"Do you think that's why he's on leave? Because of Chester?"

"Maybe."

We had made it back to the truck by then, Levi had opened up the passenger door for us to climb into and stood there staring back at the gate we just came through.

"You thinking what I'm thinking?"

"That a big plate of loaded French fries sounds amazing right about now?"

"No, not what I was thinking. Thinking we should try and contact Nora, the wife. See what she knows?"

"I like the way you think Shel. Fries would still be my first option but yours is ok too."

As we drove away talking about some late-night food I thought I saw the shape of a black truck pull out of the bushes on the Cemetery side of the road. Could have sworn a glimmer of metal bounced in the street lamp for a second. Then thinking I must be too tired or hungry, dismissed the idea as quickly as it came in.

23

A week or so had passed since the third, fourth maybe fifth not a date. I lost count at this point. Other than his "thank you" text replying when I kept my promise by sending him a quick text that I was home sweet home, and another short series of texts back and forth about Nora's phone being disconnected with no new number to be found and just a PO for an address, I hadn't heard a thing from him. I pulled the door to the office shut behind me and let out a long sigh.

"Luna my girl, time to stop thinking about this. Obviously, it was indeed, again, not a date and just a continuation of welcome to the neighborhood."

Luna glanced up at me as we strode to the car, clearly agreeing with me. I was sure she was sick of hearing about it anyway. Daily happenings at the center had been peacefully slow allowing me to make short work of what remained on the to do list that I went back over a few days ago. Other than a few upcoming rentals, my only real responsibility was to show up each day, walk around looking for potential problems. Problem was, although it was a pretty walk, it was mind numbing. It only took two hours a day tops, if we walked slowly and took squirrel chasing breaks. I was bored...beyond bored. This was not what I had imagined when I took the job. Which is what pushed me to leave today after the run though, change the routine.

Without an ounce of guilt, Luna and I were heading home to grab our stuff for a long hike to a nearby fire tower. I had called Walters a few more times, being the bigger person and all, to see if I could get a jump on anything for him for next season. Offered to work up new flyers, catalogs, a social media marketing plan, find some grants...all of which was taken with as much enthusiasm that one shows when getting a filling put in at the dentist. So, I let that ship sail.

My other new hobby that was bordering on stalking was scanning Nora O'Rourkes Facebook page to see if I could find a time to accidentally bump into her. With her phone number being off grid so to speak, Facebook was the only connection we had with her. Trouble was, since Chester's death her posts had been very few and far between. What I was scanning were posts pre-Chester's death, PCD as I had been referring to it to myself as no one else was talking to me. I hoped it would spell out a pattern of things she did or places she went. So far, from her posts PCD, I knew she liked farmers markets, loved reposting memes about squirrels and it looked like her and Chester had done a bunch of traveling. The farmers market piece would be useful had it not been late fall with snow starting to fall. Next time one of those would take place would be months from now.

So, the new plan, check the Center out, then head out to explore the area by day and try new things by night. So far it has been working for us. I had signed up for a pottery class at a cute little shop in town, the owner was a spunky woman in her mid-forties named Suzette. Initially, I had just ventured in after work looking for a souvenir coffee mug, something that would pair well with cold nights, thick blankets and a good book by the wood stove in the cabin. I left with a fun mug with moose antlers for handles as well as a spot in a class to attempt to make my own. Suzette promised that by the end if I didn't have a functioning mug I could pick one out of the store for free. I had taken a ceramic class in high school and had barely scraped by. Even the art teachers, who always had such positive things to say about everything, had a hard time giving my sorry excuse for art more than a C+. I was not fooled, that C+ was all for effort, not the final products. Needless to say, I was anticipating taking her up on her free mug offer.

Thinking about which mug I would pick after I crashed and burned during pottery class, I pulled into the cabin's drive and slammed on the brakes. Poor Luna tried to stay on the seat but gravity won and slung her onto the floor. I got out of the truck, mouth gaping at the two-story pine tree that had decided to lay down on the Cabin roof and kept going right through to the floor.

"You have got to be kidding me."

I hopped out staring at the roof and tree.

24

T WO HOURS LATER it was very clear we were not hiking. Camping perhaps in the yard, as the roof was obliterated by a monstrous white pine, but
no fire tower sunset hike. That prospect fit my mood rather nicely. Once
I got my head together, I calmly got my phone out and called Walters.
The Center provided housing as part of the employment benefits, one
quick call and I could pass this off to the powers that be, no big deal. Two
hours later I had yet to hear back from him. With nightfall not far off, I
made the executive decision to call someone to take care of it. Problem
was, I wasn't sure who that someone should be and settled on the police.

The chief of police sounded a bit sauced when he hung up on me,
accusing me of being a lousy high schooler who should know better than
to prank call the police station. Jackie the deputy must have overheard the
conversation because she called back moments after the Chief hung up.

She swung out not too long afterward, took a quick look and immediately called to have the electricity, gas and water to the cabin turned off.
The tree not only took out the roof, but a good chunk of the electrical
lines, the water tank and clipped the stove enough to knock the gas line
out of place allowing it to seep into the cabin. She gave me a 'you were

lucky speech' and I felt like I was back in grade school and more than a little foolish that I hadn't thought to do the same. Thankfully, she knew the couple who had rented the cabin to the center and was getting in touch with them to see what they wanted to do. She also called in the fire department to make sure nothing dangerous was leaking and the forestry department to get the tree out of the way for everyone else to do their job.

Hearing that forestry was coming did not make this night any better. I was still miffed that I hadn't heard from Levi. Really pissed at myself for thinking that what we had been doing was anything more than working on Harvey's meat problem. Clearly, I had read that all wrong.

I sat off to the side on the tailgate running through my head as to how I would play it. I settled on being polite but not making the initial contact. I didn't want it to look like I was hoping to see him but when the forestry department crew arrived, it did not contain Levi. Not too long after they had the tree out and the three-man crew was in the process of chain sawing the trunk into manageable chunks to haul out. The fire department sent a handful of people over to check the house and lines inside and out, and it seemed like they were wrapping up as well. They were all exiting the cabin and not in a rush, I took that as a good sign.

"Come on Luna, let's go see if someone will fill us in."

Trying not to get in the way but at the same time wanting to be in the way enough that someone may stop what they were doing to talk to me, I started up the walkway to the front door.

"Ma'am? Hold up a second, you can't go in there just yet."

My plan worked perfectly. I turned to see a kid, who couldn't have been a day over 17 I swear, holding a large pair of wire cutters looking very uncomfortable to be talking to me.

"Can you tell me what's going on, when we will be able to get inside?"

I gave him my most pleasant smile. Who can say no to a pleasant smile?

"Um, I can't. I can go get the fire chief if you want. He's inside, just a sec."

He turned his head and then did an about face.

"Um, would you mind waiting, just over there somewhere? Chief will chew me out if I let you stand here so close to the cabin before he clears it."

The poor kid looked like he was going to puke when he asked me to move. Confrontation was clearly not this kid's forte.

"Not a problem, we will wait over here for him."

Luna sat statue still next to me, not thrilled with the influx of people everywhere. I always thought she would be a good chess player the way she absorbs every detail before making her next move. She let out a low warning growl suddenly that had me searching for the cause of it. A tall man in fire garb was walking briskly over. I put a hand on her back letting her know I saw him. Her growl subsided but her body language was very much on guard.

"Hello there, I'm the Fire Chief. Sam said you were hoping to speak with me?"

He took off his helmet, smiled and reached his hand out. I was pleased when his handshake was firm, I hated when men shook hands with a woman using a dainty 'you're so fragile' shake. Nothing says 'I feel you're weaker than I', than that chauvinistic maneuver.

"Shelly. Thanks, Chief, for taking a few minutes to talk. Just wondering what was going on and when we could get in to see what smooshed, that kind of thing was."

"Chase, you can call me Chase."

He smiled again and paused, glancing back at the house.

"Well, we are just about done. Luckily you came home when you did and called right away. The gas line to the stove was leaking steadily and the electrical panel for the house was taken out, either of those things given enough time would have been worse. Everything is turned off and safe from that perspective, just waiting on the tree guys to get the pine out of the way and you should be able to get in to grab a few things."

I blew out a breath as I absorbed what he said.

"This is all not an easy fix I am going to guess."

"I wouldn't plan on staying here for a while if I were you. Do you have somewhere else to stay?"

No, I thought, but said yes. No need to tell a stranger I had zero back-up plans at the moment.

"Let me go check on a few things and see if we can get you in there to grab what you need. I'll be around for a bit and can help you get stuff to your car."

"Getting in would be more than enough help, thank you."

"Sit tight, be right back."

He reached down to pat Luna but stopped at her low growl.

"Good pup, must just be stressed. Dogs usually love me."

With that thought he retreated back to the house.

"Ease up Luna, biting the fire chief would not be in our best interest at the moment. He was just trying to be friendly."

I ruffled her ears and scratched her chest in the spot she liked best. A few minutes later Chase waved us over.

THE cabin was a wreck. This was not the first time I was thankful we traveled light as there wasn't much to gather. Nothing of mine was really destroyed, clothes were a little soggy, a few books had to be tossed and Luna's food bag was done. Other than that, not a total loss other than the roof over our heads.

As promised, Chase helped to lug what we had to the truck. I had to redirect him from trying to load everything into a little white Honda Civic he assumed was mine that was actually Sam's wheels, but was a help none-theless. He was friendly, making small talk as we loaded. Seemed like he was another born and raised Mainer who wanted to help the community that he loved. Everything was loaded as dark settled in. Jackie pulled up the driveway, parked and made her way over to us.

"Hey Chase, Shelly. Just got off the phone with the McNeilands, they're going to have their son-in law swing by here tomorrow to assess the damage and start rebuilding before snow hits. They offered you their other rental in the meantime. Bit farther out of town and a little smaller but I can assure you it has been meticulously maintained over the years."

She paused looking back at the mess the tree made.

"Poor cabin, it was always one of my favorite properties in town. Anyway, are you interested?"

"Yes, please. Do you have McNeiland's number? I'd love to call and thank them as well."

"Excellent, yes I'll write it down for you, here."

She scribbled a number down on a piece of paper along with the address to the new property. I glanced at the address, the road sounded familiar but couldn't place why it did.

"The neighbor has a spare key and can meet you there to open up in a few hours, around seven."

I glanced at my watch, just past 4:30pm, seven would have to do.

"Perfect. Thanks again for helping me with this Jackie. I appreciate it."

"No problem, if you need anything give me a buzz, my cell is on the bottom of that paper if you need it."

She shot a sidelong glance at the fire chief.

"I mean it. Call me if you have any issues. Have a good night."

Chase turned to me, one arm leaning on the hood of the truck.

"Want to grab some dinner seeing as you have a few hours to kill? I'm starving and you are homeless for a few hours."

He had a good point and other than the Center we really had nowhere else to go until seven.

"That would be nice, thank you."

"Alright then, we can take my truck. It's the black extended cab over there."

He gestured to a large, very new, very shiny truck parked in the road. I glanced at my steady eddy truck with our stuff piled haphazardly under a tarp in the bed and thought the less I drove our belongings around the better.

I nodded and clucked to Luna and started walking over.

"Whoa, hold on a second. The dog is not coming, is it?"

"Where else would she go? The cabin is not an option."

"Can't you leave her in your truck?"

"It's the end of October and dark. Would you like to be locked in the cab of a cold truck?"

My tone was sharp but I didn't care.

"Ok, ok easy now. I didn't realize you were one of those people with your pets."

I felt my eyebrows shoot up in a I can't believe you said that look which had him quickly backtracking.

"I'm sorry, didn't mean it like that either. Been a long day."

I took a breath and counted to 10 before saying anything. We both had had long days, which I could understand. He seemed genuinely sorry for suggesting Luna stay and for the pet comment.

"Tell you what, why don't you follow me and we can grab a slice at the pizza place. They have outdoor seating although I am sure we will be the only ones using it tonight."

He held his hands up in a what do you say gesture.

"Let's do that."

Easier on everyone and gave us wheels to leave if we wanted to. I sat in my truck and waited for Chase to finish talking with his crew, Rubbing Luna's ears absently. Whenever I was waiting or day dreaming I would catch myself rubbing her fur. I hoped it was as stress relieving for her as it was for me. I glanced at my watch hoping to get this show on the road soon. Sam walked up to Chase's window. I was starving and starting to regret agreeing to grab a bite to eat with the Fire Chief.

WALKING cautiously, Sam stopped at the chief's window. Chase let out a sigh and rolled it down for him.

"Yes Sam, what do you need? I'm on my way out in case you can't tell."

"Sorry sir, I... ah just thought you'd... well that you would want to know..."

"Come on kid, spit it out already."

"The tree that fell?"

"Yeah, what about it?"

Chase was flipping through his phone as he listened but froze as Sam finally got out what he was trying to say.

"The tree looks like it didn't fall, sir. It looks like it was cut with an ax."

Chase's eyes narrowed as he looked Sam up and down.

"Sammy, don't worry about it. I saw that too. Looks like someone tried to chop it down years ago and gave up. Betting those wind gusts, we had today hit it at the right time and down she went. Before you go, roll up that fire house on truck 2, better would you? Looks like children wound it up."

With that cutting remark he rolled up his window and pulled out with Shelly's truck a few lengths behind.

Sam stood there not sure what to do. The Chief was probably right, but how did a tree that was almost chopped down years ago end up with fresh sawdust all around the base and cut marks? His phone pinged with an incoming text. He read it and sighed, his mom wanted him to stop and get eggs on his way home. He hated this job but he needed it to save up to move out on his own. Loved his mom, just needed some space. A few more months and he should have enough to move downstate. With plans of doing just that in his head he started in on unwinding and rewinding the fire hose.

25

Levi had taken the call from Jackie about a tree falling on top of the McNeiland's house but was tied up with a lost hiker when it came in. He sent a few people over there and had Sal talking with the crew, keeping tabs on the progress. If anything crazy happened, Sal would call him. The McNeilands were long time family friends of his parents. Mr. McNeiland had given him his first summer job freshman year of high school, Work Site Remediation. He smiled as he thought about how that title had him bragging to everyone about his big important job. Five minutes into his first day he realized that all it meant was he was a low man on the totem pole and had to lug and clean up anything anyone else didn't want to. He worked summers for him all through high school and college, learned a hell of a lot about construction and woodworking. Even after college he had helped renovate several of their rental properties over the years and nowadays acted as their caretaker occasionally when they ditched their flannel lined jeans to become snowbirds down south for the winter.

Being a small town, Jackie knew all of that and didn't have to ask him if he could open up the cottage later. At that point his guys had already found the hiker, and feeling hopeful, he had told her he should be over there to open up around 7:30 pm. Levi flipped the collar of his jacket up and stomped his feet a bit to get the blood flowing.

Thankfully the hiker hadn't been too far off the trail and was making his way back with two of the rangers. The hiker was cold and more embarrassed than anything. Tourists did not always dress for the Maine fall weather which could have been deadly had they not found him as quick as they did. What he gathered so far from the short radio talks with his rangers was that the guy saw a moose way off the trail and wanted a picture. He walked off the trail and into the woods following a moose, a 1,200 pound animal that has a tendency to charge things.

The guy never got near the moose but while in pursuit he ended up turned around, and never made it back to the trail. He started to pack up the make shift command post they had slapped together using a piece of plywood and sawhorses. Mentally he ran through what was left as he worked. Already called off the Game Wardens and the S&R dogs. Had notified the hiker's family they had found him. He thought again at how lucky the guy had been. The only smart thing he had done was tell someone where he was going and what time to expect him back. The family called in worried when he was four hours overdue. Levi glanced at his phone. If all went according to plan he should be able to wrap this up here and get over on time to the rental to let in whoever the pine tree evicted when it fell.

26

THE PIZZA PLACE was a cute mom and pop's Italian restaurant, complete with the classic red and white striped awning that I presumed used to cover outdoor seating. Today it was just cement, no picnic tables in sight. I had stopped at the grocery store on my way over to pick up some food for Luna until I could order her regular stuff along with shredded cheese. Luna was a lot of things and a picky eater was one. She would only eat strange kibble with a solid layer of shredded cheese on top.

Chase was inside already, I could see him at a booth through the window. I had pulled into a parking spot that was just outside the window near the booth Chase was in so I could see Luna in the truck from the inside. Not what I had hoped for, but the truck was warm, she had dinner, her favorite blanket and I could keep an eye on her while we ate.

"I'll be back in a few, my dear."

I gave her a quick kiss on the nose and shut the door. The smell of warm pizza hit me as soon as I walked in making my mouth water. Chase waved as I entered and singled to the waitress.

"Smells amazing here."

"Best pizza I have ever had. They make a great chicken parm too. What are you in the mood for?"

"Anything but fish and pineapple on pizza works for me."

I took a glance at the table, he couldn't have gotten here that much before me and already had two empty beer bottles sitting off to the side.

"Let's keep it easy, cheese and pepperoni?"

I nodded in agreement as the waitress walked up.

"Can I get you something to drink?"

She was looking at me but before I could answer Chase jumped in.

"We will have a large cheese and pepperoni pizza, and a pitcher of Miller please."

He glanced at me and winked. The wink was getting irritating.

"I'll also have water, please. Thank you."

The waitress wrote it all down and I swear cast a pitying look as she walked away. Wondering what the hell that was about I turned back to Chase wondering what I had gotten into.

CHASE kept the conversation going as we waited for dinner. He was alright company, a little full of himself but not a bore. It wasn't the worst way to kill a few hours I told myself and the food was outstanding. If nothing else, this town had nailed the food options. We chatted politely throughout dinner, and heard a few more stories about his heroics as a firefighter than I would have cared to, but such was life. Amazingly, he drank the whole pitcher himself and then ordered another beer.

"So, how are things at the Center?"

"Pretty good, can't complain."

He glanced at his cell that had chimed for the 50th time since the pizza arrived. He seemed to be running out of things to say as he opened and closed his mouth a few times like he was going to speak before he actually did.

"I ran into the police chief the other day. Mentioned that you had been helping Harvey with some ah garbage?"

"Yeah, A bunch of rotting meat keeps getting dumped in the garbage can by the end of his driveway."

"What does that have to do with you? Better question, what does it have to do with the Center?"

"Well I guess it really doesn't tie directly to the Center or me but it's a stone's throw from the property line where it's been happening. In fact, the weird thing is that the spot it's being dropped is like a no man's land. No one owns that section nor who put the garbage can there in the first place."

"You don't say."

The tone he used was not one that said how surprising, it had more of an underlying annoyed tone.

"Even weirder? The same thing was happening north of here for a while, up around Fort Kent. Have you ever heard anything about it?"

"About rotting garbage? I have better things to do than worry about another town's sanitation issues. You really think Walters is paying you to chase crap like that?"

"Whoa hold up, what's with the attitude?"

"Attitude? Didn't peg you for being one of those chicks. Let Harvey deal with it. Walters gets wind that you're pissing off work at the Center to do that? He'll can you before sunrise. Waste of a paycheck that could have been used for something useful if that's what you're doing."

To say I was stunned would have been putting it mildly. Who the fuck was this jack ass? The waitress reappeared at that moment with the bill. I stood up and threw a 10 on the table and started heading for the door. I was almost to the truck when I heard him jog up behind me.

"What's your problem?"

"What's my problem? You're an ass and I made an incredibly poor decision coming here tonight."

I started to turn to open my door signaling I was leaving when he placed his hands on either side of the truck stopping me from turning or opening the door.

"What are you doing? You need to back up."

"Slow down girl, just wanted to say goodnight. Least you could do after I bought you dinner, besides you were all green light inside."

"Hold on jackass, I paid for my own dinner, no way in hell I owed more than ten bucks and no signals whatsoever were given."

"Oh chill out, no need for name calling, I'll let you go."

As soon as he said that he smashed his lips into mine and copped a feel at the same time.

"Get off of me!"

I punched his throat as hard as I could and kneed him in the nuts, wasn't a full wind up for either but he staggered back, shock all over his face. Luna was going nuts growling behind me.

"What the fuck is wrong with you?!"

I jumped in the truck and threw it in reverse before he was able to speak. I flipped him the bird as I pulled out, my heart was racing as we hit the two- lane road into town. Thank god we drove ourselves. Luna was sniffing and nuzzling me all over making sure I was ok and making it impossible to drive safely. I pulled over in the grocery store parking lot to collect ourselves. I took a few deep breaths, rubbing Luna's scruff. My hands were a little shaky. From anger or nerves I wasn't sure, a mix of both?

We sat for twenty minutes until the clock read seven.

"Let's hope this next neighbor is a cute little old bocce lady."

I reached into my coat pocket to pull out the paper Jackie had given me but came out with nothing. I checked the other one, then my jean pockets. It must have fallen out in the pizza shop when I threw my ten bucks down or in the parking lot. I took a long steadying breath, I remembered the road name and was fairly positive on the house number. We could do this. Nerves settled, we pulled out and made our way to Gunther Hollow Road.

Jackie wasn't kidding when she said it was a little farther out. Totally misjudged how long it would take to get out here, I hoped whoever was waiting on me didn't give up. I wasn't sure I was up to cold calling on random doors until I found the right one. I glanced at the clock, 7:37, I was kicking myself for not charging my phone earlier. It was uselessly sitting dead in the cup holder. The GPS would have gotten me here a heck of a lot faster. I was trying to read my map and glanced up in time to see 'Gunther Hollow' on the street sign as I drove right by. I slammed on the brakes making Luna scramble for purchase on the old seat.

"Sorry girl, we're almost there, I hope. Here we go, onto the road finally. Keep your eyes peeled for the address."

27

Levi had just gotten home. The hiker had a pretty nasty sprain that slowed the extraction process a bit. He parked in his drive, grabbed the spare key he kept for them and jogged the couple hundred yards over to the McNeiland's hoping whoever was coming to stay had waited. When he hit the gravel drive, he slowed, then stopped, looking around. Not a car in sight. "Shit" he muttered. They either left or they haven't shown up yet. He hoped for the latter. He hopped up on the porch of the little blue cedar shake cabin and dug his phone out of his coveralls. Maybe Jackie had their number. He wanted to see if this was going to be a short or long night depending on if they had already been and gone. He was just about to hit send when a pair of headlights paused at the road, then slowly turned into the driveway.

He stood to the side and waved wishing he had thought to turn on the porch lights. Guy standing in a dark driveway was not the welcoming committee most hoped for. The truck stopped and the driver rolled down the window just a crack. Odd he thought, but then again he was a strange dude standing in a dark driveway in the middle of nowhere.

"Hey, sorry I was a little late. I hope you didn't have to come back out here. My name is..."

"Levi? What are you doing here?"

"Shelly? I could ask you the same thing, what are you doing here?"

I opened the door and stepped outside as Luna hurled herself out at the same time knocking me forward. I would have hit the ground except Levi had moved to the side of the truck making my landing softer as I took him out on my way down. Luna thought this was great fun and was doing her best to get to the top of the dog pile.

"Luna, get down!"

Rolling off of Levi I tried my best to drag Luna with me.

"I'm so sorry, she apparently couldn't wait to say hi to you."

Levi was still laying on the ground with Luna dancing all over him as he rubbed her belly and gave her a friendly squeeze around the shoulders.

"It's all good, the feeling is mutual."

He smiled up at me, gave Luna a gentle shove and got himself up.

"So, what are you doing here?"

"Well if I have the right address, I'm staying here until the cabin I was staying in gets fixed."

"You're the one staying at the McNeiland's log cabin? The one the tree fell on top of? Are you ok? Jackie said she was sending someone out to stay in this one but she never said who. I figured it was someone passing through or a couple up here on vacation."

I squatted down to hug Luna.

"Yeah we're fine, the tree fell while we were still at the Center. Came home and found it then called the police. Didn't actually set foot in it until a few hours ago. What are you doing here? Did whoever was going to open up for us bail when we were late?"

"Nope. I am the person who is opening up."

He handed over the key.

"Come on I'll give you the 10 cent tour then we can get your stuff inside."

"Wait, so you live next door?"

Jackie saying the neighbor had a key was ringing loud and clear in my mind.

"Couple hundred yards to your left. You can't see my place from here but you can walk over if you two need anything. Come on Luna, you will love the bay window in the back."

He walked up the stairs and flipped the porch light on and waited for us to follow. Of all the places to end up I thought as I went tromping up the stairs behind him.

28

THE BLUE CABIN was adorable. About half the size of the one in town but I loved the look and the feel of it. The kitchen had an amazing bay window, complete with window seat, and opened up to a living room that had a big comfy couch in front of a wood burning stove. Down a short hall was the utility closet on the left, half bath on the right. Upstairs was the loft bedroom that was open so you could look down into the living room and had, what for sure was heaven sent, a huge claw foot soaker tub that was on the other side of a set of French doors in back below several skylights. I was not one to swoon but oh did I swoon at the sight of that.

I glanced over my shoulder and caught Levi watching me take in the cabin. He was leaning against the wall with his arms crossed and a grin on his face.

"What? Why are you looking at me like that?"

He cleared his throat and stood up.

"Tell you what, how about you get a fire going and Luna and I can start bringing your stuff in?"

He paused, waiting for her to say yes or no.

I looked at Levi, not sure what to say. So maybe he didn't want to date me, but perhaps I found a friend, a good friend.

"Thank you, really."

"What, no witty remark?"

I knew he was just teasing me, and I cursed myself for getting a little teary eyed.

"You, um ok?"

I blinked rapidly looking anywhere but at him.

"Yup, just some dust in my eyes. You could have cleaned a little before I got here, you know."

"Had I known it was you coming I would have placed little chocolates on all the pillows, your majesty."

He did a mock curtsy that made him look ridiculous in his coveralls.

"Oh god, please go get some bags!"

I gave him a friendly nudge on my way to the wood stove. There was a small stack of kindling in a bin next to it but nothing substantial to burn.

"Hey, I didn't even look, is there wood on the porch?"

"Enough for tonight. I can bring some over tomorrow, I have a few extra cord that I should use before it rots. Should be another bin of kindling in the utility closet as well. Be right back."

HE made a few trips from the truck to the cabin but they really didn't have all that much stuff. The last trip was only a small duffle bag that he took with him as he made a detour back to his house to grab a couple beers and a bag of cheesy popcorn. He wasn't sure if she had eaten but he was starving. He walked in and felt the warm fire. Not only was this woman beautiful but she knew how to make a fire.

"That's the last of it. God that fire feels good."

"Thank you for lugging all our crap in."

"No problem. I grabbed us a few beers and some popcorn, I wasn't sure if you had dinner yet."

"Where did you get that from? Wait, better question, that's what you call dinner?"

"I ran home quickly before bringing in the last of your stuff and some-times that's what I call dinner. It's been a busy few weeks, I haven't had time to go grocery shopping. I just got home a few minutes before you pulled in. I was out on a lost hiker call."

"Did you find them?"

"We did. Thankfully he wasn't too far off the trail, sprained ankle and more embarrassed than anything. Do you care if I stay and warm up for a minute?"

"Yeah, of course come in. This is more your place than mine."

I flushed a little, feeling still out of sorts from earlier.

He took off his boots, glanced down at his muddy wet coveralls.

"Um, this may sound weird."

It was his turn to blush a little, I was intrigued at what could possibly make him blush.

"Go on."

"Do you care if I take these off? I have long underwear underneath, I'm not going to be naked or anything, these are soaked and..."

He rushed through getting out the last part and his face was getting a similar shade of red that mine takes on at times. I tried to keep a straight face but lost it and ended up sinking down to the floor in a fit of laughter.

Wiping the tears from my eyes I looked up at him waiting flustered by the door.

"Please feel free to strip, make yourself at home and I would love one of those beers."

"So glad I can amuse you."

He slid out of his coveralls and laid them neatly on the doormat and walked over in his thick flannel shirt and tight black thermal underwear.

"I know I'm not naked but hell, I feel like it."

He sat down on the floor and handed over a beer. His legs looked very muscular under his long underwear. I took a long sip and let out a sigh as the cold liquid warmed me up from the inside out.

"Long day?"

"You have no idea. Well, actually probably not as long as yours. Missing hikers are no joke."

"Wasn't terrible because we found him quickly. His wife reported him missing when he was overdo getting home. She knew where he had started from and where he was going, that helped a ton. Too often people go out and don't bother telling anyone what their plan is. Person gets lost but no one realizes for almost a full day or more which makes the search that much harder. Every hour that ticks by, the area that they could be in increases by the size of a business card laying on a map. Every hour adds miles of ground to cover in a search."

"The woods are so dense up here, too. Easy to get turned around and not be able to hear someone yelling for you or a nearby road."

"Exactly. The most beautiful pristine wilderness I have ever seen, but that beauty hides danger if you don't know what you're doing."

Levi took a handful of popcorn and chewed thoughtfully for a moment.

"Other than a tree smashing your cabin, how was your day?"

"It was ok up until that point, then all downhill from there."

"Jackie help you out?"

"She was the first to show up, then she called in the fire department, your department and the McNeilands. She was a huge help. She didn't stay too long after everyone seemed to have their part under control. I heard her radio chirp a few times, guessing she had other calls to get to."

"The forestry crew, get in and get out alright?"

What Levi really wanted to ask was if they were respectful but didn't know how to do so without looking like a dork. It was Middle school and not knowing what to say to a girl he liked all over again was the thought that kept running through his head.

"They were great, couldn't tell you who they were. They showed up, said hi and then jumped right in. I will say it didn't take them as long as I thought it would to disassemble the tree."

"Who was out for the fire department?"

"Um, four guys total I think? I only met two of them. Sam, who can't be more than 17, am I right?"

Levi grinned.

"Sam is almost 25 but looks like he's 16 and acts somewhere around 35 most of the time. Nice guy, good head on his shoulders, tries really hard."

"He was very nice, little nervous and green it seemed."

"Who was the other one you met?"

He took a sip and grabbed some popcorn.

"The chief was there, Chase."

"Hmm, he's a bit of an ass."

"You got that right. He talked me into grabbing a slice of pizza while I waited for you to open up here. Tried to get to second base as I was getting into my truck."

"He did what?!"

I glanced up and was surprised to see the anger in his face.

"I handled it, he had way too much to drink and pinned me against the truck for a second and copped a feel. I punched him in the neck and hopefully kneed his nuts into his stomach. I didn't stick around to see how he was doing."

I took another sip of beer and glanced at Levi, not quite sure what to expect out of him. I felt a bit better about the whole thing, turns out it was a little cathartic to tell him about it.

Levi didn't say anything, just sat frozen. I swear I could hear his teeth grinding in his head.

"Hey, it's not that big of a deal."

Levi scoffed.

"It's not? No one should have to put up with that Shel, especially from the fucking fire chief! Guys is a fucking ass. Sorry I called you Shel, Shelly."

"You can call me Shel, just don't tell anyone else you do."

That got a smile out of him.

"It's not alright, but it happened and I handled it."

"The guy is a drunk and an asshole on a huge power trip. You handled it tonight but he will not let that go. Last woman he dated had to get a restraining order and moved out of town because he wouldn't leave her alone."

"I didn't date him!"

"No, you kicked his ass which may be worse. Just, if you run into him and he's drunk and acting like an idiot, call me. If I can't get there I will make sure someone else does."

I opened my mouth to argue, Levi threw up his hands and kept talking.
"I know you are alright and you handled it, but are you alright?"

He lifted his arm like he was going to touch my shoulder but wasn't sure he should, so it hung awkwardly in between us for a second before he dropped it down on Luna's head. I smiled and respected that he respected me enough not to assume I wanted his arm on me. I lifted my hand and set it on his, giving it a gentle squeeze.

"I'm good, thank you for asking. But let's talk about something else."

He let out a long breath, shook his head.

"I could use another beer. Would you like one?"

"Yeah, what the hell. Why not?"

"Okay then, be right back."

With that he stood up in his long underwear and flannel jacket and proceeded to jog out the door and through the woods. I watched him disappear out the window in the darkness.

"You know Luna, I am glad it wasn't a little old lady waiting for us. No way would she have been jogging through the woods to bring us back a beer."

29

Levi woke up the next morning groggy. He hadn't stayed at Shel's place all that late and only had the two beers. Problem was when he got home he couldn't stop thinking about her. Turns out he had had that sleepless night over a woman for the reason he didn't want. Before he left he checked all the windows and back door to make sure they were locked. He tried to do it on the sly but she caught on to what he was doing and sent him home. It made him feel better knowing she was only through the woods. Felt even better knowing she had an 80 lb dog with her at all times.

"I should get a dog. Then in the mornings I wouldn't be talking to myself, I would be talking to my dog."

Maybe a search and rescue dog, then the pup could go to work with him too. He was contemplating texting her to see if she wanted some coffee, he wasn't sure if the cabin had anything like that stocked in it.

He started walking into the kitchen but stopped short when he glanced out the front window. The ground had a fresh dusting of snow, first of the season. He opened the front door and found two perfect paw prints on his front step next to a piece of paper folded in half. He reached down and read the short note and whistled as he went back inside. He had a dinner date with the neighbor.

30

My PHONE CHIMED while I was in the middle of checking in the week-end rental for the Big Hall. Whoever named the buildings and pavilions at the Center was seriously lacking in imagination. I glanced quickly. It was from Levi asking if he could bring anything tonight. I had to admit, I was a little nervous. Not my usual play, inviting a cute guy over for a home cooked dinner but I found myself delivering the note with Luna before really thinking it through. I told him no as I had no idea what I was going to make. Luna and I lived simply, deliciously, but simply nonetheless.

"Alright, Mrs. Otto, just sign here and here, basically the form says you agree to abide by the Big Hall rules and that you know if any damage is done we will keep your security deposit."

"Fairly straight forward, thank you my dear."

She signed then handed the slips back to me and I in turn handed her the keys.

"My cell is on the bottom of your receipt, give me a call if anything comes up. I am on call for your entire event and will not be far."

"Again, thank you. We will be fine. My husband actually built this building years ago. Anything goes wrong I will blame him."

She chuckled and waved goodbye.

"The world needs more of Mrs. Otto's, Luna. Come on kiddo, let's lock up and boogie. We have a grocery store to hit."

In route to pick up ingredients I decided to make a pit stop at Rivers. Fresh snow mixed with a little bit of sun called for something chocolatey with caffeine. I had a feeling I would not be disappointed as I walked in deeply inhaling the most heavenly scent.

"Welcome to River's, what can I get you and your adorable partner?"

I opened my eyes and smiled sheepishly.

"I'm sorry I should have checked to see if you allowed dogs, took a chance."

"It's easier to ask forgiveness than permission, no truer words have been spoken."

I turned to Sal with a forestry jacket sitting at a table near the window. "Trust me young lady, words to live by."

"Oh Sal, stop. Your pup is more than welcome as long as she mind's her manners."

"Why? You sure as hell don't!"

"Sal!"

The woman burst out laughing.

"She is going to think we are a couple of kooks!"

She turned back to me.

"Dogs are always welcome at my place. I'm River."

"Nice to meet you, and good to see you again Sal."

"I'm Shelly, the caretaker for the Center for the winter."

"Likewise. Now, for sure you didn't come in here to chat idly with us, what can I get you?"

"Well I came in for something hot, chocolatey with caffeine, what do you recommend?"

"Mattawamkeag Mocha is a house favorite."

"Love the name, I'll go with that to go, please and thank you!"

I glanced at the menu as she was making the concoction.

"Hey, are all your drinks named after rivers?"

"Hah! You are a sharp one. Usually takes the out of towners quite a while to pick up on that. Figured my name is River, the shop is River's the drinks should be named after rivers."

She handed over a cup with liquid that made me want to sink into a comfy chair with a book and disappear for the weekend.

"I love it, and if this tastes even half as good as it smells I have a feeling you will be sick of seeing us."

I took a sip.

"This is amazing, thank you."

Sal pushed out a chair with her foot making a god awful screeching sound as it slid. "Whoops, sorry about that. Here, come sit for a minute, if you're going to be coming around more might as well get to know you more."

I paused, looked at the clock on the wall, did some quick math and sat down.

"Got a hot date?"

Sal said that loaded with sarcasm, I laughed and plopped down into the offered chair, Luna stood on Sal's lap loving every second of the offered belly scratch.

"Actually, I do."

I wiggled my eyebrows at her as I took a sip, which made Sal laugh. Stand-up comedy here I come I thought.

31

THE COFFEE STOP had taken a bit longer than I anticipated, but was well worth it. Not only did I have a much-needed jolt of delicious caffeine but I happened to make friends with the owner of said delicious caffeine and Levi's Assistant who most likely is Levi's boss in disguise. I couldn't picture Sal being anyone's assistant.

After much debate at the grocery store I decided the hell with it and went with cooking what I wanted instead of what I thought would impress. Luna and I were on our way home with all the fixings for bacon grilled cheese sandwiches, French fries and to make it a balanced meal, a spinach feta salad. I was almost to Gunther Hollow Rd when my cell rang. I slowed to a stop at the corner and fished my phone out from under the passenger seat. That was the problem with my old truck, the front seat was a long bench that spanned the entire cab. Anything I set on it, including Luna at times, ended up on the floor, then would shift under the seat. It stopped ringing before I could answer. It was a 207 number, not one I recognized. Living dangerously, I hit the call back and Mrs. Otto picked up.

"Oh, hello dear, sorry to bother you, it's Mrs. Otto."

"Not a bother at all, what can I do for you?"

"Well, we seem to have a bit of a problem."

She paused but I wasn't worried, couldn't be too bad as she was very calm sounding.

"Bob, my husband, turned the oven on to keep the pizza's we ordered warm until dinner."

In the background I heard an angry man yelling over Mrs. Otto.

"You told me to turn the oven on!"

"I know I told you to but I never said put the pizza's in the oven still in their boxes!"

She cleared her throat.

"Sorry about that, as you may have heard he put the pizza's, box and all into the oven to stay warm. Long story short, the building is on fire."

"What?!!"

"Not to worry, we already called the fire department and they are on their way."

"Oh my god, I'm on my way. How much is on fire?"

I was already spinning the truck around, so fast my wallet and groceries slid onto the floor, Luna dug in and managed to stay relatively put.

"Well that's the good news, only two thirds seem to be engulfed at this point. But no one is hurt! Have to look at the positives on this one, don't we?"

"Two thirds?! Two thirds, that's....I will see you in a minute!"

And with that I hung up and hit the gas.

I pulled into the Center and could see a huge cloud of billowing smoke coming from what was left of the old building near the picnic grove. I pulled up as close as I dared, which was about 300 yards off, left Luna in the truck and ran over to the blaze. My run slowed to a jog and I began searching the crowd for the Otto's. Thankfully I found them safe. Mrs. Otto was cool as a cucumber, Mr. Otto not so much. As I approached I caught the tail end of their discussion. Argument? I wasn't really sure nor did I care at the moment.

"I built this place so I can burn it down!"

"I don't think so dear."

"Well not on purpose!"

"No one thinks you did it on purpose dear."

"God Damn pizza boxes, what idiot makes a box out of cardboard?!"

"I don't know dear, come sit down, Shelly needs to talk to us I'm sure."

Mrs. Otto waved me over and patted a spot next to her on the tailgate offering me a seat. She must be crazy or on really good drugs to be sitting so calmly with a huge blaze glowing a few hundred feet away.

"Are you guys alright? Is anyone hurt?"

"We're fine, a few people have some singed hair but no one is worse for wear. The sprinkler system kicked on in time to get everyone out, just wasn't strong enough to prevent the flames from spreading once they got hold of the walls."

"Those walls were all hand scraped pine, it took us a week to do each wall just about."

Mrs. Otto was eerily calm while I could hear my heart thudding in my chest as we talked. I took a deep breath and watched the fire department put out the flames. I had no idea what my next move was other than find someone who may know what that may be. I had called Walter after hanging up on Mrs. Otto but the call went right to his voicemail. I left a short, frazzled message to call me back, after I had a bit more info I would call again and hopefully catch him.

"I suppose this means you will be keeping our deposit?"

I just stared at her. Who was this woman?!

The three of us stood in silence for the next twenty minutes watching the flames slowly die to embers, then fade into darkness. The cold snow and heat from the fire had made a rising mist giving the burnt structure a ghostly appearance. I ran back and pulled my truck up next to the Otto's and turned on the headlights to give us some light. Mrs. Otto was sitting in the driver seat of their truck with the door open. Luna was resting her head on her lap getting her ears gently massaged as we all waited for whatever was going to happen next.

Luna jerked her head up and let out a low growl. I turned and saw a fireman walking towards us, helmet with mask still in place.

"Easy girl, just someone in their fire gear is all."

"Nice that she looks out for you, we had a dog like that a long time ago, remember Scout Bob? Your dog reminds me of him."

I stroked Luna's back and waited for the fireman to finish walking over.

"Did you make the 911 call?"

He was looking at Mr. Otto, at least I think he was as his helmet with the mask was still on.

"I did."

Mrs. Otto slid out of the truck, she barely came up to his waist. He lifted his mask and I blanched, it was Chase. My fingers tightened on Luna's collar as her growl deepened and she stood on the seat ready.

"I will need to take your official statement then you can go home. Thank you for waiting for us to get everything under control."

He turned to look at me, paused, and then turned back to Mrs. Otto for her statement. I took a deep breath. I can handle this, just have to stay professional and near other people. Moving quickly I dragged Luna back to our truck and hopped in behind her.

After about ten minutes of light questions he seemed satisfied with the details, tucked his pad and pen back into his jacket.

"Alright Mr. and Mrs. Otto, thank you again for your help and for calling when you did. Couldn't save the building but your early call prevented it from spreading."

"Damn cardboard boxes, back in my day pizza boxes were made out of..."

"Cardboard. They have always been made of cardboard."

"Well they should be made of something else. Destroying buildings and the planet the way they are now."

Mr. Otto continued to grumble as he walked to the driver side of the truck.

"Thank you both, and again, we are so sorry for this and apparently pizza boxes. You have my number, please do not hesitate to call if you need anything."

And with that she followed Mr. Otto. Seeing my safety net disappear I followed suit, shutting the door on my truck and fired her up as soon as Mrs. Otto took a step after Bob.

"Now where do you think you're going?"

He reached through my window and grasped the steering wheel planting himself in a way that I would for sure run his foot over if I took off.

"You have their statements."

"Yes, but you are the one responsible for the building, are you not?"

I didn't say anything, just waited to see where he was going with this.

"You need to come with me to the station to fill out official documents regarding the fire."

He tried to open the door with his other hand but thankfully It was locked.

"No, I don't. Any paperwork you need can be mailed to the Center or dropped off at the police department."

His grip tightened and his smirk slowly changed to an angry scowl.

"I said get out of the truck. Now."

"Let go. Now."

I hoped I sounded more confident than I felt. Luna had been crouched on the seat during this whole thing watching and waiting. She leapt over me snarling and snapping at Chase. She didn't make contact with him but got close enough that he stumbled back a few steps. Just enough that I could hit the gas and not run him over.

"Thank you, Luna, good girl my love, good girl."

I had one hand buried in her fur as I looked in the rear view. He was yelling and shaking his fist. The last thing I saw as we rounded the corner and pulled out of sight was him smashing his helmet on the ground.

After a few miles my heart slowed down and so I slowed the truck as well. Would just top off my night to be pulled over for excessive speeding. I glanced at my phone, two missed calls. I hoped they were from Walter, it may be childish but I wanted someone else to deal with the aftermath of tonight. No such luck. First one was one of those phony IRS messages, like the IRS would leave a voicemail, seriously who fell for that crap?! The second was from Levi.

"Oh shit, I forgot about dinner."

I rested my head on the steering wheel at the next stop sign and counted to 10. Then 15. Then another 10.

"Time to call it a night Luna, maybe a week."

Fifteen minutes later I was slowing down to pull into the driveway and saw Levi's truck waiting to turn out of his. Not sure what to expect, but would much rather get this over with tonight, I pulled to the side of the road. I stepped out and looked up, Levi was already walking over.

"Hey, everything alright? I called and left you a message. What's wrong?"

I had started to apologize in my head but when I opened my mouth all that happened was my face turned red and tears were threatening to ooze from my eyes. It was one of those moments I felt like I shouldn't be crying, nothing happened but everything had happened at the same time. I knew if I answered him I would lose it which made my eyes tear more. Instead I held up my hand to ask for a second then spent the next 20 seconds with the heels of my hands pressed to my eyes with my back to Levi.

"Shel, what's wrong.... are you ok? Luna ok? I mean if you didn't want to have dinner you could have said so....totally joking by the way, was trying to make you laugh...did it work?"

A laugh sob escaped out.

"I'm, I'm so sorry about dinner..."

I paused and took a breath.

"I was on my way home when I got a call that the Big Building was on fire at the Center."

"Oh shit, is everyone ok?"

Levi went to pull me into a hug, then paused and I'm guessing said the hell with it and went for it. I needed one.

"Everyone's fine, building is toast. Toasted I guess would be a better description. As soon as Mrs. Otto called I spun around and went, didn't even think about anything else."

"Well yeah, who would have?"

I shrugged, still leaning into his hug.

"Either way, I'm sorry I was a no show. I can make dinner now."

I glanced at my watch.

"At just about 11:30 at night."

I trailed off, dinner was not happening. Levi gave me one more squeeze then stepped back and lowered his head until he was looking into my eyes.

"How about a raincheck for tomorrow?"

"Deal."

Levi smiled then looked at his truck then back at me.

"You got any plans?"

"Right now? No. Why do you have any plans?"

"Wanna go on a stakeout?"

I raised an eyebrow and waited for more details.

"Harvey called a few hours ago, the meat's back. I would have left sooner but I was waiting..."

He cut himself off quickly, eyes wide clearly worried he may have offended me. He really was a nice guy.

"For me?"

He smiled sheepishly.

"I'm in. Let me park my truck."

"I will follow you up the drive. He started back to his truck and turned back half way. "Are you sure you're ok? You don't strike me as one to be frazzled by a burning building."

"I'm much better now that I'm going on my first stake out."

I joked hoping to get a laugh out of him, but he just stood and waited.

"Seriously, I'm good. The fire was what it was, the lovely fire chief was at the call and a jackass."

Levi stiffened at that part but said nothing.

"It could have been worse, Luna bailed me out, nothing happened. More bullying than anything. And then on the drive home I realized I missed our dinner which I was looking forward to all day. Just a straw and the camel's back kinda day."

Levi didn't say anything but had a look on his face that said plenty for a few moments.

"I'll be at your house in 10, grab warm clothes, dark colors if you have them."

And with that he backed up the driveway and out of sight.

FIFTEEN minutes later I was locking the door behind me and climbing into the stake out vehicle. AKA Levi's truck.

"Sorry, Luna ate and I had to dig my fleece and hat out of a duffle, couldn't find the right one until the very last option."

He smiled and handed me a thermos and a sandwich wrapped in a paper towel.

"What's with this? I mean thank you, but did you run home to make me a sandwich?"

"You're welcome. Sandwich and coffee. I can't have you falling asleep on me. No telling what we will find with the menacing mystery meat."

I punched him in his arm gently.

"Oh stop, seriously thank you, I haven't eaten dinner yet."

"Not a problem. Grabbed us a few other snacks too. What's a stake out without food?"

"I'm guessing not a stake out?"

"Not one I'd want to be on."

With snacks in hand we made our way to Harvey's.

32

Pulling up to Harvey's driveway I looked around and realized just how dark it was there. Not a street light for miles, the mature trees were giants that blocked out most of the moon light. Harvey's house was the only one for an easy two miles in either direction but with the trees and bend in the driveway, the house might as well not exist. I shivered slightly as the remoteness and something else settled in.

"Cold?"

"No just a, I don't what you'd call it. Body tremor? Spooky twitch?"

I shrugged.

"Glad you're not cold. I'd offer you my favorite flannel but somebody still has it."

"Yeah, yeah, It will be returned, I promise. Washed even."

I made a mental note to search my truck and center for it.

"So, we're here, now what?"

"Well, I think I am going to back the truck up over there. See the grassy patch that disappears into the trees about 500 feet to the right of Harvey's driveway? We should be able to get in far enough that whoever is coming won't be able to see us from the road, but we should be able to have a clear view of the can."

He backed the truck up and then we pulled and fluffed the tree branches around to give us a bit more coverage. Then we walked over to the can to take a quick peak and it was indeed stuffed with meat. So much that the lid was coming unhinged. All of it wrapped and bagged like before, no tags. On the return trip to the truck Levi stopped and scooped up some mud.

"Putting on war paint, are we?"

"Something like that."

"Seriously? I was just teasing, I wasn't serious."

"Not a bad idea now that you mention it, come here I'll work yours up."

I stood there giving him the no way in hell look.

"No? Okay, your loss. More for us."

"Us? Who's us?"

Levi walked up to the truck and began to smear the mud over the lights and any reflective surface.

"Us as in you and your truck?"

"This truck and I have been through hell and high water together, we have a bond."

"I'm rethinking my being here. Ok your sidekick, "Truck", is officially undercover. Now what?"

"Now, we wait. And eat."

With that he opened the passenger door with a half bow.

"After you."

I threw in a fake swoon as I climbed in.

"My hero."

We sat in silence for a few minutes as I devoured my sandwich and he munched on beef Jerky, slipping a few slices to Luna as he went.

"So, I hung out with Sal today."

"Oh yeah?"

"Hm-mm. You sure she works for you, it's not the other way around?"

Levi smiled.

"You definitely bonded with Sal if that was your take away."

"She was really nice. Anyway, since we're on a stake out, should we talk shop?"

Levi turned in his seat so he was sitting with his back to the truck door and crossed his arms.

"Seriously, do you have a 1920's police manual you read before we hang out? Talk shop, it's like we're bounty hunters chasing down Al Capone."

I threw my balled up paper towel at him only to have it smacked back at me to bounce off my forehead.

"You're so funny I forgot to laugh."

"Oh yeah? Middle school called, they would like their joke back."

"Again, soooo funny."

He waved his hand in front of him, smirking.

"The floor is yours, let's talk shop."

"Thank you. Have you found anything out about Chester or Nora?"

Levi shook his head, finished chewing before answering.

"Nothing, which makes it fishier. Especially in this day and age? You should be able to find out a little something about anybody. Other than his obituary, there is nothing recent about Chester that I could find online. I tried getting in touch with James again but I think he blocked my number and the station is not giving out any information to anyone. I've called there four or five times hoping to get a dispatch person who would pass info along. Only one who didn't practically hang up on me was the Woman.... I forgot her name, who helped us when we went up there. She not so subtly hinted she wants to grab a drink sometime. Twice I got her when I called and I was the one who had to hang up on her."

"You could take her up on the offer, you know, take one for the team to see if you can get any info from her."

"Yeah, no. Not going to happen. I have a feeling I would end up tied up in a closet and kept captive. She is a little....much."

"Oh, come on Levi, tall blonde and armed, not your type?"

"Not even close."

When he said the last part he held my gaze longer than normal. I felt my face turning a little red and changed the subject back to the task at hand.

"Well that leaves Nora. She's gotta know what happened or have an idea why James hinted that Chester had an answer."

"Maybe."

"Maybe? Just Maybe? Come one Levi, she was his wife! Of course she knows something. How could she not? Before Chester died she was crazy on social media. Posted anything and everything they did. Now? The stuff she posts is almost like prerecorded 5 am infomercial crap. Like white noise just Facebook edition. It's like she's on the lam."

"Her Husband did just die, maybe she doesn't feel like posting stuff. That alone is not evidence that she's on the lamb. Doesn't on the lam mean on the run? I don't have my police manual handy to double check the lingo..."

I glared at him.

"Ok, so not on the lam but there is a distinct change in her pattern which could be a red flag about something."

"I will give you that. Her phone is disconnected, her address is a PO and no one is willing to tell us her actual living address. Million-dollar question is how do we find Nora?"

I took a sip of coffee and held the thermos cap warming my hands as I thought about the million-dollar question.

"Maybe we will look at PCD more closely."

"PCD?"

"Sorry, PCD Pre Chester's Death."

Levi grinned.

"You're going all out on this."

"It's kind of catchy and easier to write in my notes."

I saw his eyes light up when I mentioned my notes.

"Yes, I have been taking notes and not a word about them."

I gave him my sternest look which only made him laugh, and did not strike fear into him as I had hoped. I blamed my freckles. No one took freckles seriously.

"Alright say we look, PCD, what the hell does that even mean?"

"So, say we look at a post she did before and she has a bunch of likes. We look to see who liked it or commented on it, see if they are a frequent flyer on her page. Chances are, if they like or comment on the majority of them, they are most likely a friend in real life."

"And a friend in real life would be one we could find more easily, pin Nora down that way. Red, you just may be onto something."

I pretended to dust dirt off my shoulders.

"No big deal, just following the breadcrumbs. Day in the life and all."

Levi pretended to bow down, fawning me as he did.

"Tomorrow before our rain check dinner, we will follow your bread crumbs and see if we can't find a local friend who may be willing to get word to Nora for us. Deal?"

"Deal."

I opened the truck door, stood and stretched for a second then started bushwhacking through the brush. I heard Levi's door open then a muffled question.

"What did you say?"

"Said where are you going?"

"Oh, I have to pee."

Then in my best terminator impression "I'll be back."

33

A FEW HOURS later we were still on the stake out, sitting in his truck. It wasn't the dinner date I had imagined but it was turning out to be one of my favorites, maybe a date, maybe not a date. The time was passing quickly as we traded stories from when we were kids, college choices gone wrong and bad dates. I felt like I had known this man for far longer than I had. Something about him just clicked.

"Ok. Worst day at work."

Levi took a bite of jerky and offered me a slice.

"Hmm, you first."

"Chicken. Ok..hmmm. Oh! This is a good one. When I was in high school, it was my first job teaching swim lessons at the local pool. I had a five-year old who could barely swim at the first lesson, but by the end he was able to swim almost all the way across the pool on his own. Not pretty, but he could do it. On the last day his parents and grandparents were there taking pictures and filming. Towards the end he wanted to swim across to show off his skills. Like always I kept right next to him in case I had to grab him."

I paused, taking a sip of water.

"We were almost to the wall, and he got excited and lost his rhythm. I saw him start to falter so I put an arm under him to give him a boost. He panicked and grabbed onto the front of my swimsuit and pulled it right down. Everything came out, on camera, in front of everyone in the pool."

Levi started laughing so hard he sprayed water out of his mouth all over the dash.

"We were in the shallow end too so I wasn't under water or anything, standing waist deep. To top it off after it happened the kid froze and wouldn't let go of my suit. His mom had to pry it out of his hands. I don't know who was redder, her or me. To this day whenever I go home, Tyler, who was the lifeguard that day, who is now married with three kids and teaches middle school science, can't look me in the eye. He blushes and will cross the street to avoid me."

Levi was wiping tears from his eyes.

"Poor Tyler probably never saw a pair of boobs in person until that day."

"Poor Tyler?! That's what you took away from that story?!"

"Yes poor Tyler! Picture it, a teenage boy in a swimsuit just saw his first pair of live boobs at work? Imagine what he had going on under that lifeguard tube. No wonder he can't face you, probably still dreams about you..."

"Oh my God, stop!"

I threw the jerky bag at him.

"You're making my worst day at work worse 12 years later!

"Poor, poor, Tyler."

I smacked his arm.

"Alright, alright I'll stop."

I could tell by the teasing in his voice that he was nowhere near stopping with this one. I cleared my throat.

"Ahem, your turn. Worst day at work."

Levi paused, looked out his window for a moment then turned back to me. Smile no longer resided on his lips, a sadness now crept into his eyes.

The Job Post

"It was really early in my career. I was in training still and riding along with Sr. Rangers to get a feel for the department, policies and procedures, that sort of thing. We took a call about a guy being stupid near one of the bridges, standing on the guard rail, yelling at cars. The guys I was riding along with had been doing his job for over 30 years and hated every minute of it. I swear, I never met anyone as miserable as he was. So, we get there, and watch for a few minutes. The guy is obviously drunk and amped up. He calls it in over the radio as a drunk tourist, no need for backup and we get out and approach him. The guy is really still a kid. Found out after the fact he was 19. The Sr. Ranger I was with starts talking to him, asking questions and during the whole thing the kid starts crying, talking about how it's not worth it anymore, better off dead.

As he's talking I'm starting to really worry, thinking this kid needs help and fast. Half way through the other ranger cuts him off, calls him a cry baby and says time to cut you off and let you sober up. He grabs the bottle out of his hand, looks at me and says let's go. I couldn't believe it and basically said no. Then he called me a pussy and walked back to the truck and got it. I was sick to my stomach, couldn't believe what was happening. I ran to the truck and demanded he call in someone to help this kid and we stayed until they got there. While that was going on the kid decided that enough was enough and pulled out a handgun. I didn't see it right away, but to this day I remember exactly what it sounded like when the kid clicked the safety off. I turn around and he's holding it up to his head, I didn't think. I ran straight to him. I have no idea what I was going to do when I got to him, probably I would have tackled him. I wasn't fast enough. He saw me coming, pointed the gun at me, took a shot that caught me in the shoulder and dropped me in my tracks. I hit the ground and before I could get up I heard another shot."

Levi paused. I reached over and took his hand, gave it a squeeze and held on while we sat.

"The kid needed help, he was drunk. I know it's not my fault but I can't help wondering what would have happened if I just stayed next to him instead of running back to the truck."

"You ran back to get help that he obviously needed. If anyone is at fault it was the jerk you were with."

"I know. The department agreed with you by the way, he was let go the next day."

He took a deep breath and let it out slowly.

"That was my worst day. It was a hell of a lesson about following your instincts but one I took to heart. After that I took a handful of mental health courses, figured the more I learned the better equipped I would be to help someone if I needed to."

He absently rubbed his thumb over my knuckles. We sat in silence for a few minutes, each lost in our own thoughts until Levi changed the subject.

"Next question. Worst date, go."

I glanced at him with raised eyebrows, giving him a half smile feeling him out to see if he was ok. This man had many layers, he was more than I expected on just about every level.

"Hmm, let me think about this one. There are many that are strong contenders."

I pretended to stroke my beard as I thought, making him laugh.

"Alright, ready for this? It was a pleasant evening..."

We talked for quite a while, swapping stories that had me laughing so hard it hurt. Somewhere in our conversation I must have dozed off. Next thing I know, Luna's nudging me with her nose letting out a low growl mixed with a whine. I sat up quickly and tried to get my bearings. I glanced over at Levi who also had fallen asleep, head leaning on a balled up jacket that rested on the window. Luna, having woken me up, was now staring straight out the windshield, hair standing up down her spine still emitting the low warning growl.

"What is it girl?"

I kept staring, the hair on my own neck starting to stand up. My eyes had adjusted to the darkness, but still couldn't quite make out anything other than the silhouette of the garbage can. Suddenly I saw a flash of eyes much too low to be a person's, but moving in a way that whatever it was, was not moving normally.

"Levi, Levi wake up. Somethings wrong."

I reached over and shook his shoulder, a little too hard as it made his head slide off this coat and into the steering wheel.

"Ow, what the, what's wrong?"

He sat up quickly rubbing below his eye where it had smacked the steering wheel, looking around the cab to figure out what was going on.

"Somethings out there and whatever it is, it's... something's wrong."

Levi leaned closer to the dash peering out. Within a few seconds the eyes flashed again, moving in a very unnatural pattern. Levi grabbed his mag light and reached for the door handle and turned to me.

"Don't even think about saying stay in the truck."

"Wouldn't dream of it, was going to say in the glove box is a head lamp, grab it."

"Oh, alright."

I grabbed the head lamp a little sheepishly and threw it on.

"Ready?"

I gave a nod and we exited the truck. Levi shone his light in a grid pattern sweeping the ground looking for whatever it was. I moved over a few feet and started sweeping with the headlamp. I took a few more steps and found it.

"Levi, over here."

He came jogging over and locked his light onto where mine was shining. Not far behind the garbage can was a raccoon, barely moving now. The poor thing was obviously having trouble breathing. It didn't seem to be able to move his body very well either. Spasms kept sweeping through it. Eyes were glazed over, not even registering that we were there. Levi stood for a few seconds then jogged back to his truck. I could hear him calling something in on his radio, then he returned with a rifle. He looked at me, what he was going to do was written all over his face. I nodded and turned my head. I knew it was coming but I still jumped when he squeezed off the round. When I turned back, Levi was kneeling next to the now still critter with a pair of protective gloves on.

"What happened to it?"

"Not a hundred percent sure, but.."

He pointed over to some torn paper with meat still stuck to it.

"Looks like whoever dumped the meat this time didn't make sure the lid was secure, the raccoon got into it and ended up like this."

"From rotten meat? Raccoons and coyotes and tons more animals eat rotten meat and are just fine. Maybe puke, but not...this."

Levi stayed crouched over the raccoon then suddenly got up and walked over to the garbage can.

"What? What are you looking at?"

I walked over and stood next to him, as close as I could get without retching from the smell.

"What if it wasn't the meat? What if it was something in the meat?"

I started to say something then stopped as what he said sank in.

"What would be in the meat? Poison?"

Levi didn't say anything. The silence was making what I thought was a most likely a crappy high school kid prank suddenly something far more sinister. Every hair on my neck, arms, and legs you name it stood on end. I rubbed my hands over my arms trying to shake the sudden chill.

"In the tool box in the truck bed I have a bunch of gallon Ziploc bags. Would you mind grabbing a handful?"

I nodded and started to the truck.

"Behind the driver seat is a box of gloves."

I put the gloves on at the truck, way too big for me but better than nothing, and grabbed another pair for Levi. He was walking slow circles near the shoulder of the road. I watched and waited for about a minute and then decided just standing there was silly.

"Hey, do you want me to bag a few of the bags?"

I guessed that's why I was sent back for the bags. I had watched enough CSI in my days to know evidence goes into plastic bags.

"Yeah that would be great, I'll be right over. Just looking to see if anyone left a print or something before the ground froze."

Sounds like Levi watches CSI too. And with that thought I pulled my sweatshirt over my nose, took a deep breath and started collecting evidence.

An hour later we were sitting on the tailgate with give, gallon sized Ziplocs, each with two wrapped rancid meat chunks inside watching Jackie argue with the game wardens as to who would be investigating. Levi called Jackie first, then the wardens.

"It's almost 2 am. Do you think they will wrap this up anytime soon?"

I stretched my arms behind my back and tried to roll the kinks out of my shoulders. I had plenty of layers on, or so I thought when we began this adventure, but sitting outside for hours with the temp hovering around 15° had me hunched for too long. I laid back and rested my head on Luna's butt. I envied her thick coat. She never was cold. And if she ever was, she was too stoic to show it.

"Soon I hope."

Levi's stomach chose at that point to protest our continued stakeout.

"I don't know about you but I am starving."

"Food and coffee sound amazing. No, make that food and hot chocolate."

His stomach rumbled louder in agreement. He leaned back and stretched out in the truck alongside me. Luna lifted her head and set it on his shoulder with a heavy thump.

"Make yourself comfortable Luna, please no need to ask."

She thumped her tail a few times, never opening her eyes.

"So, what were we going to have for dinner had a building not burned down or mystery meat re-appeared?"

"A feast. Culinary masterpiece in fact."

"Oh really. That spectacular?"

"Yup. Ten-star meal."

"Hmm, give me a hint."

"It would have included bacon, cheese and butter."

"You had me at bacon... could have been just bacon and that would be a ten-star meal. Hell, at this point I'd settle for butter."

"If we get out of here in the next hour I'll cook if you make coffee and hot chocolate. Now I want both."

"Deal."

He reached over and enthusiastically shook my hand.

"You two awake in there?"

A head wearing a green warden's hat appeared next to the truck.

"Or did I interrupt something else?"

"Oh, shut up Paul. If you were better at your job we wouldn't be here freezing and starving."

"Yes, everyone is worried about you starving to death, Levi."

"Was that a fat joke? I'm calling your boss, that's harassment."

"Good, tell dad I said hi and if any evidence is messed up it's all your fault."

Levi smiled and pulled Paul into a quick awkward hug that men do.

"So, you two are brothers?"

They couldn't look more un-related if they tried. Where Levi was tall with dark hair, broad shoulders and an easy, not fat by any means, 200 lbs., Paul barely was a head taller than me with blonde hair and narrow build that had him clocking in at a buck thirty soaking wet. Although

Paul's impressive beard probably weighed ten pounds on its own.

"Yes, and obviously I got all the good looks. And manners, I'm Paul, nice to meet you."

Levi rolled his eyes.

"Shelly this is Paul, Paul, and Shelly."

"Nice to meet you as well Paul."

"So, what's the deal here Pauly boy?"

Paul leaned over Levi.

"Like I said, no manners. You have a wolf behind you, you know."

Luna chose that moment to stand, stretch and sit with a paw on my shoulder.

"Why yes I do, Luna this is Paul, Paul, Luna."

I mimicked Levi's introductions making Paul's grin broaden

"I like you Shelly and for that reason, and that reason alone, I will tell you both what's going on. I'm taking what you bagged with me to have the lab look at it and keeping the local Police in the loop. The raccoon will also make the trip to Augusta for testing. See what he got in his system and go from there. Most likely it was something he ate from the garbage, but who knows? Raccoons have a pretty big scavenging area. Time will tell. The lid is now on correctly so nothing else will be getting in. I left a message at the sanitation department to swing by and grab it first thing.

"Keep me posted?"

"If I must."

"Alright, then we're going to hit the road, thanks Brother."

"Yup. Good night Shelly, or good morning depending on how you look at it I suppose. Nice meeting you."

He turned to walk away, took a few steps then yelled to Levi as he started walking backwards.

"Hey, are you going to mom and dad's for dinner Sunday?"

"Uh, I hadn't thought about it, I'll let you know."

"Fine, be that way. Shelly, do you want to come to dinner Sunday?

Your wolf can come too, my kids will feed her tons."

Levi's look went from calm and collected to frazzled in seconds, I couldn't resist.

"That sounds lovely, what can I bring?"

"The idiot next to you. See you both around 4, good night Levi."

Paul called the last part out in a sing-song voice.

"Your brother seems very nice."

"You obviously have a warped sense of what nice is. Shall we?"

He opened up and held the passenger door for us.

"Thank you."

"See? Now that's nice."

34

Two hours later we were sitting on the floor in front of the wood stove in the little blue cottage. I had my hands wrapped around a mug of chocolate spiked coffee while Levi finished off his third bacon grilled cheese.

"You were wrong, this is not a ten-star meal. Easy fifteen."

"That coming from the man who said he would eat straight butter a few hours ago may not be that much of a compliment."

"Trust me, I have had a lot of grilled cheese, these take the cake. The outside is perfect, toasted but not burnt. What's your secret?

"Mayonnaise."

"You're shitting me. Mayonnaise?"

"Saw it on the food network a few years ago, the Mayo spreads easier than butter, adds flavor and doesn't burn. I was a bit skeptical but fate had me trying it when I went to make grilled cheese one day and was out of butter."

"But let me guess, you had mayo?"

"Haven't looked back ever since."

I took another sip of the concoction Levi had made.

"This is amazing by the way. I may never be able to drink a plain cup of coffee again."

"You can thank my mom for that. She will only drink coffee if it doesn't taste like coffee. Made sure all of us knew how to doctor it for her when we started finishing the pot before she could get to it."

"All of you, huh? That sounds like more than just you and Paul. Spill it, what am I walking into on Sunday?"

"Oh no, you got yourself into this. Just going to have to wait and see. I will guarantee Luna will look like a sausage when you leave, it will be raining food on her."

I laughed,

"It's going to be that bad?"

"Worse."

He stood up and gathered the dishes and took them over to the sink. Realizing if I sat here any longer I may fall asleep, I followed him into the kitchen to start putting things away.

He was rinsing the dishes and loading them into the dishwasher as I snagged things off the counter to put back into the fridge. The kitchen was cute. And by cute, I mean tiny. Both of us kept pausing to let the other move an inch. I had just put the rest of the cooked bacon in the fridge trying to sidestep out of the way when Levi leaned over to grab a dish towel. I found myself slightly pinned between him and the counter.

I was staring at his shirt pocket stealing glances at his forearm and could feel my face turning shades of red. When I realized he wasn't moving I glanced up, he had his head almost level with mine and was gazing at me, a slight smile on his lips.

"You smell amazing."

I laughed and relaxed a little.

"I smell like wood smoke and a wet dog."

"Nothing smells better to me."

He leaned in slowly and pressed his lips to mine for a second, then retreated a step, his eyes checking to see if that was ok. That gentle kiss had me aching for more. Without thinking I threw a hand behind his neck and pulled him, answering his question not so gently. After that he did not hesitate, he matched each kiss with his own fever, working his way down my cheek, to ear, to neck. Suddenly he lifted me off the ground and up onto the counter, running his hands on my back and hips, his lips landed back on mine teasing my lower lip. I wrapped my legs around his waist pulling him closer. I felt like a teenager with out of control hormones, I wanted more. His hands were resting on my ribs and were slowly working their way up, I let out a soft moan as his thumbs were just starting to graze...

"Whoa, whoa easy girl, it's ok."

My eyes snapped open and was about to give this lousy ass a piece of my mind when I noticed Luna had his pant leg in her mouth and was doing her best to drag him off of me.

"Luna, hey enough. It's alright, we're just...just... we're good."

He looked up at me and flashed a smile that had me ready to hit re-start. Luna was still hanging on with an added warning growl.

"Really, really good."

He rested his forehead on mine and took a deep breath.

"I'm going to regret this the moment I walk out the door, but maybe this is a good place to stop. Not stop, pause. We will finish this... if you want to?"

I could hear the want and need in his voice. I'm not going to lie, it felt good to feel wanted, needed.

"Yes. Very much so."

I let out a sigh and gave him one last long kiss.

"This is a good sign, if she didn't like you we'd be on our way to the emergency room by now."

"I was wondering about that, maybe you can have a heart to heart with her. I don't know if I'll be able to stop next time."

He snuck one more kiss in.

"Would be worth a bite or two, that's for sure."

As soon as my feet hit the floor Luna released him and sat down next to me.

I ruffled her ears.

"Thanks mom, we were just studying, you know."

I swear she let out a huff before walking back to her bed by the wood stove. Levi ran a hand up and down my arm, and pulled me in for a quick hug.

"Seriously, you smell amazing. Alright, I'm done. I'm going to go. Thank you for dinner and your help. I gotta run into work and finish up paperwork from my found hiker and the mystery meat. Ah... would it be alright if I spun by later? No pressure or anything, just a hello."

"Hmm I think we could work you into our busy schedule."

He smiled, gave a quick wave and stepped off the porch. The sun was just starting to peek out giving the snow a reddish hue. I sprawled out on the couch in front of the fire and giggled. Thinking slightly inappropriate thoughts about my neighbor, I dozed off and slept like a rock for a few hours.

35

I SHOULD HAVE stayed asleep. I knew I was going to have to deal with the charred remains of the Big Building, I just had hoped it would be on Monday. Not today. I had just stepped out of the shower when my phone rang. In my rush to answer it I slid on the bath mat smacking my elbow on the tub as I tried to catch myself.

"Ahh son of a bitch, oh that hurts!"

I stayed in a sleeping baby pose on the floor cradling my elbow. Whoever the hell named it a funny bone had a sick sense of humor. A few minutes later my phone started going off again.

"Hello?!"

I was in pain, my hello had an edge to it, I couldn't care less however at the moment.

"Where have you been!? You left a message yesterday that a building burned down and you disappeared?! I have been calling the Center on the hour for the past 14 hours!"

"Walters? Why didn't you call me back on my cell? That's the number I Called you from."

"I didn't have your cell! A responsible caretaker would have been waiting for a call when something monumental happens!"

"A responsible boss would have made a copy of my application and resume which had all of my contact info on it! And if you didn't have my cell, how in the world are you talking to me now, on my cell?!"

I hoped I sounded as pissed as I felt. Never again would I apply for a job based on a billboard flyer. Walters was silent, but you could feel the tension oozing through the phone. Like a pot just starting to boil over.

"I now have your cell number because I called the fire department who gave me the number of the Otto's who made the 911 call. They gave me yours."

He paused again, I could hear the slow intake of breath before he plowed on.

"You were hired to take care of the Center that includes all buildings, boats, lifejackets, every stapler and pen that resides on the property...not let a bunch of senior citizens burn the place down!"

"Hey, I did not tell them to put a pizza box in the oven. Nor should I have had to! That is not a standard conversation you have with anyone at any time. Everyone is ok by the way."

"I know because I had a long chat with the fire chief this morning. He actually answers his calls!"

I closed my eyes. Be the bigger person, be the bigger person. Breathe in through the nose, out through the mouth. I listened to my inner Zen and just stayed silent.

"Are you there? You better have not hung up on me, I..."

"I'm still here. I was letting you finish."

"Don't you dare smart mouth me young lady."

My eyebrows shot up in surprise, who the hell did this Walters guy think he was?

"I need you to do your job today. I am out of the state, I can't clean up your mess."

I took a very long breath, and told myself again, be the bigger person.

"You need to go to the fire department and meet with the fire chief, finish filling out the form you should have last night, then get a copy of the official report and fax it to me so I can send it to the insurance company."

"Whoa, last time I checked it was the 21st century and they have this thing called email. Your insurance company can email the fire department to obtain whatever it is they need. I gave my statement last night alongside Mrs. Otto. Your fire chief is a handsy jackass who only wants me to swing by so he can have another..."

"That's it, I have had enough. You are refusing to do your job and your negligence on the job resulted in a building burning down that could have killed numerous people. I have no choice but to fire you."

"Wait, what? That is ridiculous and you know it!"

I was floored, this could not be happening. I could feel the anger building in my chest and I opened my mouth ready to defend myself against his insane accusations. Then I stopped. I didn't need this.

"Walters, I resign."

I hung up. Luna jumped up and put her paws on my shoulders nuzzling my face. Wrapping my arms around her neck I buried my face in her fur and took a few steadying breaths.

"Fuck this Luna. We are better than this."

Luna stared into my eyes agreeing, if she could she would have high fived me, I'm sure of it.

"Alright, change of plans today my lady. We are going into town to find a Lawyer, get our own statement from the Otto's, cover our ass and then figure out what the hell we are doing from here."

36

Levi stretched and closed the lid on his laptop. Finally done with his paperwork, he sat back and finished his cold, tasteless coffee smiling. His mind was somewhere else, with someone else. He spun his chair to set the now empty mug on the windowsill then spun back, stood and headed for the door. He had just grabbed the handle when the office phone rang. Reluctantly, he stepped back and answered it.

"County Forest Department, Levi speaking."

"Hey, it's me. Got the lab report from your rotting meat."

"Well good morning Paul, why didn't you call my cell?"

"Well, I wanted to try you at the office first as this is now a very official call and the start of a very interesting investigation."

Levi sat down slowly as Paul laid it out for him.

Twenty minutes later Levi went to the door again and like clockwork, as he reached for the door the office phone rang.

"God, I hope this is Paul again."

"County Forest Department."

Five minutes later he was running out the door on his cell phone calling anyone he could. They had a missing 8 year old who was running out of time.

37

To say I felt better was an understatement. I jumped into the car to hunt down a lawyer and then realized it was Saturday. Any lawyer that I could afford would for sure not be working Saturdays and if they were, most likely would not be a great one. I then exited the car and went back inside to regroup. Something was nagging the edge of my brain and for almost an hour I couldn't get it to click then it hit me. One of my college roommate's brothers married a lawyer. A good lawyer. Last time I talked to Lainey she was talking about some national news story that her sister in law was a part of for her outstanding lawyer abilities.

Quick call to Lainey and fifteen minutes after that I was face timing her sister-in law and adorable niece. She talked to me for a while, listened a lot and put my mind at ease. Basically, she said as long as I followed the checking in/ out policy that I was trained in there really was zero liability they could pin on me. When I told her I didn't receive any training whatsoever, I was just tossed a set of keys and a few notes, she laughed. She continued to say if I really wanted to I could turn the tables claiming negligence on their part for not providing adequate training.

Killed two birds with one stone on that phone call. No need to find a lawyer or track down the Otto's. I sent Lainey a quick thank you text with a promise to visit soon as my schedule now was incredibly open. I had just sat down to figure out my next dilemma of what the hell I was going to do for work/housing/ the rest of my life as I was getting too old to be floating around the country when my cell rang and Levi's number popped up. As he talked I quickly gathered some supplies, stuffed them into a day pack and Luna and I were out the door.

38

THIRTY OR SO miles outside of town we pulled into a trailhead for a popular fire tower hike. I was relieved to see more than a dozen cars and trucks parked, most of them with Search and Rescue or EMT stickers. It looked like Levi was able to pull in the help he needed. I hoped so anyway. We followed the now beaten path through the snow to a small clearing where a makeshift command center had been established out of the bed of a side by side ATV. Levi was standing in the back of it addressing the group when Luna and I joined. He locked eyes with me for a second, gave a quick nod and continued.

"Robert Chefield, Robbie, is 8 years old. He was separated from his parents during their hike going on four hours ago. The father is en-route to the hospital, mother is getting patched up in the ambulance in the parking lot. She is in no shape to join the search but refuses to leave without Robbie. Both slipped at the summit and went over the edge while posing for a picture. The mom, when she came to, was able to get to the trailhead and flag another hiker down who alerted us. Robbie is moderately dressed for midday, nowhere near prepared for the drop in temps that are currently happening. He had on a green hooded coat with black pants, orange hat with a white pom-pom on top and had a red daypack. He's a little over four feet tall, wears a size 7 shoe, and the boot print looks like this."

Levi handed out copies of what the boot tread should look like.

"We all know that for every hour that passes the size of the area that he could be in increases. He's been on his own for over four hours. Mom said he had a few granola bars in his pack, a spare bottle of water along with whatever was left in his other one. By now he's most likely hypothermic and very scared, we need to move fast over a hell of a lot of ground. We have enough people here that I want to send out three hasty search teams and the rest will begin a grid search with Paul as the lead at Robbie's last known point."

The hiker who called us in ran to the summit to see if they could find Robbie but by the time they got there he was gone."

Levi started to hand out radios and flagging.

"We are using channel 32, radio in anything you think may be relevant and mark it with flagging. Ross, Marla and Joe start your search on the west side heading towards the river. See if he got down the rocks. That would be the direction he would have seen his parents fall. Chase, Scott and Grayson start at the summit and circle down. Parents fell to the west but he would have had to have taken an alternate route to get to that side, pay extra attention to the North trail that would be the easiest route down."

I ducked down a little as Chase and his group took off up the trail. I was glad another person was here to help find Robbie, but that did not mean I wanted anything to do with him.

"River, Seth and Shelly go east and fan out. If he ended up over that way I wouldn't be surprised if he got turned around on the old logging roads that run through there. They look like trails but they all end up back towards the beaver ponds. The rest of us will start the grid search from his last known spot."

I looked through the crowd scanning until I saw River. She waved a hand for me to come over, apparently she had been looking for me as well. Halfway to her I felt a hand on my arm and turned quickly smacking into Levi.

"Ah sorry, bobbed when I should have weaved."

He smiled but it did not touch his eyes as it normally did.

"Here."

He handed me two reflective vests.

"Will she wear one?"

He nodded to Luna.

"Yeah, for sure."

I bent down and snapped into place around her chest and belly.

"I was hoping you were bringing her, I didn't think about it until after we hung up. A trained search and rescue dog is on the way but won't be here for at least an hour. Figure it won't hurt to have Luna out there."

I could see the worry on his face, and felt the worry in his voice. I reached over and gave his hand a quick squeeze.

"He will be alright."

Levi squeezed back.

"Be safe."

WE started our hasty search in silence except for the intermittent calling for Robbie. As we walked looking for any sign of an 8 year-old boy I was once again astounded by the density of the Maine woods. Not just with how thick the forest was, but how it absorbed all sound, and swallowed paths you took just moments before. Within a mile there were almost two dozen people slowly making their way through the woods calling for Robbie, but from where I stood you would never know. Neither sight nor sound traveled far. The trees, moss and snow were the keepers of this realm and the rest of us were just visitors walking through their muffled silence.

Twenty minutes later River signaled for our group to stop.

"I may have a partial boot print, calling it in."

Seth, Luna and I jogged over to look.

"The boot treads look the same, hard to tell the size with only the top half."

Seth held the paper print up to the track, comparing as River relayed what was found over the radio.

"Other than ours that were leaving tracks, this is the first track I've seen since we jumped the stream."

River looked around.

"This is not the path, not sure why anyone would be over here who isn't Robbie. Let's fan out a little, 10 minutes then check in with each other."

I gave a nod in agreement.

"Come on Luna."

With each step I carefully swept my glance back and forth looking for anything out of the ordinary. It was starting to get dark, dark comes early in northern Maine. I couldn't help but worry about Robbie. Not only was he freezing but he had to be terrified. The radio crackle broke me out of my not helpful loop of thoughts.

"Seth to base, found another partial boot track and a gray glove, kids sized."

God, I hope we are getting close I thought. Levi's voice camp back through.

"Flag it and read me your GPS coordinates."

I gave a short whistle to let Luna know I was moving again. Figured we could keep looking, better to be moving and not thinking about the what if's. Luna was poking around 15 yards ahead of me, she never was farther than that from me. Ever. People would often ask what training method I used with her for off leash walking. I always laughed and said she trained me, refused to walk on a leash, not one single time in her entire life. She's more people than dog I would say, has always had a very intuitive nature and marched to her own drum.

The dark was getting thicker, I reached into my pack for my headlamp. "Robbie!"

Each step I could hear the crunch of the snow, the crisp crunch that only comes with incredible cold. I was scanning again, sweeping the light from my headlamp rhythmically making sure to look under heavy pine boughs when I heard Luna whine. I snapped my head up and saw her behind me, nose shoved into the snow, her whine getting more bark into it. Jogging over she had found another gray glove.

"Nice work lady."

I ruffled her ears as I called it in.

"Shelly to base, found another gray glove kid sized, flagging it now."

I was crouched down and had just started tying on the flag and waiting for a radio back when Luna came flying back over to me and grabbed my sleeve tugging me over onto my ass.

"Easy Luna, hold on! Let me get up!"

I heard Levi's voice crackle back through the radio buried in the snow. With one arm in Luna's mouth, I stretched and snagged the radio before I lost it. I let her pull me into the woods. Levi's radioed again.

"Hang on a sec."

"Hang on a sec? Shelly..."

I didn't hear the rest as we pushed through a thick batch of pine and saw a green bundle huddled against the truck of the pine. Luna let go and rushed over to the boy, nuzzling him. Robbie made a small groan.

"Oh, thank God."

I rushed over, radioing in as I went.

"Levi, we got him."

I read off the coordinates quickly then gently shook Robbie.

"Hey bud, my name is Shelly and this is Luna. We're going to get you out of here, ok? Can you answer me?"

He made another small noise, I ducked down to get a look at his face. Frosty eyelashes, blue lips and cheeks with frozen tears had tears starting in my eyes. I took off my jacket and wrapped him up in it. Luna wrapped herself behind him so her tail covered one leg and her head the other.

"It's ok Robbie, we are getting out of here."

I rubbed my hands up and down his arms hoping to create a little warmth with the friction. I finished the radio call giving a health update and hashed out a plan for extraction with Levi then connected with Seth and River.

"Alright Robbie, my friends Seth and River are on their way over. They are going to help us walk out of here."

He hadn't said anything since we found him, but his eyes were now focused instead of glazed over and his hand was rubbing Luna's neck.

"Here bud, can you take a drink of water?"

I held out my water bottle and he reached over and drank half of it.

"Excellent job, alright what I'm going to do is slip my gloves onto your hands, we're going to stand up and get my coat snapped into place around you. Does that sound like a plan?"

The faint nod he gave me was a good sign.

"Shelly! Can you hear us?"

"River, we're over here. Look for Luna. Go get'em girl."

Luna streaked out from the pines and returned a few minutes later with Seth and River.

"Oh, thank heavens. Hey Robbie, I'm River."

She gave Robbie a bear hug and Seth did the same.

"And I'm Seth. It is so good to see you dude."

"I want my Mom."

"That is where we are going. She's waiting for us in the parking lot."

I looked at Seth and River.

"We just stood up, and haven't tried walking yet. Ready to start our hike Robbie?"

He nodded, then took a few cautious steps.

"I can't feel my feet."

The tears started to well up in his eyes.

"It hurts."

"How about this, think you can hold onto my back?"

Seth crouched down in front of Robbie handing his backpack off to me. Robbie nodded. River and I helped him up.

"You alright Seth?"

"We're good, just going to take it slow. River and I will start walking back the way we came in. Can you radio in our situation?"

"See you in a few."

I waited until they were out of ear shot then made the call.

"Shelly to base."

"Go ahead Shel."

"Robbie is awake but can't feel his feet, when he tried to walk he said it hurt and was enough to bring on tears. Seth has him riding piggy back but I don't know how long that's going to work."

"We are sending an ATV as we speak. Your coordinates have you about a mile and a half off the trail over some pretty steep and rocky stuff. Get him to the trail and they will meet you there to bring Robbie back down. Let me know when you're ready for the coordinates."

I jotted down what I needed and jogged to catch up with our group.

"How are we doing Seth and Robbie?"

"Good."

Seth's good was a labored puff.

"An ATV is going to meet us here."

I handed off the coordinates to River to plug into our GPS. Robbie was clinging to Seth, head resting on his back.

"Alright, we are about a mile off. What are you feeling Seth?"

He didn't stop, my guess was he didn't want to break his momentum.

"Let's keep going. River, lead and break trail?"

"You got it."

"Shelly, can you take my hat off?"

"Of course, let me know if you need anything else or a break."

Seth nodded and kept a steady pace after River.

Twenty minutes later we heard voices and saw a sweep of a flashlight. River yelled and flagged down the duo.

"Hey guys, we thought maybe you could use a hand. We're about a quarter mile from the quad."

River smiled and turned to Robbie.

"Robbie, I'd like you to meet our friends from the Forest Service, Mark and Bill. Is it ok if they carry you from here?"

Robbie sniffed and nodded. Seth let out a small groan as he stood up after Robbie was transferred.

"You ok?"

I handed Seth his water. Luna leaned into his leg licking his hand.

"Never better."

He smiled and we started after our now enlarged group. Fresh legs make all the difference and we hit the ATV not even five minutes later. We loaded Mark and Robbie onto the ATV and followed down on foot. We walked in silence, each of us relieved and letting the three- mile hike to the parking lot relieve us of our stress and tension. We were very thankful it ended as it did.

39

By the time we hit the parking lot Robbie and his mom had left for the hospital as well as most of the volunteers. Seth turned to us, giving us each a long hug. No words needed to be said, we were all feeling the same.

"Alright ladies, normally I would say let's go toast a job well done but I am heading home to hug my wife. She's due any day, the whole hike back I kept thinking what if that was my kid?"

River punched his arm.

"Hell, if that was your kid he or she would have been carrying you out. They come from good stock, on their mother's side."

Seth laughed and gave her hat a tug so it covered her eyes.

"Rain check on that beer until after our super baby arrives then."

River turned to me.

"Seriously, his wife is the incredible hulk. Looks like a ballerina but hits like a linebacker. Until last week she was still making farm calls."

"Farm calls?"

"She's the best large animal veterinarian in the county. She will see Dogs and cats occasionally, but specializes with the big beasts. All she has to do is give the critters a look and they behave. I swear, she is part animal."

"Good to know. Do you need a lift?"

"No honey I'm all set. Rode in with Marla and Ross, the neighbors."

She looked at the sky, now streaked with stars.

"In my younger days I would have bossed everyone here back to the bar for a celebration. Now I just want a beer in the bathtub. As Seth said, raincheck for another day."

She gave me a hug, then Luna.

"And you good girl, next time you are in the shop I'll have something special for you."

She stood up.

"If Levi needs anything he knows where to find me."

She sent me a knowing glance that had me blushing a little and laughed heartily when she saw it. I sighed and muttered about small towns as I made my way over to the truck to dump our gear.

Across the lot I saw Levi talking with Paul and a few people, packing up the base. He waved at me to come over. I hesitated, I really had to pee. I mimed as best I could that I was going to use the woods. I think he got it, as he shot a thumbs up back. Luna was wagging and looking in his direction.

"Go on, you can go over there, I'll catch up to you in a minute."

A quick glance and a wag and she was trotting off to schmooze Levi and whoever was left.

I took a quick glance around and decided to move a little deeper into the woods. Wasn't I just saying how dense the forest was? Apparently that was only when you didn't have to pee. Finally I found a spot that didn't make me feel like someone was watching.

I was on my way back thinking about how I would be hard pressed to find a more beautiful bathroom than one under the stars when I felt my legs sweep out from under me.

40

P<small>AUL GLANCED UP</small> from the bag he was packing.

"Ah, the wolf is back."

Levi stopped what he was doing and dropped down onto his knees.

"Hey there pretty girl, I hear you were the one who found Robbie."

He rubbed her shoulders and pulled her in for a hug.

"Thank you."

"You know that's her dog and not her, right?"

"Bite me Pauly. You're a cat person, you wouldn't understand."

Levi kept on loving Luna. Paul chuckled and went back to packing up.

"Oh brother, you're sunk and you don't even know it yet. Wait till I tell my wife. Better yet, wait till mom sees you two Sunday."

He made a smoochy face at Levi.

"Seriously? What are you 10? What the hell Cheryl sees in you is beyond me."

He stopped rubbing Luna down when she froze and snapped her head in the direction Shelly went.

"What's up girl?"

"Oh, what, now she's Lassie?"

Luna let out a low growl and took off for the woods. Levi went after her.

"Oh, for crying out loud. Let the woman pee in peace!"

Paul paused for a second before shaking his head and following.

"Oh what the fuck."

Dropping the bag he was packing up he jogged to catch up to his idiot brother.

41

I LANDED FLAT on my back knocking the wind out of me. As I lay there trying to catch a breath my mind was attempting to figure out how the hell I wiped out. Then I saw him.

"Not so tough now are you."

Chase was standing near my feet holding a long solid branch. Now I know how I fell. I lurched up to sit and tried to scramble to my feet. He took two quick steps towards me and knocked me back again, this time sitting on me, holding me in place.

"Get the fuck off of me!"

I gave it all I had to wiggle out or tip him over. I was stuck, he had an easy 150 lbs on me.

"Hey now, you're getting me excited with all your twisting. I knew you wanted me."

I reached back with my free hand and grabbed the first thing my fingers touched. As hard as I could I smashed the rock into his head.

"Ah, you bitch!"

He grabbed my wrist and slammed it to the ground and slapped my face with his other so hard I could taste blood. He leaned his face in close and snarled.

"You should have left town when you had the chance."

I didn't wait to hear what was coming next, as hard as I could I head-butted his face then lunged to the side as he rocked back. He took another swing making contact with my ribs but all his moving shifted him just enough that I could get a leg underneath me to beat feet. I grabbed the rock and took a swing at his neck. He let out a grunt as it hit home, his hands letting go. Pushing off of him with my free leg I was able to take a few off kilter steps before he grabbed my ankles sending me crashing back to the ground knocking the wind out of me again.

I heard a crunch of snow and caught a glimpse of Luna as she barreled into him, knocking him completely off of me. She was snarling and snapping at his hands, face, anything she could get at. Any direction he moved she stayed on him, keeping herself between me and him. I got on my feet and lunged to grab the stick he used to trip me and groaned as the pain in my ribs and head dropped me back to my knees. Luna heard me fall and turned for a split second to look, giving Chase enough time to get a full swing with a mag light into Luna. I heard her yelp and saw her roll.

"Luna!"

I scrambled to get to my dog. Chase was back on me in seconds, this time pinning me by the neck against a tree. I clawed at his hands, tried to reach his face but he kept it just out of reach. I was gasping for breath and felt dizzy with the effort.

All I could think was that there was no way this was happening right now. A second later I dropped to the ground and saw him fly backwards, Levi behind him. Able to breathe properly again I took huge gasps of air that hurt like hell and crawled to Luna. Coughing and crawling I looked back and saw Levi get a few hooks in before slamming Chase into the ground and pinning his arms behind his back. I was almost to Luna, I got to my feet and ran and fell over to her. I heard feet running on snow and looked up to see Paul handcuffing Chase and Levi headed for us. He skidded to a stop and dropped down next to me.

"Shit Shel, don't move."

He reached for me but I waved him away.

"Luna, he hurt Luna"

"He hurt you! Slow down."

"I'm fine, help me get Luna."

Levi muttered something to himself about stubborn women as he reached to steady me as we maneuvered over to Luna. I dropped down next to her running my hands over her thick coat looking for injuries. She licked my hand and let out a whine as my hands went over her ribs.

"Oh Sweetie, I'm so sorry, I'm so sorry."

I kept running my hands up and down looking for anything and everything, Levi doing the same. After a few minutes he placed his hand on mine, stopping it for a second.

"I don't see any external wounds, betting her ribs are bruised, may or may not be broken. Let's get her into town and get some x-rays after we get you checked out."

Paul must have left during our trip over to Luna as he suddenly reappeared.

"Jesus Shelly."

He rocked back on his heels into a catcher position and gave me a head to toe glance. He turned to look at Levi, exchanging a heated look.

"Where's?"

"In my truck, in cuffs. As soon as we get you all out of here I'm taking him down to Bangor. No way in hell I'm letting the worthless police department hold him. He'd be walking by breakfast."

Levi nodded, he looked like he was doing his best to stay calm but anger radiated off of him in waves.

I looked down at my hands and realized how much they were shaking, how much all of me was shaking. I forced myself to take a few deep breaths, but they hurt so bad I ended up holding my ribs with one hand while the other steadied myself on the ground.

Levi shifted over and put his arm underneath mine and helped me steady up onto my feet.

"I can carry you out."

"I can walk."

I stood up straighter to make a point but gravity seemed to be extra strong today and had me hunching back over trying to find a position that I could stand and breathe in. Levi rolled his eyes and bit back whatever he was going to say. Paul looked at the group of us then took charge.

"Tell you what, I'll get Luna, Levi walk with Shelly and get the truck ready for the wolf."

Levi shot Paul a thank you glance as Paul bent down and slid his arms carefully under Luna.

"Ready or not, here we go, ugh! How much does your dog weigh?!"

Letting out a grunt as he repositioned his arms and started walking out.

The walk out felt like it was miles instead of yards. Finally, we made it to my truck somehow ahead of Paul and Luna. I leaned up against the door steadying myself.

"I just need a second, I think I have a blanket behind the seat we can lay out for her. Would you mind grabbing it?"

Levi didn't say anything, just stood still for a second then turned and walked to the other side of the lot where he and Paul had parked. He paused outside of Paul's truck for a split second, glaring at Chase. It looked like he was thinking about opening the door but settled for punching the driver door of his own truck. As Paul stepped out of the woods Levi flashed his lights twice to signal Paul to wait and started the truck.

They loaded Luna into Levi's truck then drove the 100 feet to pick me up. I started to walk over when I realized Levi was using his truck instead of mine but Paul yelled over to wait. Normally I would have ignored him and went anyway. At this moment, a few more minutes leaning against the truck to re-group seemed like a good idea. Besides, Luna was in good hands. Ones that were moving much faster than me at the moment. I closed my eyes for what felt like a second, and opened them to Levi's face hovering in front. Worry was etched all over his face. I attempted a smile but cut it off with a wince, my face was swelling and pulling at the cuts and bruises. Paul strode up and pushed Levi off to the side.

"In you go Shelly, lean on me to slide up and in. There you go. Watch your hands."

He shut the door and leaned through the window. Call me if you need anything, I'm heading down now with shit for brains. Take care of your wolf and yourself. Most likely someone will be calling you early, if not stopping up, to get your side of the story and talk you through the next steps. I'll give them Levi's number to contact you.

"Next steps?"

I looked at him like had two heads.

"You will be pressing charges, right?"

"Of course she will!"

Paul looked from Levi back to me.

"I just want this over with, I .."

Paul held my gaze for a moment, then let it drop.

"When they call, talk to them. Ask any questions you can think of, they will lay it all out for you as to what happens if you do or don't."

He paused, shifting from one foot to the other uncomfortably.

"It's your choice, but I'm betting you're not the first person he's done this too and maybe if the others had spoken up, it wouldn't have happened again tonight."

I closed my eyes and let his words sink in. I felt Levi shift the truck into drive and hoped to stay lost in the darkness behind my eyelids for a few minutes.

It was as if Levi read my mind. The ride back towards town was silent. When we hit the outskirts, he pulled out his phone.

"Seth? Sorry to bother you. Is Sierra still seeing animals?"

There was a pause, I couldn't make out what Seth was saying and had to settle for Levi's contribution to the conversation.

"Dog, Shelly's dog, Luna."

Another pause.

"Ah, I'll ah, I'll tell you about it when we get there. Tell Sierra thanks and we'll be at the clinic in about 10 minutes."

"River says she's a super human, part animal."

Levi let a half smile escape.

"River knows all. And she's right. I was hoping she was still taking calls or we would be heading to Bangor ourselves. Wouldn't blame her one bit if she wasn't. At the rate she's going she will end up giving birth mid patient exam."

He took a deep breath. I could hear his hands wringing his steering wheel and he exhaled. We finished the short drive in silence and stopped outside a two-story yellow craftsman with a chainsaw statue of a bear in the yard holding a small sign that said Dr. Sierra Jasper, DVM.

"How long before they get here?"

"Well, I'd give them 30 or 40 seconds."

I looked at him out of one eye in no mood for sarcasm. The other had just about swollen shut.

"They live upstairs, the clinic is on the bottom floor."

Sure enough, 30 seconds later the porch light went on and Seth was walking out to the truck. Levi came around and gave me a hand down, then opened the back to grab Luna.

"Holy shit, what happened to you?"

Seth kept looking from me to Levi and back again.

"I'm thinking we should have had that drink after all."

I was trying to lighten the mood, Levi grumbled. I glared at Levi as best I could with one eye. He glared back. Seth glanced from Levi to me and back again.

"Ah as fun as this is, let's get the show on the road, shall we?"

Seth gestured the way to the house giving me a once over as we walked. Levi gently hefted Luna out of the truck and marched her into the clinic. I fumbled a bit getting up the stairs and was thankful when Seth reached out to steady me, even more so that Levi was in front and didn't see it.

We walked down a short hall past a waiting room then turned a quick left into an exam room. A short, incredibly pregnant woman stood leaning on the counter in her slippers and lab coat. She stood up, one hand on her back as she pointed to the table.

"Set her on here Levi."

As soon as Levi set her down she tried to scramble to her feet. Levi made the mistake of trying to pin her and had to jump back when she snapped at him.

"Hey, hey easy girl. Settle down. Sooner you do, the sooner you leave."

Sierra had a matter of fact tone about her that had Luna bailing on her escape attempt. River was right. She could talk to beasts.

"That's better."

"Thank you so much for seeing her so late, I can't tell you how much I appreciate this Dr. Jasper."

"Sierra, please. No one calls me Dr. Jasper. At least not in the clinic."

She sent a glace to Seth that had his ears turning red. Levi, get this woman a chair and some ice. Chest freezer down the hall, second door on the right. Seth, I left my tablet upstairs, would you go grab it please?"

Both nodded and jumped to comply. Apparently, she also had powers over humans as well.

"Now that they are not hovering, what the hell happened to you two?"

She raised an eyebrow and waited. The story started to fall out of my mouth. I was not immune to her either. She listened intently, the only reaction that came from her was a spike every now and then with her eyebrows. When I finished we let the silence linger as she finished looking over Luna. Levi returned with a Ziploc full of ice and a towel, handed both to me. Sierra nodded in approval.

"Put that on your eye. I'm a doctor, trust me. You'll regret it in a few hours if you don't."

Sighing deeply, I covered my face with the ice.

"Alright, your girl here is in great shape other than I'm betting she has a cracked rib or two. I'd like to get an x-ray to make sure and to rule out any chips or floating bone chunks. Now whether they are cracked or not, the treatment is going to be the same. Rest and limiting exercise. With that being said, I'm not taking x-rays anymore for obvious reasons."

She pointed to her impossibly full stomach.

"My technician comes in at 7:30am which is... in three hours. I propose this. Let's get Luna settled in back, I can give her a mild sedative that will help her relax and start that resting process. At 7:30 she will still be groggy making it a perfect time to take an x-ray. Does that sound good to you?"

I nodded. I wanted to speak but felt the tears prickling the back of my eyeballs. I don't know if it was the stress, being tired, the whole shitty two days but I was feeling way more emotional than normal. Sierra caught my gaze and gave my arm a squeeze as she walked by making it worse.

"Seth and Levi, can you bring Luna this way?"

I gave her a quick hug then hung back to collect myself. I was being childish, nothing wrong with crying, I knew that. Told other people that all the time. Still, I hated to break down in front of anyone, hated feeling not in control of what was happening around me. I shifted and felt a stab of pain shoot through my body. Thankfully that quickly put a kibosh on my tears. Got to love pain transfers. I waited in the hallway for everyone. I was done. Mentally, physically, emotionally. A door was held open, Sierra came over with a few forms for me to sign while she reviewed everything.

"Thank you so much, I know you didn't have to see us tonight, I... I really appreciate this."

"Please, stop. This is what I do."

She gently touched my shoulder in a gesture that felt like she wanted it to be a hug but didn't want to actually hug me in my current state. Hell, I wouldn't want to hug me in my current state. Not having the guts to look in the passenger mirror I was only imagining what I looked like. I'd put good money down that my imagination was being optimistic.

"I will call with the results around 8:30 or you're welcome to swing back at 7:30 or whenever. Seth, can you walk them out? I'm going back upstairs."

"You don't have to walk us out, Seth."

He looked at me again like I had two heads.

"Did you not hear the woman? You don't argue with an almost 9 month pregnant woman. I'm walking you two out."

With a no nonsense let's get a move on gesture he gently hitched an arm around me as we started slowly down the stairs. Levi grumbled something behind us, throwing god knows what into the bushes, before jogging ahead to start the truck and open the door.

Seth shut the door once I was in. He lingered for a moment, appearing to try to decide whether or not to say something. He kept opening then closing his mouth, shifting from one foot to another. He must have thought better of it, shook his head and said to call him if either of us needed anything.

42

W E DROVE IN silence back through town stopping at the only red light. Why it was red at this time of day was beyond me. No one for miles, betting there never was at this time of night. The light turned green, but we still sat.

"Levi, the light's green."

Silence. I took a one-eyed glance in his direction, he had both hands clenched on the steering wheel and was just staring straight ahead.

"Levi?"

Without averting his gaze he rolled out of the stop getting back up to speed. At the next turn where we should have taken a right, he kept going straight.

"Um, you missed the turn."

"Not going that way."

"Ok, where are you going? I need to go back to the cottage."

"You're going to see a doctor."

"Whoa, not right now I'm not. And what the hell gives you the right to make that decision?!"

The only sound was that of the tires on the pavement.

"Levi! Stop the truck. Now."

He took a deep breath and let it out slowly, hands back to wringing the steering wheel.

"I'd tell you to take a look in the mirror but I know you can't possibly see out of your left eye, and I have serious doubts about the right. You..."

His collected deliberate speaking crumbled, he swore softly and pulled off onto the side of the road. He kept both hands on the wheel, eyes trained on the road.

"I am so fucking pissed off."

"At me? You have got to be kidding me!"

"No! Well, yes but no."

"Oh, that makes perfect sense. I'll walk."

I went to open the door but couldn't find the handle.

"Where is the door handle? Who in their right mind makes trucks and hides the friggin' handle."

"Would you please just stop!"

He reached over grabbing the door handle, opening it for me.

"Please, stop and listen."

Having my exit available now I waited to see what he had to say. That and my I'll walk statement sounded good but in reality, I wasn't sure I would get very far.

"Look, I am so sorry for what happened to you tonight."

"Oh knock it off. What the hell do you have to be sorry for?"

"For the love of...would you just let me finish?"

I gave him a head nod beckoning him to proceed with my left hand.

"I feel sick over the whole thing. I keep seeing you against that tree..."

He took his ball cap off and mashed the brim around in his hands as he continued.

"I should never have sent Chase out on any part of the search, I just, the call came in and my only thought was to find and get the kid out fast. Now your dog's hurt, you look like hell I can't stop thinking about what if we didn't show up when we did, what if..."

He flung his hat on the dash.

"I..."

"No, it's my turn. You have absolutely zero responsibility for what happened. You can't control what other people do and the only one to blame for tonight is currently riding with Paul in cuffs. I made the choice to go on the search and I would make the same one again. I feel horrible that Luna's hurt but that's on him. You can't live life not doing things because maybe some asshole is going to do something stupid. You live and prepare yourself as best you can for what comes your way. Good and bad. For what if's, I always travel with a wolf."

"She really doesn't look like a wolf."

I snorted out a laugh.

"I was going to mention that your game warden brother may need a bio class or two."

Levi nodded in agreement and blew out a breath.

"Not my fault, my fault, doesn't matter. What does is that you cringe every time you take a breath, you've been holding your ribs all night and you look like you were in the ring for a few rounds with Mike Tyson."

"Ah but I still have my ears so not a complete KO."

"You are the most exasperating woman I have ever met."

I went to wink and remembered my eye was swollen shut.

"I really, really would feel better if you had a doctor see you."

I closed my eyes, well I closed the little bit that was open, and leaned back against the seat.

"What time is it?"

"Ah, 5:30."

"Make a deal with you. Take me back to the cottage. Let's get a few hours of sleep. I want to be at the clinic at 7:30 when they x-ray Luna. After that is done, and I've talked with Sierra, then I will go see a doctor. Besides, who in the world is open at 5:15 AM that's not an easy two -hour drive?"

Levi paused for a moment, thinking then then stuck out his hand. Then re-positioned it in front of my good eye so I wasn't groping around in the dark for it.

"Alright Shel, you got a deal on one condition."

"What is your one condition?"

"I'm staying with you and you're going to listen when we get back to any and all medical advice I have."

"I'm already in pain, your medical knowledge sounds painful, I don't think I can take any more."

"I'm glad to see your sarcasm didn't get hurt tonight."

I kept my eyes closed as we turned around and headed for the cottage.

43

GETTING OUT OF the truck after sitting for a bit was a hell of a lot harder than getting in was. The four steps up the porch might as well have been Mt Everest. His medical advice turned out to be a couple of ibuprofen, a ham sandwich and a mercifully cold beer that I alternated between holding on various parts of my face and sipping as he carefully dabbed off the blood. Under an hour later I felt myself drifting to sleep propped up on the couch, Levi stretched out on the floor promising to wake me up in an hour and a half.

Next thing I knew I felt something nudge me. Then whatever it was gently shook my arm. I went to open my eyes but couldn't. I jerked up only to have my body remind me of what happened and ended up slowly rolling to the floor onto my knees, one arm wrapped protectively around my ribs. I groaned, my face firmly planted on the floor.

"Can you help me up? I really have to pee and I can't see."

"Up you go, nice and slow."

He slowly let go as I regained my balance sitting on the couch and handed me ice wrapped with a towel.

"How bad does it look?"

"On a scale of 1 to 10? Around 35."

"So not so bad then."

"Maybe it's a good thing your eyes are swollen shut. Actually, let me get you a warm wash cloth too. Not sure which will help faster, try one on each eye."

I leaned back trying not to move. If this was how I felt after one scuffle I had no idea how professional fighters did it day in and day out. Turned out one eye was more stuck shut from crusty eye gunk and not all the way swollen shut like the other one. Satisfied I could still somewhat see, it was time for the next test. Walking.

"I'm getting up and using the bathroom."

Levi walked ahead to turn on the lights. He even lifted the lid on the toilet.

"Do you need any help with...any other part of...this."

Out of my good eye I could just see him waving his hands in awkward circle motions making me laugh. Oh God it hurts to laugh. Once I started I couldn't stop.

"Are you ok? I can get someone else to help you if you don't want me to."

I waved him away.

"Stop, just go, you're making me laugh. Hurts to laugh right now."

I snorted, trying to stop laughing.

"Coffee. And snacks for the drive."

He gave me a salute and hightailed it out of the tiny bathroom.

WE got out of the cottage in record time for most senior citizens. I didn't have coffee to make which at first felt like the start of a horrible day. Then Levi reminded me River's opened up an hour ago. As he put it in park out front I said a quick thank you to whoever deserved it for blue collar towns and people like River who make the day a little brighter.

"I'm going to wait here."

"If you want to make it to Sierra's before lunch that would be a good idea."

He pretended to walk like me towards the entrance. I sincerely hoped he was hamming it up as that was not how I ever wanted to look like moving. Not even at eighty.

THE bell over the door chimed as Levi walked into Rivers. No one was in line as he entered, Levi sent a mental thank you to whoever was listening.

"Hey River, can I get...."

River set two large coffees to go on the counter with a bakery bag.

"Right ones yours, left is Shelly's. Put your wallet away, it's no good here today."

She paused for a second.

"Paul stopped in on his way home."

"Thank you."

She gave him a half smile then waved him away.

"Go on, get out of here."

She went back to getting the day's baked goods on the shelf as he left.

I was resting my head on the window when Levi climbed back in. The smell of what he handed over was heavenly.

"Thank you for that, oh and please tell me there are muffins in there."

"You will have to thank River; all of this was on the house. I have no idea what any of it is."

"Really? Why would she..."

I stopped as the reason sunk in.

"Paul stopped in on his way home from Bangor. River's solid, she won't gossip about any of it but will always have your back."

He took a sip.

"And makes the best cup of coffee. What more could you ask for in a person really."

"This is really good. Mine has whipped cream in it, whatever it is."

"What? I was jipped. I take back every nice thing I just said about her. Stingy miserly witch, that's what she is."

A snort escaped as I held back a laugh.

"I'm begging you, do not make me laugh."

"I will do my best to be incredibly boring today."

With that he turned on talk radio and headed the truck to the Sierra's.

44

WE ARRIVED JUST in time for Luna's x-ray which came back with no breaks. After a thorough check up with Sierra, Luna was free to leave with us under the condition she rest to let her bruised ribs and pulled muscles in her legs heal. Armed with a homeopathic pain reliever and a script for stronger stuff if the homeopathic wasn't quite cutting it, we left with a promise that we would come back for dinner and a check-up in a few weeks. As we walked out I strongly suspected dinner in a few weeks would have another addition at the table. Levi got Luna comfortable in the backseat of his truck while I very slowly climbed in.

"Alright, deal is a deal. Your turn."

"What are you talking about?"

"Oh no, don't play dumb we made a deal. Luna gets checked out first then you."

I rolled my eyes.

"It's Sunday. And 8:30 in the morning. No doctor will be working today unless you're taking me back in to see Sierra."

I leaned back smugly. Clearly, I had won this one. Levi started the truck humming a tune.

"Why are you smiling?"

He shrugged and turned up the talk radio as he pulled away.

LEVI failed to mention his mother was a doctor. A retired one as of six months ago but a doctor nonetheless. Although I was more than a little annoyed at being trapped in my agreement, I had to admit being seen by a doctor in her home office with a fresh cup of coffee on a comfy couch was not the worst thing in the world.

"In my medical opinion you're lucky that all you have is swelling and moderate to severe bruising to your face and ribs. Unfortunately, the only thing that will cure either is time and rest. Take an over the counter Tylenol or Ibuprofen if you feel you need it but if you actually take it easy you should be fine without it."

"Thank you, Dr..."

"Betty, please. A friend of Levi's is a friend of ours."

"Thank you, Betty. You have a beautiful house by the way."

It was an older home that they had obviously done renovations to over the years. Enlarged doorways gave everything a connected feel without being completely open. Wide pine floors stretched throughout each space while white wood paneling adorned the walls with accentuated pops of vibrant green from all of their house plants tucked around everywhere. It had a farmhouse meets greenhouse feel. I liked it.

"It's a work in progress and now that I'm retired most likely will continue to be as inspiration strikes. Much to my husband's dismay. He'd much rather get it settled then leave it that way until we die. Ah, but where would the fun in that be?"

She opened the door and gestured for me to follow.

"Smells like breakfast is ready."

She eyed me suspiciously.

"You are the type of woman who eats bacon aren't you?"

"On anything but ice cream. I draw the line there."

She smiled approvingly.

"Good. Can't fathom why anyone would not eat bacon. Life's too short."

Luna was relaxing with a rawhide on a giant dog bed next to a black lab who was also gnawing away at one. She thumped her tail when she saw me but made no move to get up. Levi was flipping pancakes on a beautiful orange gas range while his dad was plating bacon.

"I am in love with your stove."

"My wife is a doctor/ designer or so I am told."

Chuck hurmped a little as he said it.

"Pop of color is what she wanted in here. I said go for it, didn't realize that meant an orange stove. It's like we're living in a Crayola box of crayons."

"Oh stop. You love this stove."

Betty swatted him with a dish towel as she walked by.

"Ignore him, he likes to grump. Grab a seat anywhere."

I took a seat near the dogs.

"That's Murph."

Levi gestured to the lab with his spatula.

"Hello Murph."

I ruffled his years then Luna's and watched Levi work alongside his parents. Their easy conversation and seamless dance around the kitchen as each finished up a part of breakfast spoke volumes about their relationship. Levi came around and placed a heaping plate of pancakes, bacon, fruit and what appeared to be fresh bread at each spot around the table.

"Your breakfast."

"Why thank you. Looks and smells amazing everyone, thank you."

Everyone sat down and then on cue the backdoor opened and Paul came in with a chocolate lab in tow.

"Smells amazing. Morning Mom, Dad. Hey Shelly."

"Hi Levi, nice to see you Levi. Oh, nice to see you too Paul."

Paul shot Levi his middle finger as Levi finished his one-sided conversation.

"Paul, Levi knock it off."

Betty had amusement in her eyes as she scolded her grown children.

"There's another bone on the lazy-Susan for Milo."

At the word bone Milo started dancing in place, tail wagging furiously.

"How are my grandbabies this morning?"

"Oh, their normal selves. Causing trouble."

Paul handed an ecstatic Milo his bone and sat down with us.

"Want a plate, honey?"

"No thank you, all set. I've been snacking since yesterday. Long night."

"So we've heard."

I squirmed uncomfortably in my chair as everyone stole a glance in my direction.

"Cup of coffee sounds amazing."

Paul snagged a slice of bacon off Levi's plate as he walked to the coffee pot. Levi in turn tried to trip him as he walked by.

"Anyhow, Levi, did you tell them about what the lab found in the meat?"

"The mystery meat by Harvey's house?"

My hand froze en route to my mouth, the question coming out as I thought it. Paul nodded.

"No, I haven't gotten around to it yet."

"Well, what did they find?"

I looked from Paul, to Levi, to Paul and back to Levi.

"Come on guys, the suspense is killing me!"

"The raccoon basically overdosed on heroin."

"Seriously?"

"Yeah not in the actual meat but inside each wrapped chunk of meat was a container stuffed in the center that had heroin in it."

Paul shook his head as he spoke as if he couldn't believe what they found.

"How much did they find?"

Betty and Chuck chimed in asking the same question at the same time. I smiled thinking shared thoughts must be a side effect of being married for so many years.

"Just shy of 1,000 grams."

"Is that a lot?"

I felt it was a good thing my drug knowledge was limited and didn't hesitate to ask.

"That would be right around one hundred thousand dollars-worth."

"Holy crap!"

I set my fork down as I wrapped my head around that.

Levi rocked his chair back on its legs, rubbing Murph's ears as he did.

"Think about it too, Harvey must have called me about rotting meat at least six times in the last year. If each of those times had the same amount?"

"Then you're not talking about a small-time drug dealer."

Chuck stood up and grabbed a pad of paper out of the drawer.

"This is something a hell of a lot bigger."

"Exactly."

Paul locked eyes with his dad.

"When did you get the results back?"

"Yesterday afternoon."

"Why didn't you call me? This is the kind of thing I need to know as soon as you do."

"I did call you dad. It went right to voicemail."

Chuck scowled and pulled out his phone.

"No you didn't, I would have... oh I have a voicemail."

He handed it over to Betty.

"Here open that up."

Without saying a word, she dialed into his voicemail to retrieve the message. Paul shook his head, looked at Levi and pretended to shoot himself.

"Dad, I just told you what I said in the message."

Chuck shushed him as he listened. Paul threw his arms in the air and stood up.

"I need more coffee. Anyone else?"

I raised my mug to accept his offer.

"Everything is delicious Betty, thank you again."

"You are welcome, anytime. So, Levi said you're staying at the McNei-land's cottage. Cute place isn't it?"

The earlier amazing coffee turned sour as I swallowed and remem-bered the earlier part of my day yesterday.

"Well, it is cute but I'm pretty sure I'm not going to be there much longer."

Levi's head snapped up from his conversation with Paul and Chuck.

"Why's that?"

"Did you hear about the building fire?"

At her well duh expression I chuckled.

"Of course, you have. Apparently, I am taking the fall for Mr. Otto putting cardboard boxes in the oven and turning it on. I was fired as of yesterday."

I shrugged my shoulders not knowing what else to add.

"The cottage was part of my employment package."

Levi shifted over to rejoin our conversation, spinning a chair around backwards as he straddled it.

"That's bullshit. How the hell was that your fault?"

"Beats me but Walters made it clear that I was done."

Levi started to say something but Betty cut him off.

"I agree with Levi, bullshit is what that is. Walters is a slimy guy, never liked him.   What are you going to do?"

I took a breath and blew it out.

"Honestly? I haven't really thought it through.   After I got off the phone with him I called a friend of mine who has a lawyer in the family to cover my butt, see what I needed to do if anything.   Then Levi called about the missing kid and my planning kind of stopped there.   Forgot about it until now."

Paul and Chuck had left the kitchen and were making phone calls in the other room. Levi was rooted to the island torn between what Paul and Chuck were doing and my conversation with Betty.

Betty started to clear the table. I finished my coffee and started to follow her lead. Mid reach for a plate Levi swooped in and blocked me trying to grab what I was going to take.

"Sit down, I got this."

"I have a bruise, I'm not dying thank you very much."

I glared at him as I grabbed a stack of dishes nudging him out of the way with my elbow. Betty smirked at her son. I rolled my eyes which turned her smirk into a deep laugh.

"The cottage was part of your employment package?"

I nodded yes to Betty as I started washing dishes.

"Walters can't kick you out with the snap of his fingers, any type of arrangement legally has to give whoever is living there notice before evicting. With that alone you have an easy two weeks I bet. In all honesty, you most likely could stay as long as you want. McNeilands don't rent that one too often."

"Good to know. Hey, you wouldn't happen to have their number would you? I know you're right but I would feel better talking with them, laying it all out on the table so to speak. I already feel guilty staying there, just waiting to see what happens would drive me insane."

Betty shot a pointed look at Levi. Levi crossed his arms and stared back. Betty put her hands on her hips and really gave him a stare.

"Mom, cut it out. I'm thirty-two. That crap only works on kids."

She kept staring. My eyes darted from mom to son and back trying to figure out what was happening. Levi crumbled.

"This is ridiculous."

He threw up his hands and stalked over to the sink to dump his coffee out.

"I have their number."

My eyebrows shot up as I took over the staring game.

"I am the caretaker of the cottage for them when they're out of town. I live next door, it just, it makes sense."

Levi went to take a sip of his coffee but having just dumped it paused awkwardly mid sip before deciding to refill his cup.

"Look, you don't need to call them. They won't be back till spring anyway and I know no one else is going to rent it or they would have told me."

I kept the silence as I continued to stare. I laughed inside as his face blushed a little. Finally, someone else's turn. A few more seconds and he cracked.

"Fine. I'll give you the number, it's on the fridge at my house."

Betty snorted. I shook my head. Paul and Chuck reappeared from the dining room.

"Gotta run, hon."

Chuck gave his wife a long firm kiss and feisty squeeze that made everyone in the room blush.

"Dad, come on! Get a room."

"This is our house, we are in a room."

Chuck gave Betty one more smooch who giggled and gave him a gentle shove away.

"And that's why no one just drops by anymore."

Paul turned to me with a solemn expression.

"Never stop by without calling ahead. Trust me, we've all been through years of therapy because we wanted to 'drop by' after moving out."

Levi cringed slightly and changed the subject.

"What's going on?"

"Well seeing as this chucklehead took so long giving me the lab results..."

"Gotta answer your phone dad!"

The yell came from the back hall where Paul was pulling on his boots.

"I just had the unit on patrol swing by to secure the rest of the meat but they radioed back that it's gone. We're going to look to see if anything was left behind, and figure out what's next. Could use a hand if you're not busy."

"Well on that note I am declaring Sunday dinner is cancelled for tonight. You're on your own when you get back Chuck. Murph and I are headed out to see the kids."

Paul poked his head back into the kitchen.

"Where? To my house? At least call my wife first before you show up."

"Already knows I'm coming darling."

"How? You just canceled dinner. Literally a second ago."

"I've known since last night I was canceling dinner when you didn't come home."

"How the Hell.. How'd you know I didn't come home?!"

She placed a hand on his cheek and gave him a quick kiss on the other.

"Sweetie, if I relied on you three men in my life to keep me informed I would know nothing and be aggravated. I like being happy. Off to see the grandkids."

With that she waved goodbye over her shoulder, whistled for the lab and left. Chuck looked at his son solemnly.

"Paulie, women have strange abilities that us men folk will never understand. Just go with it and life is easier."

"My wife didn't even text me this morning, and she talked to my mom?"

"Just let it go Paul.   Let it go."

Changing the subject, he turned his attention to us.

"So, what do you say, you two coming?"

45

Not wanting to be the slow poke I headed out to the truck while the guys finished doing whatever they were doing. Turns out getting Luna in the truck was a bigger deal than I thought. I finally gave up on the idea of lifting her in and went into Mcivor mode. Thankfully, Levi's parents' trash can and recycling bin were empty and Levi had a bunch of sweat-shirts in his truck. As I stuffed the sweatshirts around the tipped garbage can to keep it from rolling I made another mental note to return his shirt. A few minutes later I was sweating a hell of a lot more than I should have been for a low 30's morning but Luna had a set of stairs. Levi walked out as she settled into the back seat, took one look and muttered something to the sky.

"You were saying?"

He dragged the bins back to the garage where I had found them.

"You could have waited."

"Didn't need to."

"Yup, I can see that. Point has been made."

I couldn't tell if he was sincere or being an ass. Having nothing nice to say because of that, I left it at that and we rode in silence. Silence except for the talk radio.

WE spent the next two hours looking for anything that might have been left behind. I got the same treatment as everyone else on the ground and it felt great. It actually hurt like hell, my body was in full protest, but mentally it felt great. After about another hour that felt like five hours, everything was wrapping up. The truck seat could have been a deluxe feather bed, it felt good sitting still and not moving. I put my shades on and closed my eyes for a few minutes while Levi was talking with the last of the Game Wardens. Not having found much of anything, the search had been abandoned and a shift schedule had been established to swing by and keep an eye out for another drop. Chuck hoped that whoever was using the rotting meat as a decoy didn't know that the drugs were discovered, as we only took five hunks, and would make another crack at it.

"Ready to roll?"

Levi hopped into the truck startling me out of my drifting doze. I bit back a grimace when I sat up too quickly, the ribs were still protesting sudden movements.

"Ready Betty."

"I think I would be a Freddy or an Eddie, not a Betty."

FORTY minutes later the truck came to a stop in the cottage driveway. The empty sight made me realize my truck was still at the trailhead from last night. I let out a long sigh wondering when this week would end. Levi turned off the engine and, clearing his throat, turned to face me.

"Look, don't take this the wrong way. I... I. oh hell. I want to stay here. With you. Tonight."

I didn't have a chance to say anything before he barreled on.

"Not because I think you need someone to take care of you. I just, I care about you. No strings attached. Not expecting anything. I will sleep on the couch, do my own dishes, hell I'll even wash Luna's."

He had one hand resting on the steering wheel, the other arm slung around his head rest, eyes locked with mine waiting for an answer. That was him I realized. He would wait, not push. Tease and poke to get his point across but would respect whatever I said next. I leaned over and kissed him.

"Give me an hour, I need to shower. And you're cooking the frozen pizzas I have."

"Deal. I'll even throw in a beer or two. Be back in an hour."

46

It was going to take every bit of will power I had to turn the shower off and step out. Small cottage it may be, but, oh, the shower made up for it. Rain shower head, body jets, little stone floor tiles. I never saw what the big deal was that people made about gorgeous bathrooms with all the bells and whistles, until now. I had been living in denial. Relishing one last blast of hot water I turned it off, stepped out and heard rustling downstairs.

"Levi? Is that you?"

More rustling and clanking. No sign of Luna, which was either good or bad. Given the amount of steam that was trapped in the bathroom my hour had to be well past. I was giving it a 95% chance that it was indeed Levi downstairs making dinner. I leaned my head over the loft railing as I wrapped a towel around myself to verify my hunch. Levi looked up as I looked over and walked smack into the wood caddy by the door.

"Oh fuck! Ouch, ahh!"

I couldn't help it, I let out a laugh.

"Laugh it up woman, this is all your fault."

"My fault huh?"

"Walking around nearly naked like that? Luckily I wasn't carrying a knife, I could have killed myself."

"Har har. I'm sure the sight of my knees and ankles is a lethal weapon."

He picked himself up making a big show of it, dusting off invisible dust.

"You should lock your doors by the way. Anyone could have waltzed in here."

"It is a rough neighborhood. Would hate to have a moose in the living room, you know how they get."

"Very funny. Seriously, what if someone of the human variety came in while you were showering? Then what?"

"I'd show them my ankles, have the poor bastards KO'd in no time."

He shot me a stern look then rolled his eyes.

"Hey now, If you roll your eyes like that they are going to get stuck, didn't anyone ever tell you that? Besides, I knew this tough forest ranger was coming over. He would have taken care of any moose intruders."

Before he could get another word in I hiked my towel up an inch to show off just a smidge of thigh as I turned to get dressed and heard the very satisfying clatter of logs on the floor.

Twenty minutes later I was sitting on the couch in my favorite flannel PJ pants and tattered college sweatshirt sipping an iced cold beer watching a good looking man take a frozen pizza out of the oven with purple oven mitts. Life was good.

After dinner I indulged in another beer, because it was for medicinal purposes. I shifted to stretch my legs out on the couch for a second. Levi set his beer down and gently grabbed my foot, setting it on his lap.

"May I?"

"May you what? Tickle me? Not if you want to keep your teeth."

"That's what you think of first when a guy sets your foot in his lap? Being tickled?"

The swelling in my face was just about gone making it much more effective to give him a warning look. Without another word he started to rub my foot with his thumbs in slow deep circles. I couldn't help it, it felt so good I let out a deep sigh of pleasure.

"Apparently I've been hanging out with the wrong guys. This feels amazing."

Levi chuckled.

"Well, what can I say, I'm quite the catch."

"And so modest too."

"Yup, they broke the mold when they made me, good looking."

"Good looking, huh?"

He raised his eyebrows suggestively, heat back in his eyes. He held my gaze for a moment, making my pulse quicken before he cleared his throat and changed the subject.

"So, what are you going to do now? Really no reason to rush out of here..."

"I don't really have a plan in place."

I sighed deeply as he switched to my other foot.

"I texted my uncle, the one that has the ranch? He said I'm welcome back anytime. He could use another guide and someone to help in the kitchen on the weekends."

Taking another slug of beer, I mulled that idea around for a moment as it was the one that made the most sense.

"Or, I might see what I can find on the east coast. Problem with that is not many places will let Luna tag along. The ranch is Luna approved. I don't know. Time will tell I guess, but I'm not rushing. Still want the McNeiland's number to give them a heads up and see what they want to do. I may be a lot of things, but a mooch is not one of them."

"Not rushing is a good place to start."

He seemed lost in thought for a moment, staring into the wood stove as he rubbed my foot. As quickly as he left, he turned back giving me that slow sexy smile that had me grinning back.

"So, how are you feeling? Still tough as nails?"

"Very funny. Why do you ask?"

"Well, your feet are fully relaxed, and if you're feeling up for it I was going to..."

He slid his hand up my calf massaging as he went.

"Shift my area of focus."

"Hmm, is that so?"

"Hmm, that is so."

He leaned forward and kissed my PJ clad knee, then my hand, my wrist. When he hit my elbow, I burst out laughing. He smiled and planted his lips on mine. His lips pressed gently, slowly taking and teasing. At that moment I let my brain stop thinking and fully enjoyed the company of my neighbor.

47

The fire had died down to embers giving the room a faint glow that matched the sun peeking in through the windows when a banshee's scream shot me out of a deep sleep. The couch where we drifted off was modest sized at best. How we both fit without falling off all night is a minor miracle in itself. Now, gravity's grace period had officially ended as I found myself tangled up in the blanket on the floor under Levi as he frantically scrambled around in the dark searching for whatever was making that god awful noise. Finally, it stopped. Levi rolled over on the floor and pulled me in.

"Sorry about that, forgot to shut it off."

"Shut it off?"

"My alarm."

"That was your alarm? What the hell is wrong with you?! Why in the world would that be your alarm?! It was like...like hell chickens screaming at you."

"Oh, it wasn't that bad. You get used to it."

I stared at him in disbelief.

"I don't know if I can sleep with someone who wakes up to that every day. Nope. Just checked, it cannot happen."

Levi propped himself up on one elbow while the other hand slowly walked his fingers down my hip.

"Problem solved, we won't sleep."

And with that he rolled me on top of him and officially started our day.

THAT afternoon I caught myself staring out the window, watching the wind make little snow tornados with the powder that was on the ground. I don't know how long I had been standing there. I had gotten stuck in a loop thinking about the mystery meat filled with drugs, my lack of employment and then Chester had popped into it. Something had been nagging at my brain and I just couldn't get it to click. Levi had left a few hours ago for work after making a run with me to pick up my truck from the trail head. I sent him a quick text that I was heading out to Last chance. I was willing to bet the farm that maybe Chester had also found out that the meat was a decoy for something else. If my hunch was right, finding out all that I could find out about Chester and what he knew was the next step in solving this mystery.

The drive to Last Chance was beautiful. Lots of windy wooded roads that would break open occasionally to show off a sliver of a lake or rock outcropping. It took longer than I remembered but chalked that up to still being stiff and sorer that I wanted to admit. Out of the two of us Luna seemed to be bouncing back faster but was still moving gingerly. Finally, I threw on my blinker and pulled into the parking lot. Half a dozen cars and trucks were parked in the lot giving me a little hope that even though it was fairly early for bar goers, I might be able to find what I was hoping for. I tugged a baseball cap over my pony tail hoping the brim would hide what was left of the bruising. Luna sat up looking hopeful about joining me. I hesitated then thought what the hell and opened the door for her to hop out. Glancing at my phone to see if Levi had replied I realized I had forgotten to charge it again. It was dead. Tossing it on the charger and locking the door behind me we headed in.

Just like last time every head in the place snapped up as we walked in. It may have been all in my head but the atmosphere was not warm and welcoming. Luna was walking close enough I could feel her side pressed up against my legs making me think that maybe it wasn't just in my head. Hopping up on a bar stool I scanned the room as I waited for the bartender to finish talking with the only other guy at the bar. They looked familiar. Bartender for sure was here last time, the other guy I was fairly certain was as well. In fact, in the same spot even, but no sign of James. I had hoped by chance that he would have been here and maybe would open up a little more. I swung the stool around to face the bar as the bartender approached trying to decide how I wanted to play this.

"Hi."

He grunted in response. So much for small talk.

"So I was in here the other night, not sure if you remember me.."

"Are you going to order anything?"

"Ah yeah. I'll take a pint of whatever's on tap. Please."

Thinking this may be my only shot I leaned over the bar as he was getting my drink.

"So anyway, last week when I was here I was talking with a guy named James. Think he comes by here pretty regularly. You wouldn't happen to know if he usually stops by any time soon."

The bartender eyed me warily as he finished pouring the beer.

"Or maybe I could leave my number for him?"

"What, that guy you were with not cutting it for you?"

"So you do remember me! And no, not like that. Just trying to figure something out and I think he may be able to help me."

I swiped some hair that had fallen out of my ponytail up and under my hat to get it out of my face.

"Hell of a bruise you got there."

I shrugged, playing it cool.

"Should have seen it a few days ago."

I was trying to make a joke, to ease the tension a little but it seemed to have the opposite effect on him. He tossed the bar rag he was holding over his shoulder and leaned in closer to me, forearms resting on the bar top.

"Look, I don't know what's going on but I do know this. After you were here? Next day a big guy comes in, dark glasses, hat pulled down low. Started asking me what you and your friend were doing here and who you were talking to."

"Wait, what? Who? Who was the guy?"

"Don't know, hadn't seen him before. My opinion? It's nobody's business who is here talking to who so I says nothing, hoping I'll get rid of the guy. Loose lips over there?"

He gestured to the other guy I remembered seeing who was now sitting slightly slumped on his bar stool.

"He told him how you were talking to James and how he thought it was weird that James gave you the address to the cemetery.

Slumped over guy straightened up a little as he turned to face us.

"I thought it was funny, thought it would make the guy laugh and lighten up when he heard James duped a couple of schmucks into going there instead of wherever you were trying to get to."

He slumped down lower and stared into his almost empty glass before throwing it back.

"James was a friend. Good guy. Didn't want anything to happen..."

Looking at the guy I wanted to feel angry but felt sadder as it looked like that stool was like a second home to him. I turned back to the bartender.

"So, what if the dude heard that? I'm not following you here."

"Big guy leaves. Day later James' house goes up in flames. He was lucky to get his family out alive."

"What? You're saying the big guy did it?"

"All I'm saying is houses don't burn for no reason."

"What did the police report say? They had to investigate after putting it out, right?"

The bartender scoffed then started to dry glasses with much more force than I thought necessary.

"Yeah they put it out alright. Arrived just in time to douse the last embers laying on the cinder block foundation. Closest department is 15 miles from his house and they didn't get there until it was almost over."

I took a long pull on my beer, trying to ignore the sense of unease I was getting as I digested all that he said.

"Well where's James now? Do you know how I can find him?"

Bartender shook his head, crossed his arms giving me a very firm stare.

"Packed what they could salvage and left town. Let them be. They don't need any more crap from anybody and from the look of what you're trying to hide under your hat? I suggest you do the same."

The hairs on my neck stood up a little. What happened to James coupled with the drugs that were found in the meat was making for a hell of a higher stakes game of who done it than I had bargained for.

The bartender had shifted his attention back to the game on the TV and started wiping down the spotless bar top. I glanced at Luna, she was sitting at my feet back to the bar watching the rest of the people with an alert wariness. Not wanting to outstay my welcome I gave a quiet whistle to signal to her we were on our way out.

I placed a couple of bucks on the bar for a tip, turning to go I stopped and leaned over towards the slumping guy.

"Do you know where I could find Nora?"

Without hesitating or looking away from the TV he answered.

"Oh she's been staying with her cousin Vivian over on Dovetail. Leaving tomorrow and meeting up with James and family to lay low for a while."

"Travis! What the hell is wrong with you?"

The bartender looked like he was going to strangle Travis with his bar rag.

"Ah shit, I did it again."

He laid his head on the bar, body deflated more than before if that was possible.

I took that opportunity to make a beeline for the door. Glancing back as we exited I could see Travis still slumped over and the bartender talking on his phone with feverish hand motions.

AFTER locking the truck doors for good measure, I turned my phone back on to type in Dovetail in the map app I had. I was willing to bet good money that this would be my only chance to speak with Nora before she disappeared along with James.

"Woah, 5 missed calls, and... all from Levi."

I glanced at the clock in the dash. All within the last 15 minutes. Hitting the call back I turned the engine over and pulled out. I wanted a little space between me and the bar. Levi picked up on the second ring.

"Shelly, why didn't you answer your phone?"

"Hello to you too. It died, had it charging in the truck. Just turned it back on. What's up?"

"What's up? What's up?! I called you and it went right to voicemail."

"I just told you it was dead."

"You texted me you were going to Last Chance. I called you and it went right to voicemail. What's up was that I was thinking that something bad had happened!"

"Well the worst was that my cell died. Sorry to disappoint."

Levi let out a long sigh. We sat for a few seconds in silence.

"Just please, from now on, charge your cell."

"Look Levi..."

"Please. Charge your damn cell. Are you still at the bar?"

"Okay, okay. No, I was just leaving and heading to a road called Dovetail. Got a lead on Nora, she's skipping town with James."

I filled Levi in with the cliff note version.

"So, here's my take. Either the bartender is crazy paranoid or there is someone doing some scary shit to people who had some connection to the murder meat."

"Murder meat? Who's been murdered?"

"Ok, so no one yet officially but the Chester thing seems fishy and if James hadn't gotten out in time that would for sure have made it murder meat material."

I cleared my throat.

"Either way, I think we need to talk to Nora. As in yesterday."

I could hear Levi drumming his hands on the steering wheel.

"Let's see what Nora has to say. What's the address?"

"I didn't get one and I don't think I'll get one if I go back in and ask."

"No, don't go back in. Do you know anything about the cousin?"

"Vivian. Her name is Vivian and she lives on Dovetail."

"That could be all we need. Ok, I am closer to her than you are, the quickest way would be back towards me anyway so I'll wait here for you and see if I can't nail down an address."

"Sounds like a plan, see you in 30ish minutes."

"Drive safe Red."

48

By the time I got to Levi he had found an address for Vivian. It's a little scary how much info you can get off the internet about someone with a few details. We left my truck in a scenic pull off almost an hour ago. According to the GPS we were just about to Vivian's doorstep.

"Should be the next house on the left. Yes, there it is. The one with the teal door. 1178 Dovetail."

Levi parked the truck across the street and we both sat in silence looking at the cute little cape.

"Alright Red, what's our play here?"

"You're asking me?"

"You got us this far didn't you? You seem to have a knack for getting info out of people."

"Wow, I think that's a compliment."

Sitting there I pondered Levi's question. How did we want to do this?

"Pull away."

"What? Why?"

"This may sound crazy, but what if the bartender is right and someone is harassing anyone who asks about Chester. I don't want to be the reason anyone else's house starts on fire. We can't park here."

"Shel, we don't know why James' house started on fire. Maybe he lit candles and fell asleep."

"We also don't know that it wasn't caused by someone trying to cover their tracks. I told you what he said about the response time. No one showed up to help until it was over. Seriously, for that to happen it has to be someone who can cover that crap up."

"Or someone's."

Levi pulled away from the house and drove in the opposite direction we came from. About 15 minutes later he slowed down as we passed what looked like the start of a trail head.

"What about in there?"

I rolled down my window to get a better look. It was well beyond dusk and I could barely see anything not in the headlights.

"You think we will fit?"

"It will be tight, but no houses around on either side of the road and I should be able to back in far enough headlights of anything driving by shouldn't reflect off the truck.

"Work's for me."

Few minutes later we were tucking branches around the truck to make sure it blended in while we were gone. When we stood on the road looking in? No one would ever know that a truck was hidden a few feet up the trail.

"We should probably keep off the road, right? Just in case?"

Levi paused before answering and dug out a compass from his backpack that he snagged out the truck's lock box in the bed.

"Wouldn't be a bad idea. A majority of the distance between us and Vivian is a pretty wooded area. Should be able to shoot a bearing and cut through those trees. Will dump us out onto Dovetail for sure. Worst case scenario we just have to walk a block or two to get to her actual house."

"This won't be creepy at all. Two strangers and a large dog hiking through the woods behind her house at night, to talk to her about her dead husband. What could go wrong with our plan?"

"Oh, just about everything."

With that cheerful thought the three of us stepped into the darkness to bushwhack to Vivian's.

49

I<small>T SHOULD HAVE</small> taken us an hour tops to get to Nora. Twenty minutes into the hike we hit a peat bog. Correction, I stumbled into a peat bog. Levi and Luna veered around it somehow. I lost a boot and added over an hour onto what I now was calling a slog. By the time we hit pavement I was numb. My foot was killing me even after putting both of Levi's socks on it to keep walking and even though wearing his jacket most likely had kept me from getting severely hypothermic, I felt terrible that he now looked frozen as well. I didn't care who we were spotted by at this point. I wanted to go home and be done with this mess.

Finally, we stumbled out onto the graveled shoulder of what had to be Dovetail. Levi turned to me rubbing his hands together.

"We made it. How are you feeling?"

I nodded my head in a very small yes motion. That was all I had in me. Luna leaned into my legs and gave Levi a yawn.

Looking slightly concerned Levi pulled out his phone.

"Ok, MapQuest says we are about 400 yards from her house. I say we follow the road the rest of the way, hopefully get you out of the wind and then I can run back to grab the truck."

I forced my lips to move as they seemed more inclined to shiver than speak.

"What about Chester?"

"Ending up with hypothermia and frostbite is not worth whatever we may find out about Chester."

"Getting this far and not at least making an attempt at talking to her would be ridiculous and a waste of possibly my fingers and right big toe."

"Don't joke about frostbite."

"Who says I'm joking?"

Levi rolled his eyes and hitched his arm around me as we walked the last 400 yards to Nora's as fast as we could, which should have been faster but my legs were not moving how my brain wanted them to. A thick row of spruce trees was brushing up against the side of the road but seemed to stop ahead. Hoping that was our destination I turned slightly to go around the last spruce and just about had a heart attack as someone slammed a trunk a few feet from us. I wasn't sure who was more surprised, us or the woman who now had one hand over her chest and the other bracing herself on the trunk of her car.

"Holy hell, you two. Scared the actual shit out of me."

I recognized her in an instant. It was Nora.

"Are you ok? Your hair is frozen."

I had a million things I wanted to ask her but nothing came out.

"Is she ok?"

Levi realized who we were talking to about then, I saw his eyebrows shoot up then he threw his arm around me, pulling me in close.

"We're so sorry to bother you. She fell in a peat bog about an hour ago, would it be ok if she sat in your garage to warm up while I ran and went to get the truck?"

Nora was already pulling me into the garage by the sleeve as she talked. Gently pushed me into a lawn chair and then pulled a thick wool blanket off a shelf draping it around me.

"What the heck were you doing in a peat bog in the middle of the night? You must not be from around here girl, stupid shit like that will get you killed."

She then turned to Levi.

"You on the other hand should know better. I know I've seen you around before and your hat says you work for the Forestry Department. Why in the world were the two of you tromping through the woods, in the dark, in November?"

Levi shifted uncomfortably from foot to foot, hands in his back pockets. I cleared my throat and went for it.

"We were looking for you Nora. Wanted to ask you about Chester."

Nora's face went from concerned, to stunned, to seething. She took several quick steps over to the far corner and came back gripping a well-loved baseball bat.

"Both of you, get the hell out of here. Now!"

She smacked a shelf with the baseball bat to make her point. Truth of the matter was I was too frozen to move and I really didn't think she was going to club us. She looked like a wild animal that had been cornered.

"Nora, I am so sorry to barge in on you like this but we need your help. Something is going on, something that Chester knew about and whatever it is or was, it's still happening."

"You were the two that talked to James at the bar."

I nodded my head.

"His house was burnt to the ground because he talked to you. They already killed my husband, what do you think they will do to me for talking? Please, please just leave."

"That was not our intent in talking to James, if we knew that was going to happen we would not would not have talked to James in the open like that. That's why I'm thawing out in here, we didn't want anyone to know we were here talking to you so we parked a few miles back deep in a trailhead and bushwhacked through the woods."

Levi squatted down next to me and looked up at Nora as he chimed in.

"Nora, we know you're leaving town which honestly sounds like your best move at this point. Give us five minutes, help us figure out what we need so no one else has to go through what you have."

Nora's shoulders slumped, her death grip and batter's stance loosened as she sat down on an overturned bucket. Cupping her head in her hands she nodded yes.

"Who killed Chester, Nora?"

"I don't know. He didn't fall while taking photos, that's for damn sure. He knew that trail inside and out. Would never, ever, have gone without telling me where he was going just in case something happened."

She wiped her eyes with the backs of her hands, took a deep steadying breath.

"He wasn't out taking photos. His camera is still in its case, in my trunk. How the hell would he be taking photos without his camera? The one they found on him wasn't his. No one would listen to me. No one believed me. Not even James until she called."

"She? The killer is a woman?"

"No. No, well at least I don't think so but who knows? She called the day of the funeral. Everyone had finally left, it was just me and James sobbing into our whiskey. My cell rang. I answered it, threw it on speaker so James could take over the talking when I couldn't take any more. Figured it was some distant family member or friend, they had been calling since they found...found Chester. But it wasn't. It was a woman I didn't recognize. Said that the autopsy report they gave me was edited. She said that the original report stated that Chester... that he was dead before falling off the cliff. That the broken bones from the fall clearly happened after he was already dead."

Nora choked back a sob. I didn't know what to do or say, Levi and I sat like stone statues. The silence around us felt heavy. Nora pressed the palms of her hand against her eyes as she continued.

"She said Chester had to have died hours before going over the cliff face. Someone had planted the body and that I needed to be careful. Then she hung up."

"Nora, I... I don't know what to say, I can't imagine going through what you have gone through..."

My stomach was in knots listening to Nora, I couldn't imagine how she must have felt. Levi was up and pacing, thinking.

"Do you know who called?"

"No. After she hung up, James called in a favor and had the number traced. It was a secondary line at the coroner's office. The corner was, is, a man over there. No one should have been working at the time the call came through, it was a Sunday night after dark. No females are on staff either. But it was for sure, a woman who called. James didn't want to dig too deep as to who made the call, didn't want what happened to Chester to happen to me or someone else, whoever she was."

Levi squatted down in front of Nora who was still slumped on the bucket.

"Nora, is James a part of this?"

"James? No, no way."

"How can you be sure?"

She scoffed.

"After she called I lost it. I started screaming at James to tell me what the fuck was going on. I threw anything I could get my hands on at him, demanding he tell me what was happening. I expected him to yell back, throw something, tell me I was crazy."

She paused there looking almost through me as she spoke.

"He didn't. He broke down alongside me, sobbing saying how sorry he was. Told me that it was a case they had been working on for over a year. Said Chester wanted to drop it months ago, was getting jumpy and was worried they were in over their heads. James just couldn't let it go.

He said Chester told him he was being followed. He felt like someone was watching him all the time. James laughed it off, teased him for being paranoid."

"What was the case they were working on?"

"Honestly? I don't know. He would never tell me, and told me not to look. I promised that I would not look. Said not knowing was safer. James said he wanted to believe that what happened to Chester was an accident, and almost had himself convinced until she called. Until her call unraveled everything he had been telling himself otherwise."

After a very long pause, I gently took Nora's hand in mine and squeezed it until she looked up at me.

"What happened then?"

"James went into work the next day and closed the case, solved it or whatever they do to say they are officially done with it. Came over, helped me pack what I couldn't live without, and told me to lay low until I heard otherwise from him. That's what I did. Until the other night, when his house was burned to the ground for talking to you two. Then he called and said to get out. Take the scenic route and meet him at a place we all would be safe."

"Where are you going to meet him?"

Nora smirked and shook her head no.

"You seem on the up and up but that line from whatever movie it was keeps running through my head. Trust no one. I confided in you but I don't know if I trust you with my life or the lives of my friends."

"Fair enough."

I glanced up at Levi, not sure what to do or say next. Catching my glance, he dropped down on a chair next to me shifting Nora's attention to him.

"What can we do to help? Seriously, name it. You can take my truck if you need it."

"I don't think driving around in a marked forestry truck would be the best getaway vehicle. I'm leaving tonight. Just don't get caught when you leave and don't fall into any more peat bogs."

"Don't worry, I am making him walk in front this time."

That got a small chuckle out of her.

"Nora, thank you so much. Be safe, and here."

I grabbed her hand and a pen I found on the floor and wrote my number on her palm. "Not trying to be weird here, but call us if you need anything. I'm Shelly, this is Levi."

She nodded as I handed the blanket back to her and we started for the door.

"Wait! Just wait one second."

She disappeared into the house, reappeared a few minutes later with a leather book with rubber bands around it.

"Here, take this."

"What is it?"

"Chester's work log. What he used whenever he was on a case to keep track of his observations, thoughts, hunches. You know, cop crap. I promised James I wouldn't look for information and I didn't. But I never promised that no one else would. Take it. Hope it helps."

Levi tucked the book into his inside jacket pocket. We thanked Nora and slipped out the back door and headed directly into the woods. Once safely inside the tree line we paused and watched Nora back the car out of the driveway and leave. For good.

"I want to wait a few minutes to make sure no one is following her or us."

"Ok." I sat down on a log, arm around Luna and we waited in the dark. Each of us lost in our own thoughts hoping no one was following Nora or us.

"Levi, what the hell have we gotten ourselves into?"

He sat down next to me, wrapped an arm around me that I leaned into.

"I have no idea. No idea."

50

THE RIDE HOME was quiet. Blessedly warm. With the heat cranked all the way up I was finally able to feel my feet. Luna was sleeping with her tail draped across Levi's legs, her head resting on mine.

"Are you going to read Chester's log?"

"I want to. Feel like it's burning a hole in my pocket thinking about it."

"Curiosity killed the cat."

"What? Why would you say that, right now I mean. I know it's a saying but geez Shel. Don't go poking the bear."

"It just came out. No filter. Finding yourself in the middle of a drug death rotting meat ring of doom does that to a woman."

"Don't take this the wrong way, but I don't think you should read it Shel."

"But you should?"

"Yes."

"Well that makes zero sense."

"Look, you don't have to be a part of this, you can just walk away to be safe."

"Don't you think whoever burned James's house down knows both of us were talking to him at the bar?

"You don't know that. What if they don't?"

"What if they do?"

Levi didn't have any retort for that one.

"What were you planning on doing, reading it and then going after whatever info's in the journal solo?"

"No, not solo."

"With who then, the cops?"

"No, not the cops. At least not any around here, doesn't seem like they all are on the up and up."

There was a long pause in our not yet an argument but more than a regular conversation.

"Ok so who are you planning on working with?"

"Paul."

"Paul? Paul?! Are you kidding me?!"

"What's wrong with Paul?!"

"Nothing! Everything! He has a wife and kids! You're worried about me reading it because whoever is being an ass might be an ass to me but you're willing to throw Paul's family into the crossfire? Your family?"

Levi had his jaw clenched and was flexing his grip on the steering wheel then smacked it with one hand before he ran it through his hair making it stick up in a series of spikes.

"Shit. I hadn't thought about that. Shel, I don't know what else to do here. This is not your normal forestry department detail."

"Little out of my pay grade as well."

I ran my hands up and down Luna's fur as I stared out the window at the darkness. There were no street lights, just dark all around except for the small swatch the headlights took care of.

"Here is my take on this."

Levi nodded in my direction, giving me the I'm listening.

"If Nora still had the book, I'm betting no one else knew about it. Otherwise she wouldn't have had it still or she would be really missing or worse. Which means no one knows we have it or would be worried that we do."

"That makes sense. Continue Sherlock."

"That makes you Watson, my lowly sidekick."

"Pretty sure Watson was the one that solved most of the stuff, Sherlock just took the credit."

"Either way, hear me out. We lay low for a few weeks, letting the dust settle. We read the book together and if we find something then we find a contact that we trust or better yet, a few of them, and give only the info that's needed. No need to mention the book at all."

"We could work with that. Still need to be careful, but we can work with it."

"Settled then, lay low and look at it together."

Levi nodded then reached over to give my hand a squeeze.

"I bet Paul knows a few guys on the up and up, I'll ask him for some advice on who we can trust if we find anything that's more than a hunch."

We sat in silence long enough to listen to two songs on the radio before my mind couldn't stay silent any more.

"Or..."

"Or what?"

"Or we read the book tonight, get a better idea of what we are dealing with then lay low for a while having a better picture."

"Nothing wrong with the first plan you know."

"No, but the second one sounds better don't you think?"

"Second plan is a risk."

"How? Same plan, same level of risk, just we have a better idea of what the hell is going on sooner. Makes it safer actually when you think about it."

Levi stayed quiet for a moment, then nodded his head.

"Ok. We read the book, see if there is anything to see but, and seriously Shel no shitting around on this, but whatever we find we sit on it and carefully choose who to tell it to."

"I am on board with that, 100%."

"Ok."

"Ok then. Sooo your house or mine?"

Levi turned his head slightly to give me a are you serious? Glance.

"Mine, I actually have food in the fridge."

"Why should I stock my fridge with food when I know my hunky ranger neighbor has plenty?"

Levi let out a laugh.

"Oh, I'm onto you now Red."

51

A FEW HOURS later I was sitting on the couch, my legs stretched out with my feet on Levi's lap. I took another handful of cheese puffs and closed my eyes. Levi was re-reading a section of Chester's notebook that we both had had a hard time deciphering. It had a few sentences that were hastily written with a slew of numbers written here and there. My head hurt from what if's we had been throwing back and forth.

"What if it's a license plate number?"

I opened one eye and peered at him.

"What's a license plate number, the 10,000 numbers listed on that page?"

Levi threw a cheese puff at me.

"Seriously, what if it is? He has a bunch of numbers written down yes, but they all are in their own groupings. They all start with the same three numbers. What if he had a partial plate number and was trying to figure out what the rest of it was to pinpoint the perp?"

"Perp, ha! Now look who's going all detective on me. No longer can you tease me for my cop shop talk."

I took a swig of my beer and thought about Levi's thinking. I had to admit, it sounded somewhat legit.

"Ok, so how did he only get part of the plate? Why didn't he get all of it?"

"See Red? Makes sense, right? My theory? Well, I have two. Maybe three. What if he only got part of it because whatever the perp was driving was getting away? Maybe he was only able to see the first three. Or what if the perp smeared mud over the plate to keep it unknown but half of it fell off leaving only the tail end covered."

"Both plausible I will give you that. What's the third theory?"

"The third? Maybe he had crappy eyesight and left his glasses at home."

I chuckled.

"Also a legit possibility, Levi."

"Now check this out, one of the last entries in the book."

I scooted over to get a look.

"Looks like names of, what cities?"

"No, they are names of parks or conservation areas and look at this one. This one is just outside of Fort Kent."

"Where Chester and James were working on the case and look, that's the road that runs by Harvey's house."

"What if these are all other drop sites?"

Levi let out a low whistle as he ran his hand through his hair.

"Shit, if that's the case there are...15 different sites on here. Think of how much can be stuffed into one can."

"No wonder whoever is doing this went after Chester and James. So, what do we do now?"

"Shel, what we do is be careful. Don't give them a reason to come after us too."

"Well we have to do something. We can't just do nothing."

"What we have now are hunches, guesses, nothing concrete."

"So then let's check out our hunches and turn them into facts."

"Did you not listen to anything I just said about being careful?"

"Levi, it's not like they can kill us all. Would be a major red flag, don't you think?"

"Red flag to who?! James and Chester were cops and they were scared of this. Hell, Chester is most likely dead because of this."

"I just...I feel like the creep who's doing this, wins if we don't do something."

Levi had gotten up and was pacing in the kitchen, Luna had taken over his spot and was keeping my feet warm.

"What if we found someone we trusted and gave them the names of what we think are the other drop sites? At least see if those check out?"

Levi let out a long sigh and slumped down on the couch next to me.

"I could call Paul to see if he knows anyone out in those areas who's not a cop but has the ability to check and stay under the radar."

"Are you sure you want to call Paul?"

"No. But he would have more contacts than I would. I'll see if he can swing by tomorrow."

"What are you going to tell him? An edited version?"

"As much as I don't want to, I think I'll give him the full picture in hopes it will make him be careful."

"That seems sensible to me. And he already knows a large part of it, the drug part and as far as we know, no one's been messing with your family right?"

"No, I would have heard about it if it was happening. Do you want to come over too when he does? I could be persuaded to make dinner."

"Hmm tempting offer, but I have an interview tomorrow night, remember?"

"Ah yes the interview with Harvey to be slave labor at his kennel. Feel free to give me a call if you accidentally drink too much cider again."

I punched his arm.

Ha, ha Levi, it was an honest mistake. Could have happened to any-body."

"You're the first person I know of and I've lived here all my life."

I punched his arm again and got up to refill the cheese balls.

52

LAYING LOW WAS not as exciting as I thought it would be. In fact, it was downright mundane. At first it was hard to not talk about it all. Hard to not go looking for more information. Paul had come up with some people he trusted in the other areas we thought were being used as drop sites. One of them installed a trail camera at one that caught a truck lingering twice that had aspects that matched some of the cryptic notes in Chester's log but mostly just caught teenagers doing teenage things. Other than that, it had been really quiet on the rotten meat front for over a month.

With no real leads we had settled into a weird rhythm that worked for us. He did his thing, I did mine and if all was good in the world we found ourselves tangled up in front of a wood stove a few nights a week.

I had gotten a hold of the McNeilands and worked out a deal where I cleaned a few of their other rentals as needed and could stay at the cute cottage until their first summer rental landed in late May. Harvey, the last person on the planet I ever thought I would work for, had deemed me worthy after my interview and brought me on a few days a week to help him with his dogs. First it was basic pooper scooper duty. Now that's just the start of each day.

I smiled as I pulled my hat tighter thinking how strange the world can be, then stepped off the brake letting the team take flight. I loved the rush of mushing. Everything about it. The entire fiasco of taking a chance on this town months ago brought me to this and this made it all worth it. Harvey let me take out the B and C squad as he called them. Nothing B or C about these dogs I mused. His A squad was made up of his competition team. B and C were the dogs for sale. As much of a hard ass front he put on, in realty, he was a big softie. He didn't like running the B and C squads because he got too attached. "Haw!" I leaned into the turn and laughed about my first turn attempt almost a month ago. I will admit I was a tad cocky stepping up to the runners and deserved my yard sale of a crash as I was whiplashed around attempting to take a turn far too fast. Harvey was not only a fanatic about his dogs. He turned out to be a pretty good coach as well. Tough one, but that only made me learn faster.

"Easy now, easy. Hup, hup."

My mind closed out all thoughts other than the dogs. Had to focus on the dogs. Watching the trail, each dog's gait for any signs of stress, anything that might distract the team, complete tunnel vision with feeder tubes was how Harvey described it. I looked at him like he was nuts the first time, but understood it now. A quick 15 miles later we pulled back into the yard for a cool down trot around the perimeter. Like clockwork, Harvey opened the door and let Luna out to run alongside. He walked out to the center of his drive watching the dogs, his own tunnel vision check he did after each run.

"How'd they feel?"

"Like a ticking time bomb. Not even winded."

He chuckled and nodded as we circled around him.

"This crew's young. Another month we'll start pushing the distance and speed."

He looked everyone over a few more times, gave me a nod and pointed to the barn where we harnessed and unharnessed the teams.

"Whoa, ease up. Whoa."

Once they stopped, I set the brake firmly in the snow, thinking that's one mistake I'll never make again. Rubbing each dog down as I walked by checking for any soreness before getting to the leader, Tilly. A bit more aloof than the rest, she gave me her two tail thumps then waited to be escorted to the barn. She knew the drill and had her own tunnel vision of sorts. She was going to make some musher's dreams come true, nothing in the world this dog liked more than to be on the trail.

A few hours later Luna and I waved goodbye to Harvey and loaded up. Before pulling out I sent Levi a quick text, "Moe's?" By the time I got to the end of the driveway I heard my phone go off.

"Round of cricket, loser buys. See you in 20."

Smiling, I ruffled Luna's ears.

"I think he enjoys having his ass whooped at darts my dear. We're going to Moe's."

Luna's ears perked up, she too enjoyed Moe's. Not for their darts or local beers, but because the head cook now kept a dog bed behind the bar for her to lay on under the heat lamp as she munched on stock bones. Queen Luna, as I liked to call her, had servants wherever we went.

After a quick freshening up in the truck, brushing my hair and adding a smidge of deodorant we sauntered into Moe's. A quick look around confirmed we had indeed beat Levi. At the bar I ordered two beers, broke a couple of bucks into quarters for darts then froze. Luna stood pressed against my leg, a low growl rumbling out. Chase was glaring at us from the far side of the bar, the blonde woman he was with turned to stare for a second before tossing her hair back and running a hand down his arm to redirect his attention.

"Easy Luna. Stay here."

Holding her collar firmly just in case, I kept staring back even though every bit of me wanted to get the hell out of there. I felt if I broke eye contact first he won, that was my pride talking. My brain was attempting to reason with my pride by pointing out we were not in second grade anymore, staring contests did not gain you status. Pride won and I stood, staring until he turned back to the blonde. I let out a breath I didn't know I had been holding and jumped out of my skin as I felt a hand slide around my waist.

"Hey Red, sorry didn't mean to scare you. Unless I threw off your dart game, then it was fully intended."

Levi's smile quickly faded as he looked at me.

"You ok? Shelly, what's going on?"

Luna growled louder and looked from Levi over to Chase. Whoever said dogs can't talk clearly never had a relationship with a dog. They speak volumes.

"Did he come over here? Did he say anything to you?"

The sexy playfulness his face had when he walked in was erased. At that moment Chase and company sauntered by and headed out the door. As he passed he flipped us the bird with a sneer. I tightened my grip on Luna and placed my other hand on Levi's leg hoping it would have the same effect.

"No. He stayed over there until just now, stared me down a bit but that's it."

I took a slug of my beer to steady myself.

"Should have gone over there to warn the woman what slime ball he is."

"If he comes near you or tries to make contact, call me right away."

I raised my eyebrows at him as I took another slug.

"I happen to like you... a lot, deal with it. Call somebody if he does and then call that cop you talked to from Bangor. You have a restraining order against him, he knows it and I hope to hell he follows it."

He shook his head and locked eyes with me.

"Pisses me off beyond...anything that he walked away with a warning."

I stared at the door that shut behind them, waiting for it to swing back open. I relaxed when it stayed firmly shut.

"I think your brother nailed it. No one's ever said crap about him or the crap he pulls."

"You're still carrying the bear spray I gave you, right?"

He wanted to give me pepper spray but, if I was being honest, I was being stubborn after the whole thing. Didn't want to feel like I was rearranging my life because of that night. We compromised on bear spray as it had useful applications while hiking with Luna.

"Never leave home without it."

"Liar."

"Scouts honor."

I held up what I thought was the Boy Scout hand signal which made Levi relax a little and laugh.

"Oh yeah? Where is it?"

"In the glove box of the truck."

"Lotta good it will do you there, liar."

"I said I never leave home without it, I didn't say I had it duct taped to my leg."

"Hmm, that's an interesting idea. So....just where would you tape such a thing?"

"Wouldn't you like to know?"

I leaned in and gave him a quick kiss and felt that rush whenever our lips brushed. Wanting to wash out the negative energy I went in for a second, deeper one that left his eyes wanting and his voice a bit husky.

"You have me thinking now Shel, I am thinking all sorts of things."

His hands were resting on my hips, giving a gentle squeeze to pull me closer.

"You want to go somewhere else? I bet River's still serving food."

"No, let's have a drink and play some darts. No reason that jackass should ruin our night or make us change plans."

I grabbed my stack of quarters as I leaned in to whisper in his ear.

"Well, maybe we could change plans slightly. Let's get dinner to go, the loser will be charged with more than just paying."

I reached around him for my drink giving his neck a teasing nuzzle.

"I don't plan on losing by the way."

With that Luna and I headed to the dart board by the Queen's bed on the patio.

53

I COULDN'T HAVE asked for a better day. The fresh two inches of powder had made the 5-mile snowshoe loop up to the fire tower and back something out of a book. No, a poem, the way the snow clung to every branch with the sun glistening off of it was a, one hundred percent packed with emotion, poem. Levi dropped the tailgate, shed his pack and grabbed our thermos of coffee. I dug out our snacks while fighting off Luna who knew I had a beef bone tucked in there for her. Clearly, I took too long as she took matters into her own paws and shoved her head into my pack exiting with her trophy and hopped into the bed of the truck. Levi stroked her back getting a steady tail thump of approval from him.

"I think I won her over. I would have been happy with her tolerating me but I do believe she likes me. She really likes me."

"Well Mikey I put in a good word for you, you're welcome."

I hopped up onto the tailgate on the other side of Luna handing over his sandwich. "Bon appetite, Monsieur, house specialty. PB and J on wheat."

"And it complements this fine vintage of lukewarm coffee perfectly."

I leaned over Luna resting my head on his shoulder loving the warm sun on my face.

"I love today. The view from the fire tower was incredible. Little bit of history wrapped up in winter magic."

I glanced up at Levi who was staring at me with a funny look on his face.

"What? Why are you looking at me like that?"

"Nothing. You're just, you catch me off guard. In a good way."

I raised an eyebrow giving him a look as I took another bite.

"Anyway, what's with the extra collar on Luna? The name tag is blank, not going to do you any good if she gets separated from you."

"Oh, contraire handsome. It's a tracker collar. The tag is actually a little GPS. Got an app on my phone so I can pull up and see exactly where she is."

"You're shitting me."

"Nope, real deal. A couple of years ago we were out in a crazy thunderstorm guiding a trip at the ranch. I don't know if she got spooked or just turned right when I turned left but I lost her for about an hour. Scared the crap out of me. She finally found me but once was enough. The guy that lived down the street from my Uncle trained and competed with tracking dogs, he recommended this and I have to say it's worked great."

"Kinda like big brother watching over you."

Levi was flipping the tag round looking for I don't know what.

"Interesting idea though."

"I have to say you didn't strike me as the conspiracy type."

I nudged him teasingly.

Levi leaned in close, whispered in my ear.

"They're watching us right now, you know."

"Oh, you know what I mean. Take it off of her if you want to look at it. I only put it on when we are going for long hikes."

He unclipped it and took a closer look.

"This thing really work?"

"Here, I'll show you."

I grabbed my phone to pull up the app but soon realized the battery was dead.

"Ah crap, give me your phone."

"Keep telling you, you should keep that thing charged."

He handed his phone over.

"What if you need it in an emergency?"

"I have an in with the Forestry Department, they'll come get me."

"No, we don't rescue people who refuse to charge their phone. We have a stubborn slash stupid clause in our bylaws."

"Keep it up buddy, keep it up. Ok here, so this is the app...and now you are logged in as me. Has pretty accurate topography lines and you can zoom in. See? There she is."

Levi pulled out his GPS and compared the coordinates.

"Wow, pretty much exact."

He hopped down with the collar in hand and jogged into the woods, then darted out onto the path and then back over some rocks.

"This really works!"

I had to laugh as he ran back and forth a few more times yelling out to us each time it seemed to surprise him that it was working. He jogged back over and hopped up on the tailgate.

"If only my lost hikers had a dog with one of these, man life would be perfect!"

"Aw, where would the fun in that be? "

"I'll take it easy over fun any day. Want this back on her?"

"No, thanks. Actually..."

I leaned forward twisting to shift my coat around.

"Can you put it in my side zippered pocket? I have jelly all over my hands."

"I do these kinds of things for my nieces and nephews."

He zipped it in, then tugged my hat down and zipped my coat up.

"What are you doing?"

I pushed him away as I laughed and choked on my sandwich.

"My amazing uncle routine. Zip treasured item into pocket, fix hat, zip coat. Happy kids, happy siblings, happy uncle."

"You're so weird. Lucky you're cute."

He glared at me.

"Sexy. Handsome. So much more than cute."

"Cutie patootie."

"Moving on."

He cleared his throat and started picking at his sandwich crust.

"Do you miss living out west?"

"Parts of it. Miss being with my family. Thought I would miss the grandness of the Rockies but honestly? The east coast has grandeur all its own."

We sat in silence for a few moments. I closed my eyes, turning my face to absorb the sun.

"Think you'll move back come spring?"

I could feel the unease in his question, not sure how I felt about it.

"It's an option. A good one too."

I turned to look at Levi, then hoping to lighten the mood, gave him a cheesy elbow to the ribs.

"What, you're going to miss me Ranger?"

"Hell no. Just trying to decide when I can make my move on the next lucky lady."

"Honest and upfront, I like that in a man. I'll give you plenty of notice and even write you a letter of recommendation."

"Appreciate it but no letter is needed."

He stretched in an exaggerated muscle pose.

"My reputation precedes me."

"Hmm, well then I better get all the time I can."

I hopped off the tailgate and whistled for Luna. We tossed our gear into the bed and lifted the tailgate. As it clicked shut Levi's hand paused on mine. I turned waiting for a snappy comeback that I had come to love but found a serious Levi instead.

"All joking aside, you can have all the time you need Shel. Years sound pretty good to me."

Those words floored me, warmed me and scared the shit out of me. All of that must have shown on my face as Levi laughed, leaned in and gave me a long, toe tingling kiss.

"No pressure, just wanted to throw that out there. Load up buttercup, as an official ranger sworn to keep people safe while venturing outdoors It is my due diligence to check you for frostbite. Head to toe."

Thankful for the lighthearted lifeline I rolled my eyes as Luna loaded up. One thing for sure, I had a lot to mull around. As soon as I shut my door Levi's cell phone chimed from on top of the dash. Levi was silent for a moment as he read the text, then let out a long breath.

"Everything ok?"

"Are you up for a detour?"

"Sounds ominous, do I get to know where before deciding?"

He glanced up, smirked, and then grabbed a pen and napkin from the center compartment. Quickly scribbled something on it before starting the truck and handing me the napkin.

It read 'Meeting Paul at the hunting cabin, meat info- shh big brother'. Chuckling, I gestured for him to proceed.

"You're so weird."

"Pfft you like it."

Rolling my eyes as big as possible I turned up the radio and relaxed to 70's rock as we headed toward Paul and his meaty info.

54

THE HUNTING CABIN was more than a slight detour. Almost two hours later, most of which were down long unmarked dirt logging roads, we had landed. The cabin was as described by Levi, four walls with the necessities. A True hunting cabin, it was sparsely decorated with a set of bunk beds, stove, sink basin without running water and a wood stove that was cranking as we walked in. Paul was sitting on a lawn chair in front of the wood stove with his feet up on a cooler.

"Hi Shelly."

"Hey Paul, nice digs you got here."

"Come on in, I'll give you the 2-cent tour."

We plopped down into the open lawn chairs, Levi kicked Paul's feet off the cooler and grabbed us each a beer. Luna stretched out in front of the wood stove like she owned the place.

"And the tour is now over, you've seen the entire place."

He handed over a church key which I happily accepted. Levi was driving after all. I tapped his beer bottle with mine to cheers.

"So, brother, what was so urgent that we had to drive all the way out here to hear it?"

"Urgent? No, I was just pulling your leg. Meg and the kids are visiting her parents down in New Hampshire. I was going hunting in the morning and decided I wanted some company.

Paul pulled out a deck of cards and started shuffling.

"Texas hold'em?"

"Paul, you're a jerk."

"I didn't say I wanted your company Levi. Grouchy old man you are."

"I'm old? Then what does that make you, ancient?"

"Wise. It makes me wise and full of knowledge."

"Full of horse shit is more like it."

Paul stood up and turned his chair so the back was to Levi.

"Shelly, how the hell do you put up with his ass?"

"Your mom pays me to."

Paul laughed out loud.

"I like you more than him so I will tell you what I found out about our garbage meat."

"You just said you didn't have any info."

"No, I said it wasn't urgent. I've had info for like a week now. Just didn't have time without extra ears hanging around to share it."

"I can totally make your death look like a hunting accident. You know that, right?"

"Isn't he cute when he's mad, Shelly?"

Laughing I waved hands in front of me.

"I'm going neutral on this one, just call me Switzerland."

"Alight fine, we'll stop poking the bear. Know how to play?"

I laced my hands together and cracked my knuckles.

"Blinds or antes?"

"Ha! Let's play. Levi, are you joining us or going to pout in the corner?"

Levi kicked Paul's boot as he spun his chair around and plopped down.

"Fine, deal me in. But spill it. Don't want you to forget any details when your ass is being handed to you by Red over there."

"Aw thanks Levi, but I'm going to hand you yours too."

I sent him a wink as I arranged my cards.

Paul grinned as he passed out the rest of the chips.

"Brother, you're in trouble. That's all I can say. Ok here is what I know after sending some info out into the world."

"About freaking time, Pauly."

"Do you want me to continue or not?"

"The floor is yours, your highness."

"Like I said, grumpy old man you are. I was able to secure some eyes in the field at three of the other sites we were thinking were drop sites. Two of them ended up with a barrel full of rotting meat. They took a chunk of meat out of each, one had drugs inside it, the others had rolls of bills."

"Did they try to trace the bills?"

Paul paused from shuffling and looked up at Levi.

"They tried, but they were clean."

I looked up from studying my hand as thoughts started falling into place.

"What if the cash was to pay whoever left the drugs. What if whoever is doing all of this uses the same system to sell the goods and collect the fee."

"Shelly, you would be a hell of a game warden."

I sent Paul a mock salute before continuing on my train of thinking.

"So, four of the drug stuffed meat chunks have gone missing and one was full of money, right? Isn't it a little odd that whoever is doing this hasn't noticed that those are missing or whoever just doesn't care?

"Maybe they have a mediocre book keeper."

Paul flung a card at Levi at his suggestion.

"I think they have noticed, which is another reason I waited to tell you two about this."

"What do you mean?"

"Billy, the one who pulled the cash meat out, thought he was being followed a night or so after he took a hunk to the lab. Instead of going right home he took the scenic route through town and a big black truck took all the turns he did, just hung back."

"Did he get a good look at whoever it was?"

"No, unfortunately once he decided that he was for sure being followed he called it in for backup then tried to do a quick double back and confront them. Whoever it was bailed before he could catch more than a couple of numbers off the license plate. Most of the plate was covered in Mud."

Levi and I stared at each other.

"What, am I missing something?"

Paul was looking back and forth from me to Levi. Levi cleared his throat.

"We have some more information than what we told you."

Paul folded his arms and rocked back on the legs of his chair staring at Levi.

"You know how we told you we tracked down Nora? The wife of the cop that died in Fort Kent?"

Paul nodded.

"She also gave us her husband's journal, his work journal. It has a bunch of notes that all circle back to the case they were working on when he died."

"Which was?"

"Another rotting meat case."

"I want to read it. Why didn't you tell me this sooner?"

I had gotten up and opened a bag of popcorn Paul had on the make-shift table as Levi started filling Paul in. Not wanting Levi to take all dagger stares from Paul I jumped into the conversation.

"Paul, we went to Last Chance to talk to James about what happened when we had a hunch. Not six hours after that? His house burned to the ground. When we caught up with Nora she was packing for the hills. We didn't want you or your family to get dragged into it by asking too many questions."

"What about you two? It's ok for you two to get dragged into it?"

"You're the only one who knows we have it. Only four people know it exists which is also why we didn't say anything to anyone else."

"Well now I know, I want to read it."

Levi nodded.

"Then turn it over to someone else, someone higher up who will be able to do something but has the resources to stay safe."

Paul went back to shuffling cards as he thought.

"I think I have someone in mind who can do just that. Don't happen to have it on you, do you?"

"No such luck. It's tucked away behind old forestry invoices in the records closet at the office."

"Better spot than in your glove box. What was with the secret looks you two shared when I brought up the truck with the license plate hidden?"

I grabbed tissue and a pen, scribbled what numbers I could remember on it then passed it to Paul.

"Here. On a few of the pages Chester had just random sets of numbers scrawled. Our main thought was that it was a license plate that he just couldn't get all of. These were the numbers, in that order, that were part of each sequence."

Paul rocked back on his chair as he stared at the napkin.

"I think you're right. These two numbers, the 6 and 8 were the ones he pulled off the plate. Couldn't get the rest but now we have three numbers to go off of, 6,8 and 1. Let's all be a bit more careful from here on out. If we feel like we are being followed, no matter what, I mean it, we call one of us and stay on the phone until we meet up with each other at a very public place."

"Sounds good dad."

"Oh, shut up Shelly, you know what I mean."

"See? I'm not the only one who tells you to be careful. One time in my life I agree with Paul."

"I meant you too asshole."

"Aw, l love you too, Pauly."

"Alright, enough with this crap. Let's play."

55

I HUNG UP my phone and turned back to the kid behind the counter. "We will take the 40lb bags instead."

He nodded and started to ring me up. Harvey had sent me a few towns over to snag supplies for the kennel. The size bag of kibble he normally gets was out of stock. Not wanting to guess then have to drive back out for its replacement I called to get Harvey's take on it.

"Oh, and I need one of those sealed feed containers as well please. Largest one you have."

He nodded, printed the receipt then called in my order over the intercom. Harvey usually got the 20lb. bags to keep it fresher longer as he only fed half kibble and the rest soft food he had shipped in from God knows where.

"Pull around the back and we will load you up."

"Thank you very much."

Loaded up and heading back I cranked the radio up loud. Luna had stayed behind with Harvey giving me the opportunity to blast my eardrums out on the ride there and back. I didn't need to hear in my 50's, there was technology now that could take care of that.

Sitting at a red light I queued up my GPS. I had the option of the fastest way or the shortest mileage. Shortest mileage took me the scenic route through what looked like on the map a long stretch of nature preserve. Glancing up, I realized that the sky was blue with perfect fluffy clouds. The scenic route.

Thirty minutes or so later I was very glad I had chosen this route. It was stunning and I hadn't seen another car since leaving the town line. It was cold out, the weather man had been warning us of the area getting a snow storm in the next day or two, but today the sun was calling my name. I cranked the heat in the truck all the way up and rolled my window all the way down and stuck my hand outside letting my fingers dance to the radio. Suddenly a truck came barreling out of the woods.

"Shit!"

Slamming on the brakes and cutting the wheel hard to the left I ended up catching the shoulder and spun almost a 360 before getting the truck to stop.

"What the hell was that?"

The truck that almost T boned me had slowed down then kept going.

It was a black truck.

That had come out of the woods.

Completely over almost dying, I threw the truck in reverse and backed up to where I had seen it come out. As I jumped out and started up the trail I was racking my brain to pinpoint where I was on a map. If I was where I thought I was, one of the suspected drop sites was over this way. If it was, a garbage can shouldn't be too far in.

Sure enough, a couple hundred feet from the road off to the side of what probably an old access road, sat a can. Taking a deep breath, I carefully lifted the lid and found what I wasn't sure I was hoping to find or not find. Wrapped meat. Betting it was rotting. I was still holding my breath and didn't let it out until I was far enough away to test my hunch.

Jogging back to the truck I hopped in and pulled up the GPS. The road I was on was a straight shot, no roads to take in any other direction for at least another 50 miles.

What if I could catch the truck? See who was in it.

Without weighing the pros and cons, I made a mental note where I was on the GPS then floored it. It was almost 15 minutes later of doing well over the speed limit, thinking for sure the truck was gone, that I caught a glimpse of it taking the next turn. Speeding up as much as I dared to, I made it around the bend and now could clearly see the truck. The stupid black truck that almost ran me off the road. License plate covered in mud completely. Letting up on the gas I kept what I hoped was a safe, not too obvious I am trying to follow you, distance behind.

Knowing I had at least another 5 miles before another road intersected I tried to get every detail I could off the truck.

Black Dodge, extended cab with a cap over the bed. Had a hitch in, license plate fully coated in mud, so much so no way it just happened like that. I couldn't see the driver; the back window was really tinted. I thought about trying to pass the truck and get a glimpse but thought that would be too obvious as we were already 15 over the speed limit.

When the road gave way to another road, the truck took a right and so did I.

I stuck with the truck for another 20 min as it weaved around a little town. I wasn't sure of the name. I was starting to get a little nervous that whoever was driving would have fully noticed that I was following when I lost the truck. Another car had squeaked in between us and I had gotten stuck at a stop sign behind it. Once I went through, no truck was in sight.

"Oh crap."

My heart settled a bit, taking a deep breath, I made a left and started to wind my way back to the main drag.

Sitting at what had to be one of the only traffic lights in town, I glanced in my rearview mirror and two cars back was a black truck.

Not good.

"Ok Shel, lots of people have black trucks in this neck of the woods. Bet it's not the same truck."

Talking to myself made me feel better. The light turned green and I started heading back. The two cars in between us peeled off after a bit leaving just the truck and me who stayed the same distance back as when the cars had been between us. Far enough I couldn't make out the driver, but I could see that the license plate in front was obscured by mud.

"Oh shit. Shit, shit shit."

I drummed on the steering wheel thinking about how this was going to play out. Maybe it's not following me. I made a series of quick lefts basically driving in a square. The truck stayed with me the whole time. For sure it was following me. Meaning it knew I was following it.

Digging my phone out of my bag I hit Levi's number. After several rings it went to voicemail.

"Levi, call me."

Hanging up I dialed Paul. He picked up on the third ring.

"Hell-0."

"Paul, Shelly. Ah want to meet me in a really public place?"

"You ok?"

"No, not ok. Bit off more than I can chew, found some more meat, tailed a black truck and now it's tailing me."

"What part of what you just said is being careful?"

"Paul! Lecture me later. What the hell do I do here?!"

"Where are you?"

"Not super sure, was running an errand for Harvey and on my way back this all happened."

"Ok talk me through where you were and where you are now."

THANK God Paul has an excellent sense of direction I thought. He stayed on the phone with me for the next 80 minutes until I pulled into the much more populated area of Freeport. As I ran through what had happened from start to finish at least three times, Paul took notes and asked questions on the other side. He had me take the busiest roads he could think of to get there, ones as he put it, would be real hard to run a truck off the road without being seen. Real comforting Paul.

"Ok I'm in Freeport now what?"

"Find the busiest parking lot in front of the LL Bean store you can, one with lots of people and not a lot of parking spaces and as close to the front door as you can.

"Ok then what."

"Grab everything that says who you are. Got a hat and sunglasses?"

"Yes. Put those on, tuck your hair up, and try to hide the red."

"Done."

"Walk fast, but not fast enough to draw attention, to the front doors and head for the boot section. I'll find you there."

Taking a steadying breath, I jumped out of the truck and went for it.

The store was massive and thankfully, full of shoppers. I didn't look back to see if I was being followed, just made a beeline for the boot section.

As I entered the boot section I slowed down slightly looking for Paul and almost jumped out of my skin when a hand tapped my shoulder. Paul was standing inside an employee only door I walked right past. He motioned for me to follow and we slipped in closing the door behind us.

"Paul, what if whoever was in the truck saw us come in here?"

"Not possible, truck is still in the parking lot circling."

"How do you know?"

"Buddy of mine Greg, is head of security here. He's watching the camera feed, texting me updates. Whoever is driving is staying in the truck and parking far enough away that we can't get a read on the driver. But whoever it is? They are close enough they could see you leave in the truck you were driving."

"Here, put this on. Guessed at your size."

Paul handed me a gray hoodie with the LL Bean logo on the front, and a bulky winter hat that I could easily stuff all my hair into.

"Now what?"

"Now we are going to meet Levi for dinner and wait for the truck to give up. I'm starving. Oh, eat carefully, we have to give what you're wearing back. It's on loan."

"Basically If I stain it, I buy it?"

"Yup."

"Wait, does Levi know we're here? I called him but didn't get through."

"After I got you on the phone I texted Sal and asked her to have Levi text me. Said it was a code brown."

"Code brown?"

"As kids when we were messing around when shit hit the fan we called it a code brown. Mom would have killed us for saying shit. As adults, we kept the code. Only use it when we really need one another. I didn't want to hang up on you so relayed it all best I could via text via Sal. He's here and meeting us a few blocks over for some steak."

"What about the truck?"

"Greg's shift just started. He'll keep watch and let me know when the truck leaves or doesn't. Figure out what we do from there after depending on what whoever is driving does."

We snaked through the employee side of the building and came out on the back side that led right into the walkable shopping district. Pulling my hat down a bit I kept stride with Paul as we weaved through the wave of people milling around. Couple of blocks later Levi fell into step alongside us. I slipped my hand into his as we all kept walking.

"So Red, remember when we all agreed we would be careful?"

"You have to get in line, Levi, Paul has dibs on the first lecture."

Paul let out a snort as he held the door open for us.

"We eat first, lecture after."

"I think we need to start with the definition of being careful."

"You two are hilarious, you know that? I did exactly what you two would have done and you know it."

Paul rolled his eyes.

"Yeah but we both are issued firearms. What do you have, a pocket knife?"

"Bear spray thank you very much."

"Yeah? Where is it?"

"Oh shut up Levi."

Then my phone rang.

"Oh crap. It's Harvey. I was supposed to be back hours ago with his dog food."

"What are you going to tell Him?"

I answered the call and held the phone away from my ear as Harvey's voice rang through.

"Hey Harvey, sorry. I got lost."

56

LATER THAT NIGHT it was a long drive home. The black truck had waited for quite some time before leaving. We stayed another hour after Greg had called to say the truck had left just to be safe. Levi drove behind me. The thought was that whoever was doing this, if they knew who we were, would have put the two of us together after talking with James at Last Chance. We hoped that Paul on the other hand had not been connected to any of this, but had him drive home thirty minutes behind us just in case. Other than being jumpy as hell, it was an uneventful ride back.

It was after 11 by the time I had picked up Luna, convinced Harvey I wasn't a total incompetent fool and would be back on time the next day, that I finally walked through the front door of the cottage shaking off the insane amount of snow that had accumulated on me from the short walk from the truck to inside. Luna, reading my mind, leaped up on the couch, closed her eyes and let out a long content sigh. Following her lead, I ditched my boots and did the same. Levi knocked twice then came in a few minutes later.

I was dozing off and opened one eye as I heard him come in.

"You have a heck of a security system Red."

"She's ferocious, don't let her fool you. You also have bribed her with pepperoni. That earned you insider access."

"So, if someone bad came in, all they would need is a bag of pepperoni to neutralize your defense?"

"No, she would get them first then eat the pepperoni."

"Right. Not sure I believe that."

As if on cue Luna let out a low growl.

"See? She doesn't mess around."

"Regardless, did you check all your window and door locks?"

"Levi.."

"Humor me tonight, please. We tempted fate enough for one day."

"Did you hear anything from Paul?"

"Just that he sent the new info from your adventure today to his contacts he's been working with."

I closed my eyes and sank back into the couch.

"Can't they run the plates knowing it's a black dodge truck now?"

"They could but it would come back with God knows how many files to sort through. We have three numbers but we don't know the order. Even with narrowing it down to a black dodge, there are thousands of vehicles that it could be if we ran just what we had. Not to mention we're not even positive the truck has Maine plates. If it doesn't? We just added months and months of searching through DMV records.

"Too bad we were not the FBI. I bet they have a machine that could take that little info and make it exactly what we need it to be.

"If only."

We both sat in silence for a while, each lost in our own thoughts and dog tired. Rolling onto my side I propped my head up on my hand.

"Levi, why don't we call the FBI? Wouldn't they want to know about the crazy amount of drugs being man handled and really sketchy large sums of money?"

"Well... I... don't know."

"I mean we are not trusting the local police, this whole thing is really beyond you, me, Paul and the whole warden service combined."

Levi pulled out his phone.

"What are you doing? Calling the FBI?"

"Seeing how one would contact the FBI. Well I'll be damned."

"What?"

I sat up and scooted next to Levi so I could see what he was seeing.

"The FBI has local offices across the country and can be reached 24/7 by calling a toll free number."

"Think they will take us seriously?"

"Can't see why not, wouldn't you Red?"

"Honestly? Debatable. The whole thing sounds like a bad movie."

Levi tossed his phone on the coffee table and stacked his feet on it.

"Let's call in the morning. If they sound skeptical then we have Paul call as well. Maybe they have to investigate all tips no matter how crazy. Like some kind of FBI code."

"Maybe they'd send out the real life version of Mulder and Scully."

"Pretty sure what we are dealing with has nothing to do with aliens, ghosts or anything X-Filesish. Just people."

"Think I would rather deal with aliens at this point."

"You and me both Shel, you and me both."

Not sure how long we sat there, I fell asleep at some point and woke up to Levi tucking a blanket around me and whispering he was going to work.

57

Tᴜᴇsᴅᴀʏ Lᴇᴠɪ ʜᴀᴅ left before dawn, giving her a light kiss on the shoulder as he slipped into his Carhartt's. Mother Nature had been hinting of more snow for a few days. What started as a strong weather pattern traveling across the great lakes turned into what the year-round residents of Maine call a Nor'easter. With the temperatures hovering above freezing the first blast was freezing rain followed by heavy winds. The winds wreaked havoc on the heavy frozen tree branches snapping off giant limbs and uprooting towering pines. Tuesday started with clearing some trees that took out power lines, blocked a road and decided to smash down smack in the center of a car.

Today was Friday and he had yet to leave. He took a sip of his burnt coffee, grimaced, and then threw back the rest. He wasn't drinking it for the taste anymore, needed it to stay awake. The winds brought the snow. Feet of snow. Four to five feet in some spots and it just kept coming. Plows couldn't keep up. Trees couldn't stay up. Roofs wouldn't hold. It had been a round the clock nightmare.

After day two the separate department lines faded across the county as to who was supposed to do what. Now whoever was available did the next thing that needed doing.

"I got a little something on my desk if you want to spice that up kiddo."

Sal had been there since Tuesday as well, acting as dispatch out of the Forestry office coordinating the chaos.

"Don't tell me things like that, technically I'm your boss."

"Ha! What are you going to do, fire me? Please do! I'll start my re-tirement early."

"I thought we agreed not to mention the "R" word anymore."

"It's coming Levi, better stop hiding from it and start looking for some-one to pull on." She was right. He'd been ignoring the ever looming red circled date for months. Now instead of six, there were only three to go.

"Maybe we'll be snowed in for the next few months. You just might have to stay longer, Sal. Can't argue with Mother Nature."

"Watch me."

She took a long sip of her coffee and seemed to be enjoying it.

"Are we drinking the same thing?"

Sal just smiled and took another sip.

"Never mind, don't answer that."

"So, since we are the only ones in the office and I'm sick of hearing myself on the radio, what's the deal with you and that beautiful woman who's keeping you company?"

Levi bit back his smile, he'd been waiting for this conversation. Pur-posefully avoided bringing Shelly up as he knew it would drive Sal crazy the longer he said nothing.

"Who? You? I've tried to woo you away from that husband for years now. Are you saying it finally worked? You're going to run off with me?"

"Don't push me. I've been three days without a shower and I'm actu-ally looking for ways to get fired at this point. Spill it."

She sat on the desk with her arms crossed giving him that mother stare, the one that's supposed to make you confess to whatever horrible thing you did to your sibling.

"Nothing more to say, she's a beautiful woman whose company I enjoy."

Sal just stared. He stared back. He would win this one. He took another awful sip. She didn't move a muscle. He could hear the clock ticking in the background. He started to shift from one foot to the other then willed himself to stop moving. How long could she do this? The clock ticked louder as each minute passed. Then he crumpled. He stood up and stomped over to the sink dumping the contents of his cup that should never be labeled coffee and shifted over to attempt to make something palatable.

"Sal, there's nothing else to tell. What do you want me to say? She's smart, beautiful, funny. She Loves the outdoors more than I do. Has a great dog. Independent as hell."

"And?"

He normally didn't mind her pushing things but this was starting to tee him off. He glared at her over his shoulder.

"And...?"

"And what?! What am I supposed to say? I love her? She might leave in a few months, move back out west. Then what? Hell, I've hinted at it to her but she doesn't do a damn thing about it. Why? Most likely because she doesn't feel the same way! But how the hell am I supposed to know?"

He had spun around mid-rant and was facing Sal, threw his arms in the air in exasperation. All the women in his life seemed to be destined to drive him up a wall. Sal burst out laughing.

"Glad you think this is so funny."

Sal walked over to Levi, placing a hand on his cheek.

"Sweetie, if a man loves a woman he should tell her straight and simple. Women don't want a hint at love, they want honesty. You get what you give."

She patted his arm.

"Feel better getting that all off your chest? You've been brooding for months."

"I don't brood."

"Honey, if it was a sport you'd have a gold medal by now. Don't over-think this. When this is all over go home, shower and lay it out for her like you just did for me. But without the tone."

And with that she brushed by him and turned the coffee pot on as she headed back to her desk.

58

THE LAST THREE days have been kinda fun. Snuggled up with Luna, binge watching movies in between shoveling and bouncing back and forth between the cottage and Levi's house making sure all was weathering the storm alright. Levi's house had the nicer kitchen and an amazing solarium off the back of the house but the cottage had the deep, deep soaker tub. When it came down to which house to sleep over in, the tub won every time. I stretched my legs out splashing a little water over the edge onto Luna who grumbled her disapproval.

"Sorry Lady Jane. Two more minutes and I'll hop out. We can start our wild Friday night".

I just laid my head back and closed my eyes when my cell rang. I sloshed more water onto Luna as I leaned over the edge to wipe my hands off before grabbing it. I had hoped it was Levi as I hadn't talked to him since the storm began. Sent texts back and forth but that's not quite the same. Saw Harvey's name appear and frowned thinking something had to be wrong for him to be calling at 8:30 at night.

"Harvey? Everything alright?"

"God Damn meat's back! Dogs were getting all worked up so I went down the drive looking for whatever it may be and the can's filled again and a couple of coyotes were trying to get at it."

I thought fast as Harvey didn't know the real contents of the meat and I for sure didn't want him messing with it or whoever was on their way to snag whatever was hidden this time.

"Harvey, it's still storming out, are you back inside?"

"Yeah I'm not an idiot."

I rolled my eyes and took a breath.

"Did you call Levi or Paul or the police?"

"No! Nothing gets done when I do."

"Then why did you call me?"

"I like you better than the rest of them combined. Besides, you will do something about it. You understand how special these dogs are. Can't risk them with rotten meat and coyotes."

If only you knew the half of it I thought.

"Ok. Look, stay inside, I'll get a hold of Levi and someone will be over to keep coyotes away until they can grab it all."

"If no one's here in 20 minutes I'm going back out there to get rid of the varmints myself. Dogs will keep this up all night!"

To make his point he must have held his cell phone in front of a yowling husky. Wincing, I moved the phone away from my ear until the noise lessened.

"Harvey, I'll come over and shoo everything away. Just stay inside and calm the dogs down."

Hoping to play on his emotional side I threw in a cherry on top.

"You know they are ten times as worked up when you leave them when they are like this. Stay and soothe them, I'll take care of the rest."

"Thank you, Shelly, I knew I could count on you."

I heard the click as he hung up and seriously wondered if I had just been strung along by a puppeteer as I dialed Levi. Call went right to voicemail. Last time you harass me about not charging my phone I grumbled under my breath. I tried the Forestry department next, but got a busy signal.

"Well Luna my girl, either they are swamped with calls or the power is out."

I rested a hand on her head as I mulled over my next move. I glanced at the clock.

"It's not even nine. Bad things don't happen until after midnight. Right? Right."

I grabbed my coat, keys and shot Levi a quick text that the meat was back with a side of coyotes and I'd text again when I got back.

"Alright Luna, let's roll."

I ran over the game plan in my head again as we drove. Drive by, honk the horn and scare off any unwanted critters then hang out with Harvey until the storm ends and I get a hold of Levi or Paul. Safe, practical and not interfering with an ongoing investigation as I would never step foot out of the car. Just a law-abiding citizen driving down a road honking at wild-life. We rounded the bend before Harvey's driveway, snow was coming down steady still, almost a white out. I was looking for coyotes as we got closer and almost didn't see the white van on the side of the road.

"Oh Shit!"

I swerved missing the van by inches and instead caught a patch of ice and spun the truck into the ditch somehow missing Harvey's mailbox. Once I had my heart under control, I took a quick glance praying all I did was end up in the ditch. Sideswiping an idiot in a white van in a snow-storm was not how I wanted to end this day. Blowing out a shaky breath I slipped out closing the door before Luna could follow. She whined, I just shook my head no. All I needed right now was for someone else to slide around and hit Luna. I strode over to the van to make sure everyone was alright and if they were, then I was going to lay in and give them a piece of my mind. Who the hell parks like that on a night like this?! I saw two people off to the side, not moving. Oh god I thought, I hope they are just in shock, probably have a flat tire or something. When it rains it pours, I thought.

"Hey, you guys alright? Sorry about getting so close to you. It's a blind turn on a good day, not to mention a crappy day like this."

I stopped a few feet from them, still not a word from either. The back of the van was open, wrapped meat stacked neatly inside. All the hair on my neck stood up. I hoped to hell I looked calm and collected, inside I was screaming oh shit over and over.

"Alright, well just wanted to make sure you were ok."

I started to take a few steps back. I could hear Luna barking and pawing at the window. I was about to turn and book it when I heard the metallic click of a gun safety being taken off and an all too familiar voice saying not to do anything stupid. When it rains, it pours.

59

Lᴇᴠɪ sʜᴏᴏᴋ ᴏᴜᴛ his coat, kicked his boots against the door frame before going in. Everyone was in a piss poor mood, he didn't want to add any fuel to the fire with Sal. She didn't clean the Forestry Department but she liked it looking "presentable" as she put it. With everyone being in a mood it pissed him off that he was trying not to piss her off.

"At least one of you wasn't raised in a barn."

Levi gave Sal a quick salute before bee lining it to his office. He chucked his coat on the chair and threw his hat on the table. His office, his rules. He pulled his phone out, saw it was dead and hooked up the charger then sat down with his head on the desk, arms hanging down to the floor. He wanted a bed, a beer and a soak in a hot tub. No, change the order, beer while soaking, then bed. He had just spent the last eight hours cutting up and hauling out the biggest pine tree he had ever seen out of the main intersection of town then helped dig out two cars that had no business driving around in this mess.

He used to think pine trees were beautiful. Four days of storm clean-up and he hated every last one of them. He heard footsteps and looked up to see Sal handing him a hot cup of coffee. She handed it over without a word and left. He looked around at all his crap he chucked everywhere and felt more than a bit childish. Since she had already left, he yelled a thank you down the hallway and went to grab his phone. Thankfully it turned on. His hand froze as he went to take a sip reading his text. He called her, but she didn't pick up. He tried again. And again. If it would have gone right to voicemail he would have felt better, which would most likely mean she forgot to charge it. He dialed Harvey, felt his stomach knot as he heard what he feared most. Not waiting for Harvey to finish he grabbed his keys and ran out. Yelled to Sal to send him whoever was free as he blew back through the office.

60

My head was killing me. As soon as I heard his voice I tried to use one of those self- defense moves they teach incoming freshmen at college orientation. All It got me was, I'm assuming, the butt of his gun to my head.   Little blurry after that.   Lots of arguing that ended up with me thrown in the back of the van, hands tied and someone's nasty ass sweatshirt that reeked of BO thrown over my head. That was what felt like hours ago. I was fairly certain I was in the back of the van as it was freezing. Even If my hands were free I wasn't sure it would do me any good at this point, everything felt numb. Suddenly the van lurched to a stop. I heard the doors open and slam shut, then felt a blast of crisp air hit me as the back doors squeaked open. Laying still I hoped they thought I was asleep or dead and just grabbed the meat and left.

"Get up."

I was going for the full performance as a possum.

"Cut the shit, get up."

A groan escaped as he kicked my leg. Next thing I knew I was being hauled up by my shirt and dragged out into the cold.

LEVI paced back and forth in front of her truck trying to calm down and figure out what the hell had happened. He was positive nothing good, no way would she just leave Luna. Then there was the blood. A splatter of red against the white, where the footprints screamed some sort of scuffle. He followed the tracks all around the area, he could pick hers out easily, the others belonged to individuals much larger. His throat damn near closed when he realized her tracks disappeared near the blood and signs of someone being dragged took their place. Those tracks led to tire tracks. Tire tracks led four miles down to the next intersection then any tracks in either direction were replaced with sandy scrapes from the plow truck that had rolled through recently.

He had already grilled Harvey. Harvey hadn't heard or seen anything. He had circled around and around looking for something to point him in the next direction but there was nothing. No meat. No truck. No Shelly. His phone chimed and had him frantically pulling it out of his pocket. Text from Paul.

"Fuck, fuck fuck!"

He threw his phone at his truck then cursed himself as he dug through the snow to find it. Luna whined and in a move that would have made Houdini proud tried to free herself from Harvey. Luckily it was not Harvey's first rodeo.

"Easy girl. Same to you Levi, throwing a fit will not help anyone out."

Levi glared at Harvey as he dug.

"Any updates? Something on your phone has set you off, might as well share it."

Levi pulled himself up out of the snow, phone in hand and praying it still worked.

"Nothing to share. That's the goddamn problem."

He kicked his tire for good measure and stomped over to Harvey and Luna.

"Paul, my brother, just texted. He's at least 40 minutes out. Was out on a search and rescue one county over. Fucking Sheriff's not answering his phone, Jackie hasn't seen nor heard from him in a day or so. She's over at the hospital getting generators up and going. My guys are all doing something and I can't even tell them to drop what they're doing because I have no fucking idea what the hell happened or what the fuck to do!"

Luna started another escape attempt, not at all thrilled with his rant.

"Easy now, easy now."

Harvey murmured as his hand tightened on the makeshift lead he threw around her. Levi reached down and felt the rough rope Harvey had used.

"Seriously? You couldn't find anything better than a rope to hold her?"

Levi began to loosen it a little as all her struggling had made it tighter each time she performed a stunt.

"If she was wearing a goddamn collar I would have used a leash but your girlfriend obviously doesn't take the pride in her animals that I thought she would!"

Harvey huffed that last part out, annoyed. Levi could care less. Then his hands froze.

"Collar. She's not wearing her collar."

He yanked out his phone.

"If this is broken I'm..."

He sucked in a breath and held it. The app was still logged in from their hike.

"Harvey, you're a genius."

He leaped into his truck, sent snow and gravel flying as he spun it around, dialing as he went.

"Sal, I found her. Texting you the coordinates, send it to Paul, Jackie and give Campobello Island guys a heads up. See if they have anyone available."

61

"START WALKING."

His voice was more of a snarl. Perhaps it should have scared me. Instead it pissed me off and made me dig my heels in.

"I would if I could fucking see anything!"

"Just move it, now!"

He gave me a shove that had me teetering a bit.

"Fuck you, not taking a step until this nasty ass shirt is off my face."

I heard him start to move towards me, I dropped down on the ground as fast as I could. He must have gone for another shove, or worse, and ended up on the ground near me.

"Stupid bitch!"

I braced for whatever was coming next.

"Hey! Don't even think about it. It's got to look like a hiking accident. If you kill her here it will only make shit worse. Take the goddamn shirt off her head, not doing any good anyway. She already knows who the hell you are. You're the jackass who couldn't scare a fucking girl enough to leave so much so that she started following you around! If you had just done your job we wouldn't have gotten into this!"

"I did the same thing I did with all the other bimbos you hired at the Center. You should never have hired her!"

Last time I ever apply for a job posted on a flyer, was the strange thought I had as the sweatshirt was finally, and not so nicely, ripped off my head. It took a second for my eyes to adjust. I stayed on the ground while I tried to figure out where the hell I was. Knowing they fully intended to kill me but planned on making it look like an accident made me feel a smidge of hope. I had a little more time. Time to do what? I had no idea. Seething down at me was my good friend Chase and my former boss, Walters.

Funny thing about Maine. The dense pine trees, moss and rocks mixed with snow act as a super sound barrier making wherever you are cut off from the rest of the world. That remote feeling was one of the main things that I loved about it. Looking around I was starting to realize it may be the main reason my chance of walking away from this was slim. I was crouched on the ground looking for an out as they continued to argue a few feet from me. As I started to shiver I forced myself up onto my feet to move a little, generating some body heat. Getting up was no easy feat, I was colder than I realized and my hands and arms were numb from being tied behind me. Once I was on my feet I had a moment of triumph before Chase's arm sent me sprawling face first into the snow.

"Stay down. Get up and I'll knock you back down harder each time."

Tears burned my eyes as I rolled around to get back into my kneeling position, I bit the inside of my cheek to keep them from spilling over. No way in hell I was giving him that satisfaction. Resigned to that thought, bravery or stupidity kicked in.

"If you really want this to look like an accident just let me go."

"Shut the fuck up right now."

Chase lifted his arm again in a warning.

"Think about it. It's gotta be right around 20 degrees out, I have no idea where I am and if you take a second to look before you smack me around again you can clearly see I'm freezing. Let me wander off and let Mother Nature do her thing."

Chase kept his arm raised as he thought about it. Walters ended that quickly.

"Nice try sweetie. Not taking a chance you may live long enough for some witless landscape photographer to stumble upon you as they take their 1000th picture of this shitty place looking for whales."

It was worth a try. Wait, whales? I looked around again. Where we were was thick forest. I wracked my brain, we had been in the van long enough, maybe we were in the Northern part of Maine, North East. Had to be near the coast for whales.

"Grab her. Let's get this over with."

Walters started walking into the woods. Scrambling I tried to get my feet underneath me before I had help but Chase was faster. My face hit the snow before I was dragged up by my elbow and jerked along after Walters. We trudged along like this for twenty minutes or so. That was my best guess anyway, until we came to what would have been a very scenic outlook under normal circumstances. The woods gave way to rock that overlooked a gray and angry ocean 50 or so feet below. The spot we stopped was just about the center of the oval shaped outlook. Looking down, the edges were steep, rocky or non-existent and plunged right into the water lapping over the tops of boulders. Left side looked like it had a slight slope for a few feet before the land cut away in an interesting overhang above the water.

I half fell, half flopped as Chase shoved me back to the ground. Walters cut the zip ties from my wrists then gestured with his gun in the direction of the edge.

"Alright, do it. Break her leg."

"Whoa, what?! Guys, let's be reasonable here."

Chase laughed and took the crow bar Walters was holding out for him.

My mind froze for a split second, then started chanting this can't be happening, shit ,shit, shit. Then self-preservation kicked in. I ran as fast as I could to the left.

"You're just making this harder on yourself!"

I could hear the glee in his voice as he jogged after me.

"Nowhere to go but back towards us."

I glanced over my shoulder while running, took a sharp turn to the overhang then jumped.

62

Levi had his truck pushing over 90 miles an hour. Even with that it felt like it was taking years. He kept fighting the thoughts that had his stomach clenching with dread. Sal had finally gotten through to Jackie who had called ahead to the local police in the area that the GPS said Luna's collar was.

The only time Levi slowed down, even though every fiber in his being argued against it, was to identify himself to the local cops who had pulled him over and rush through the cliff-note version of what happened and where they were going. To save time, or because Levi was already pulling away mid conversation, one of the officers jumped in to ride with Levi to navigate the tracker. "How much farther are they?"

"5- 10 minutes tops. Take the next right, then a quick left. We're on the upper side of the park now. Nothing up here, not a damn thing other than trails and cliffs. Are you sure this thing works?"

"Positive."

"Then why the hell would they drive up here if they are carrying what you think they are with a hostage on top of it? It doesn't make any sense."

"Please shut the hell up, I'm trying my damnedest not to think about why or what they are doing. Just tell me when we're there."

"Take the next right and get ready, the last of the road ends just up there. Looks like the beacon is a bit farther, they must be on foot. If you're good with it, park your rig sideways across the road by the gate. They won't be able to drive out of here unless they drive over us. Short jog in from there. I'm Cal by the way."

Levi grunted and did a quick park job as the officer advised.

"How far is the rest of your team?"

"Ah, maybe 5 minutes behind."

Levi nodded as he loaded his gun.

"I'm not waiting."

"Nope, didn't think you were. Here's your phone, trace is still up. You take point, I'll hang back and cover your flank."

Levi nodded and they set out.

63

PAIN WAS SHOOTING up and down my leg. The only good thing was I hardly noticed the pain from the spurting gash above my eye. Interestingly enough I had felt the first hit as I landed on the cliff face sliding for a few short seconds until being air born again, then nothing until I fought my way to the surface of the ocean. The current was strong and from what I could tell, swept me farther down the coast then I thought I would end up. Groaning, I tried swimming in to shore. Maybe I would be in less pain if the water had been deeper where I landed. On the other hand, I don't know if I would have been able to swim to shore if I had been out any deeper. Current was fighting me with each half assed stroke I took. I could barely see between the blood dripping into my eyes and my vision blacking each time my useless leg bumped into a rock.

No matter where I landed they had to have seen me by now, getting my body as high out of the water as I could and into the rocks that jutted out like teeth around the base of the cliff as fast as I could was my only shot.

Feeling optimistic I hoped my moving so slowly would make them think I was dead and just bobbing in the current. Fast apparently was not going to be an option. What felt like days later, I wedged myself in between two boulders with most of myself out of the water? I was hoping I was hidden from view. If not, hopefully they were a good shot and it would be quick. I was starting to regret my choice to jump. Yes, I would have most likely been dead by now, but there was no way I was making it through the night. Instead of being beaten to death I was going to either bleed out, freeze to death or drown when the tide came in. Maybe all three. With that cheerful thought I passed out.

LEVI paused to take in the scene before breaking the cover of the underbrush. He could see Chase pacing near the cliff's edge waving a gun around and yelling at...he knew that guy, just couldn't place him. Both had guns. The trace on the phone wasn't moving, the icon for Luna was indicating it was nearby. No more than a few hundred yards yet, he couldn't see Shelly. In the van maybe? He hoped to hell she was, but the trace said otherwise. He looked again at the area in front of him, then back at the screen. His breath caught as he realized what the beacon was telling him. No, no, no, no! He shook his head, no. He stood up to get an answer fast when a branch snapped behind him. He spun, weapon drawn to see Cal along with three others. The cavalry had arrived. He lowered his weapon a smidge and dropped alongside the group.

"The bigger guy is named Chase, he's the fire chief and has some law enforcement training. The other guy is familiar but I just can't place him."

"Any sign of the woman they took?"

"No".

"Trace still on?"

"It... it shows..."

He gazed towards the edge of the cliff.

"Gotcha. Ok we'll spread out and pin them between us, the van and the cliff. If all goes well they'll lay down and we'll arrest them then help you get your girl back."

Levi nodded. As much as he wanted to take Chase down himself, getting shot or worse was not going to help. He had a trained team with him, better if he used it.

They spread out, staying in the tree line. They began creeping in, taking the time to be silent even though they most likely wouldn't have been heard over the yelling match between the two men near the edge of the cliff. When he was about 10 feet from the clearing Levi paused, crouching down, and looked to his left waiting for the go signal from the rest of the team. After what felt like years, everyone advanced with a flick of Cal's wrist.

64

A WAVE CAME up and smacked me out of my sleep. Coughing out a gallon of seawater, I rolled over so I didn't choke on it all. I have no idea how long I was out for. All I know for certain is I am fucking freezing and have to move or drown with the incoming tide. Everything was numb and didn't hurt quite so much. Major downside was I was so numb it took extra energy to get my body parts to move like I needed them to. I tried to stand up hoping the numbness would mask it all but pain shot through me taking my breath away and knocked some of the good numb out. After the wave of pain subsided and I no longer felt like I was going to puke, I took a look around. The rocks were picturesque Maine Coast line, but not so large they were impassable. They gave way to a stone beach a few hundred feet to my left. Scooching up into a sitting position I tested my arms to see if they would hold my weight. They were sore as hell but would hold me. My left leg was shot and I had a strange lump under my jeans that I was purposely ignoring. My right leg wasn't a whole hell of a lot better but I could push a little with my heel.

"Alright, take two. I got this."

Then in a weird crab walk, inch my inch, I made it up and out of the tide onto a higher rock. It hurt so much a few times I thought I was going to black out again. Knowing the tide was creeping up on me was incentive to keep pushing on after a brief rest. The jump from the cliff should have killed me and I would be damned if I was going to let the ocean do me in.

Catching my breath, I crab walked out a few more feet.

As one, the line of officers and Levi stepped out of the cover of the pines. Advancing quickly Cal shouted out the required police lines. In the few seconds it took to reach the van Chase tried to make a run for it but was cut off by a flanking officer. A brief scuffle had him face down with his arms zip tied behind him. Before Cal had pulled him to his feet he was choking out his story, painting Walters as the one who masterminded everything. Walters took a glance over the cliff then tossed his gun to the ground before dropping to his knees. The polar opposite of the sniveling Chase, he went silent and didn't say a word to anyone. Levi left the lead officer to handle the bookings and took the liberty of taking the other officers to start a hasty search. Levi flipped through the van fast, finding a chunk of her hair that had gotten caught on a paneling hook inside, but nothing else. Biting back his anger he left the hair as evidence. Over his dead body was either one of them going to walk away from this without an orange wardrobe? Hopping out of the van he found himself a few strides from Chase. Before he knew it Chase was on the ground and Levi's fist was cocked back to throw another punch.

"Where is she?"

Chase rolled around trying to get purchase under his feet while coughing up blood. Cal took advantage of the space in between the two to slide in and prevent Levi from taking it too far.

"Cal, move! I..."

"Levi, walk away. You're crossing the line on this one and you know it."

Levi gave Cal a shove, Cal didn't say anything, gave him a warning look and kept shifting to block Levi.

"Don't be an ass!"

Trying to keep his cool and not give into the rage he was battling he tried to drag Cal aside and ended up in the dirt. Cal had swept his legs out with a fluid grace that would have made Jackie Chan proud.

"Keep it together. We will find her. You keep hammering on him and he's got a better chance of walking away from this. You know this Levi. Don't give him an out."

Levi scrambled to his feet wanting someone, anyone to bleed to make him feel better. His head snapped around when he heard the shout from one of the officers making the hasty search.

"Down on the rocks, looks like blood and a piece of something, coat maybe about half way down."

Walter was sitting on the ground a few yards away from Chase looking 20 years older than he actually was. He locked eyes with Levi then let out a breath that took another few years with it. Staring at the ground and bracing for whatever was coming next, he said two words that would haunt Levi for months.

"She Jumped."

65

THE NEXT FORTY minutes felt like days to Levi. Where Levi had frozen up upon hearing Walters say she jumped, Cal immediately began organizing a search calling in more officers and volunteers to cover land and sea. For that, Levi would be forever grateful. He could hear voices echoing up and down the shore line, all yelling for Shelly then a few seconds of silence to listen for a response. There were voices above him, voices behind him, voices coming from the water and the blood chilling sound of the divers each time they resurfaced to regroup. They were the only ones not yelling, waiting for a return call. It was idiotic but Levi hated them for that. Hated that they had to entertain the idea they may be searching for a body. It had taken time to assemble everyone, lay out a plan. The search had only officially been underway for twenty minutes or so. Positive thinking had gotten him through the first fifteen minutes. The minutes that followed drained the remaining positive from him, replacing it with fear. Cal strode alongside him, giving his shoulder what was meant to be a reassuring squeeze.

"Search dogs just arrived. They will be able to comb the rocks better and faster than we ever will."

Levi nodded, keeping his gaze locked ahead of him.

"Hey, from what you've said she's tough as hell. There's a chance, a good chance, we will find her. In one piece with a heck of a story to tell at the bar later."

He gave Cal another nod and a half smile and kept searching with the rest of them.

I had gotten myself high enough that the waves were not threatening to drown me at the moment. Fighting the urge to pass out again, I had my eyes closed willing myself to stop thinking about my leg when I heard the sound of claws on rock, then felt a nudge and hot breath on my face. I cracked one eye open and ended up getting licked across both eyes for my effort. The rhythmic panting and tail thump on the rocks was like music to my ears. Help had arrived in my favorite form. Letting a breath out I hadn't realized I was holding, with my hand around this wonderful creature's leg, I finally gave in and the world went blissfully dark around me.

66

THE NEXT BITS are a bit fuzzy and to be honest, I prefer them to stay that way. I worked my way back to the surface of cognizant a few times over the next lord knows how long. Once was when another dog joined my initial four-legged rescuer with a human who shook the bejesus out of me to get a response. The next time was for a few seconds in an ambulance, getting yelled at by someone who looked like they were 10 years old. Then finally I crawled out of my sleepy cave and found myself in a hospital bed with Luna wedged next to me and Levi sleeping contortionist style in a chair next to the bed.

I didn't have to say anything when I woke up, Luna inched her way up my chest and burrowed her face into my shoulder. Whoever said dogs can't show emotion never had any connection to anyone or anything. Even a pet rock. I stroked her fur and buried my face in her neck soaking up her earthy scent.

"You are a sight for sore eyes my girl."

I glanced down at my leg making my brain realize the dull ache coming from that region. "Looks like we are going to have to postpone our rock climbing for a while Luna."

She thumped her tail and sighed letting me know my joke was only so-so.

Levi turned his head to look at us, then his brain fully woke up and had him half falling out of his seat as he scrambled to get up.

"Well, it's about time. You know if you didn't want to hang out anymore you could have just said so. Cliff jumping seems a tad melodramatic."

Even though my face hurt like hell I grinned. This guy had my number.

"Didn't want to see you cry. Figuring faking my death would be a much easier let down." His face smiled, his eyes still held worry.

"Shel..."

Gingerly he rested his forehead on mine, squeezed my hand. Luna grumbled, making me laugh and groan at the same time.

"So, what's the good word for me busting out of here?"

"Well, that depends."

"On?"

"If you can convince the doc that you're going to take it easy and heal."

"Do I want to know how bad?"

Levi gave me a smile that didn't reach his eyes.

"Oh, stop it already. I'm not dead and obviously not dying as I'm not hooked up to anything in here. Give it to me straight or I'll go find someone who will."

"Yup, going to be a piece of cake convincing everyone that you will take it easy. Alright, you asked for it. Broken leg, femur, three cracked ribs, bruises everywhere, concussion and you were moderately to severely hypothermic when they found you."

I let that information sink in for a moment.

"So you're saying I should go for a half marathon in a few weeks?"

"Affirmative. Probably should push for the full."

"Good, we're in agreement then, training starts tomorrow. So, what happened?"

Levi went on to tell a tale that was so bizarre, had I not lived it I would have been asking when the movie was coming out in theaters. Walters and the Chief of Police had been running drugs for years on a much smaller scale. Somewhere along the line Chase somehow caught onto what was happening and instead of blowing the whistle, decided he wanted a nest egg of his own. Three heads are not always better. Chase had been the one to figure out the garbage can drop zone being on no man's land and expanding to spots outside of town but it all started to go sideways from there. Chase was ambitious and pushy for sure. What started out as purely a local gig, morphed into one that had drop zones across the state? As soon as Walters and Chase hit the back of a squad car, both started pointing fingers to the Chief of Police. Then all three masterminds threw each other under the bus as fast as they could hoping for a plea bargain.

With Chase's help, the amount they were trafficking ended up being five times what Walters and Chief had planned on. They almost quit then and there, but somehow Chase pulled it off. He would get word that it was dropped off, then wait for a good time to empty the garbage can and head straight for the border where he met some shady contact on the other side to make the exchange. After the success of the first one, they all got cocky and each time the amounts grew, the locations multiplied and drop offs became more frequent.

"So, who were they getting the drugs from originally? Who stashed it in the meat to begin with?"

"That part's still a mystery. The three of them all claim they don't know where it comes from. A different person on a different burner phone each time. Like I said, Walters had been doing this for years, like decades. The person he got started on this with way back then has been long gone. The head of whatever this was changed hands a few times as far as he can tell but after the first guy he never knew who was at the helm. He just kept getting contacted and paid so he went with it."

"Oh yeah, I never got to tell you. The FBI hotline? I called in on the first day of the shitty snowstorm."

"Did they believe you?"

"I wasn't sure but after the search and rescue dogs found you two FBI agents showed up and took over the arrest."

"Was it Mulder and Scully?"

"Noooo, the polar opposite. No theories, no what if's just transferred Walters and Chase into their cars, asked me a few questions then gave me their number and asked If I would call them when I had a chance."

"Good to know the FBI is only a phone call away and has decent response time. Why didn't we call them sooner?"

Levi shrugged.

"Now we know, but I hope we never have to again."

I grimaced as I shifted.

"I second that. So, what was in it for the Chief?"

"Walters pulled the Chief in to help make it easier for himself and honestly, the only reason he became the Chief of police was to be the one arresting instead of being arrested."

"Jackie's got to be thrilled that he's gone. Does that make her the new chief?"

"For now she is and hopefully she will be officially once this all settles."

"Well at least something is right in this world."

I went to shift to my other side and gasped as the pain smacked into me. Levi jumped up to help me maneuver making me feel like I was 5 and 85 all at the same time.

"Like I said, it will be a piece of cake convincing everyone you will take it easy."

I glared at him and grumbled a thank you as he flipped my pillow and tucked the blanket back around me.

67

A FEW MONTHS later, after lots of physical therapy for my leg, and making official statements for the FBI, I shut the tailgate of my truck after squishing the last of our bags inside. Luna was in the passenger seat already waiting. She always knows when we are leaving. Eerie, really. Before I even start packing she always makes a break for the truck and just sits in it and waits, just to make sure she's not getting left behind. This dance had been going on for about a week. Packing a little each day then dragging her out of the truck as she was not convinced we weren't leaving yet. Today there would be no dragging, today was the day.

"I made you a sandwich for the road, threw in some Cheetos for Luna."

Levi tossed the lunch bag on the front seat as he came around to the back.

"Thanks Mom, hope you left me a note too."

He wrapped his arms around me, pulling me in close.

"No note, don't like you that much. Prefer your sister, she always gets a note."

Tightening my hold on him I let out a sigh. I was going to miss this. Hell, who was I kidding, I was going to miss him. He was running his hands up and down my back, the two of us stuck in the moment.

"Sure you have to go? You could take Sal's position. Could have off every Friday if you wanted."

"Tempting offer, but this makes sense. My uncle really needs a hand, it's a good gig and it will be nice to be back with my family for a while."

I wiggled out of his arm and ducked around to the truck door. Reaching around the seat I pulled out a newspaper wrapped package.

"Got you a little something."

"Wow you went all out on the wrapping. I think you love me, Shelly."

I rolled my eyes at him.

"Here, open it."

Levi carefully unwrapped the crappy wrap job I had done, then grinned.

"Found it when I was cleaning out, thought you might like that back."

"My favorite shirt. Thought I had lost this to a homeless person months ago."

His smile faded a little as he stood there then caught his composure as quick as he let it slip.

"Here."

He threw it behind me and tied the arms around my neck.

"Keep it. It will give me an excuse to come and get it in a few months. Man can't live without his favorite shirt."

Had to admit I liked the sound of that.

"Are you going to come visit me? All the way to Wyoming?"

"Still don't believe the cowgirl thing, have to see it with my own eyes."

"Well if you make it out I will give you the full Wild West experience. Even will splurge and get you one of those plastic Sheriff badges we give the kids on their last day."

Levi pretended to stroke his nonexistent beard.

"That will definitely score me some points with the ladies around here, how can I say no now?"

I Punched his arm. He bent down and gave me a long kiss that said volumes. Took a lot of willpower to hop in the truck and shut the door. Levi leaned on the door, tugged the hair that had escaped from under my baseball hat.

"All kidding aside, I have quite a few weeks of vacation and comp time racked up. Can't think of a better place to spend it."

"Think we could make room for you in the cabin, right Luna?"

Luna let out a deep sigh, she was ready to go. One last kiss then Levi straightened up and double tapped the side of the truck.

"Text me when you land. Drive safe and keep that wolf close by."

"Aye, aye, captain."

I shot him a wink then we backed out of the drive. We made it to the one traffic light in town. It was red. No one was around. Waiting on ghosts again. Then my cell rang, making me jump out of my seat.

"Jesus, why the hell am I so jumpy."

Looking at the caller ID I smiled.

"Hey Uncle Jerry, we are just heading out."

'Well, that's what I'm calling about. You sure you want to come out here kiddo?"

"Yeah...of course I do."

"I'm calling BS on that one. You didn't sound like you really wanted to the last few times we talked. Heart wasn't in it. Don't get me wrong, we'd love to have you out here. You're a great work horse."

"Ha, thanks for the compliment, I think."

"You know what I mean. There is always a spot out here for you, you know that. Just wondering if you may need something else."

"I thought you were short-handed?"

"No, I never said that. You kept saying it so I didn't argue with you. I said, we'd love to have you back whether we need you or not."

"Aunt Jane put you up to this?"

"Can you tell she's standing over my shoulder listening in? She just smacked me in the head. Here, talk to her."

"Hiya kiddo."

"Hey Aunt Jane."

I smiled and pulled over to the side of the road thinking this may be a long chat.

"Feels like you're running back to the safety of the ranch."

So much for a long chat, Aunt Jane was cutting to the chase.

"I'm not running. I'm coming home. Big difference."

"There's coming home and running home. Big Difference."

"What makes you so sure I'm running home?"

"All the other times you circled back you were excited! We could hear it in your voice when you talked on the phone. Hell, last time you came back you had already planned out three weeks of rides you were going to take and grilled us on all the new horses and who was working what. This time? Not a word about any of it. You're coming back because you are not sure what else to do and you're worried that staying now will make it harder to leave down the road. Tell me I'm wrong."

"Aunt Jane..."

"Tell me I'm wrong."

I let out a long breath.

"What if it's a mistake?"

"What if it's not?"

"But what if."

"Honey, what do you have to lose? You always have a job out here. This opportunity is not going to pass you by. Can you say the same for whatever and whoever is making you want to stay?"

"I'm not that girl that chases a guy. I can be solo and do just fine."

Aunt Jane laughed.

"Shelly Ann, staying to see if a relationship grows into something deeper is not chasing a guy. It's taking a chance, it's living life."

"And if it doesn't work out?"

"Then at least you know and won't be haunted by the what if's for the rest of your life and if it didn't work, we would drink and trash talk him until you felt better."

"I love you."

"Love you too. Call us later this weekend, let me know when you are coming to visit."

She emphasized the word visit then hung up. Feeling lighter than I had for days, I turned the truck around and ruffled Luna's ears.

"Time to be a little bit brave."

Luna thumped her tail and stuck her nose out the cracked window.

68

THE SHORT DRIVE seemed to take forever and not long enough at the same time. Taking a steadying breath, I pulled into Levi's driveway and shut off the truck. I saw his head in the window looking out then the door opening as he came out and leaned on the porch post.

"What did you forget?"

I hopped out of the truck and walked to the bottom step, shoving my hands in my back pockets to keep them from flapping around while I talked.

"I brought your shirt back."

Levi's face dropped a little.

"Shel, you can keep it."

"Oh, I plan on keeping it, but you're right a man can't live without his favorite shirt."

"What are you saying?"

"What if I stay?"

Levi seemed to freeze for a second then stepped off the porch.

"Is that what you want?"

"Yeah, it is what I want. Hoping that you do too."

He reached over, pulling me in close for a long slow kiss.

"I'm going to take that as a yes."

"Nah, I'm good. Figured I'd get one last smooch in."

"Oh well in that case I'll be going."

I turned to pretend to leave, Levi grabbed me and spun me in a circle.

"Oh no, you are staying right here."

Laughing I ruffled his hair.

"I was hoping you'd say that as I'm homeless at the moment. And jobless. Hell, I'm one heck of a catch."

"Got that right Red. You know what I was doing when you left?"

"Lining up your next hot date?"

"After that."

"What?"

"I was booking a flight out to Wyoming."

"Really?"

"Really. You left and as soon as you were out of sight I knew it was a mistake."

Wrapping my arms around him I felt like a complete sap as my eyes welled up a little, then felt better when I looked up and his were no better. He stepped back, let Luna out of the truck then took my hand as we headed inside.

"Good thing I came back when I did. Saved you a plane ticket."

"Well not quite. I officially have a flight out tomorrow."

"You weren't messing around were you?"

"Nope. You know, I still don't believe the whole cowgirl thing. Bet I could bump the tickets out a few weeks, grab another. What do you say, take a vacation head out west?"

"You in some cowboy boots and a hat? I think I can get on board with that."

As we went inside I realized for the first time in a long time, I felt home.

About the Author

Kristin Welch was born and raised in Buffalo NY where she currently lives with her family, an assortment of humans and critters. *The Job Post* is her first novel.